Unlovely

Celeste Conway

MeritPress | fw

Published by
Merit Press
an imprint of F+W Media, Inc.
10151 Carver Road, Suite 200
Blue Ash, OH 45242. U.S.A.
www.meritpressbooks.com

ISBN 10: 1-4405-8279-3
ISBN 13: 978-1-4405-8279-0
eISBN 10: 1-4405-8280-7
eISBN 13: 978-1-4405-8280-6

Printed in the United States of America.

10   9   8   7   6   5   4   3   2   1

Library of Congress Cataloging-in-Publication Data

Conway, Celeste.
    Unlovely / Celeste Conway.
        pages cm
    ISBN 978-1-4405-8279-0 (hc) -- ISBN 1-4405-8279-3 (hc) -- ISBN 978-1-4405-8280-6
(ebook) -- ISBN 1-4405-8280-7 (ebook)
    [1. Love--Fiction. 2. Ballet dancers--Fiction.] I. Title.
    PZ7.C7683Un 2014
    [Fic]--dc23
                                            2014027069

Cover design by Frank Rivera.
Cover image © wavebreakmedia/Shutterstock.com.

This book is available at quantity discounts for bulk purchases.
For information, please call 1-800-289-0963.

Dedication

For the dancing girls,
Maureen, Liza, and Marlo

Acknowledgments

Many thanks to my imperturbable and steadfast agent, Erica Rand Silverman, for loving this story in all its incarnations and for bringing it home. And to the brilliant Jacquelyn Mitchard, my editor, for being light and right about so many things.

At midnight, do they glide forth to
gather on the high road,
and alackaday to any youth who
comes upon them!
He shall dance, he shall embrace
them in unbridled frenzy,
and he shall dance without rest
until he fall down dead.

Elementargeister (1837)

Chapter 1

They were back in town again today. Six of them. He counted. All decked out in their summer-colored dresses—yellow, white, and petal-pink—glints of jewelry here and there and those fluttering flowers in their hair. As usual, they stopped off first at the chocolate shop, disappearing one by one under the brown-striped awning and into the bluish shade.

Harley had to wonder how they managed to stay so thin with all the chocolate they ate each week. And thin they were. It was almost unreal. They made him think of willow trees with those wispy arms and long, long legs. Necks so fine and fragile it seemed like some kind of miracle that they didn't snap with the weight of their heads. Not that their heads were very large. They were actually quite tiny heads, but the glossy hair, wound round and round in those knob-like buns, had to weigh something, didn't it? And it all looked so precarious.

From where he sat in the cockpit of the sailboat, he could see when they came out again. The shops of the town ran right along the promenade, their windows facing the sun-washed dock where Harley's boat was tethered in a row of sleek, white yachts. The *Alma* was neither sleek nor white. Its hull was black, and the cockpit was full of coiled ropes and messy pails of fishing gear. Harley lived here with his dad, or had, at least, until starting at Colby College last fall. He was back for the summer, just like the bright, white sailboats and the gauzy girls from the fancy ballet school up the hill.

The girls had been coming here for years, and sometimes he felt he knew them all. There was the sleek-haired leader of the group, whom he and his buddies called Princess Ice. The dark one they'd dubbed Conchita and the pale one, Vampire Sally, with the jet-black bun and crimson lips. Then there was Spy, the tall brunette, who wore her sunglasses rain or shine. And the tiny one who never grew. Her they called Moon because that was the shape of her weird little face.

The book on Harley's lap fell closed as he shifted slightly to watch the girls. He squinted his eyes. Yeah, there she was. The new one. He hadn't imagined her last week. Though they all looked alike in a certain way—the pinned-up hair, the board-straight backs, and the funny, toes-out way they walked—this one popped from the rest of the crowd. It was partly, of course, that rare, pale hair. Although Harley, in truth, had never been into the blonde-girl thing. But this was a blonde beyond all blonde. Not yellow or gold or honey-streaked, but that near-white hue that little children sometimes have. Added to that was her perfect skin. Even from far across the dock, he could see its glow, peaches and cream, that old cliché, set off from the blue of her breezy dress. He'd decided she was nice as well. Not as aloof as the other girls. He liked how curious she seemed, looking around at all the sights—the shops, the harbor, the details of the seaside street. That little one, Moon, seemed to cling to her side. Across the water, he caught the sound of Moon's high voice as she held up her bag of chocolates. "Yummy, yum. Try one of these!" Sometimes they'd laugh, and the blonde girl would incline toward Moon, the yellow flower in her hair grazing the top of Moon's red head.

"Dream on, loser!" A rowdy voice broke into his thoughts, and Harley grinned as his buddy Red Legs swung over the railing and onto the boat. "Good idea. The book, I mean. Makes you look smart. As if you can read. Too bad they don't know you're even alive."

"Back at you," laughed Harley. "What's the deal? You on a break?"

"No such luck. I got to do a pickup. Some asshole at the heliport."

"Well, maybe you'll get a big old tip."

"Yeah. Fat chance. Don't you know the formula? The richer the guy, the cheaper the tip. How do you think those guys stay rich?" Red Legs gave a jerk of his head, tossing a flap of limpid hair. "So you coming to my place tonight? Everyone'll be there. I ordered up a keg."

"Sounds fine," said Harley.

"'Course, Mairin will probably be there, too. It might be weird, but—"

"I'm okay with Mairin."

"Yeah?"

"It just didn't work out. It's no one's fault."

"All the same, nobody thinks she's right with Smits. Everybody says the same."

"Smits is okay," said Harley, though he knew it wasn't true.

For a couple of seconds, neither spoke. Then, "Hey, look there," said Red Legs. "It's the pretty little ballet boys." Harley turned, following his friend's fixed gaze. At the end of the sunny promenade, a wharf led out to the pale-gray, shingled yacht club. There on the deck some of the boys from Ocean Watch Academy were goofing around, balancing on the pilings and doing acrobatic tricks.

"Bunch of assholes," Red Legs sneered. "Anyone can do that shit." And he stood on one leg and stretched the other out in back, practically falling down. "What's the point? You know what I mean? I'd like to see them haul a sail. Or catch a fucking fish."

Harley laughed—Red Legs looked like an idiot—turning again to watch the boys. They might seem slender from afar, but he knew how totally ripped they were. He remembered a T-shirt he'd seen on one of them last year. On the front, it read, *Real Men Don't Lift Weights*, and on the back, *They Lift Women*. He'd had to envy the contours under-neath that shirt, the bulging pecs and the sculpted arms. Still, Harley didn't like these guys. They were full of themselves. Conceited. Always showing off—like now. And they got to hang out with those willow-tree girls. At this moment, in fact, they were waving their arms and heading in that direction. One of them, in tight white pants and a flouncy shirt, was walking on his hands. The girls didn't move to meet them. They just stood there in the yellow sun that struck their hair and seemed to love them with its light, making the boys come crawl to them.

"Shit," said Red Legs, watching the scene. "How do they stand those faggy creeps?"

"They aren't faggy," Harley said. To anyone else but his good friend Red Legs he might have also mentioned that the "f" word wasn't used these days, and no way would he have used it himself. But he and Red Legs went way back. Even beyond the hazy days when they were mates on a black, rogue ship and gave themselves their pirate names.

"Just watch that guy," Harley said instructively. "The blond one there. In the blue-striped shirt. Tell me he's not into girls." Harley knew the boys by sight, almost as well as he knew the ballerinas. And over the years, he'd seen that blonde with about a hundred different girls. He was tall and lean with one of those chiseled faces like a model in a magazine. He was fooling around with Spy right now, trying to flick her glasses off. Spy kind of spun when his hand came close, her pink skirt twirling in the air.

"Well, maybe not him," grudged Red Legs. "But the others look like fags to me."

"You're hopeless," said Harley, shaking his head.

Aside from the blond there were four other guys: one short and dark with a gymnast's build; an exotic type in a black beret; another with a ponytail; and the wiry one, all dressed in white, who'd been walking on his hands. They were working hard at getting the girls' attention. And though they weren't like Red Legs and him, not in any way or shape, Harley knew they weren't gay. The girls had started to play a game, dangling chocolates in front of them and then snatching them from reach. Then Spy started making the boys do tricks. Beg and dance around like dogs. Leap for the chocolates she tossed in the air.

"Weird," said Red Legs, watching them. "Tell me, man, would you ever grovel around like that?" Harley had to wonder. He pictured himself that close to those girls. Imagined that he had different hair—thick, gold curls like the guy with the chiseled face and lips, instead of the scruff he actually had. Tried to picture his okay-normal body in tight white pants and a gypsy shirt slit wide open down the front. That part was hard, but he gave it a shot. Now, what if that girl, the new one with the corn-silk hair, told him *Leap*, and tossed a chocolate for him to fetch . . .

"Hell, no," he answered Red Legs, but in his mind he was already flying into the sky. The interesting thing, the thing he noticed once he landed back on earth, was that *she* wasn't taking part in the game. Even cute little Moon was into the act. But the new girl had sort of pulled away and was watching from a distance, a few yards back from the laughing group. Harley was beyond intrigued.

"Well," said Red Legs, checking his phone, "as entertaining as all this is, I have to get back to work." He turned to leave, and just before hopping onto the deck, glanced at the cover of Harley's book. "So you're coming tonight? It's definite?"

"Yeah, I'll be there," Harley replied. Red Legs swung over the rails of the boat and onto the wooden dock. He paused there for a moment, tossing a swag of mud-brown hair. "I'm worried, Blood." He threw out Harley's pirate name. "When the fuck did you start reading poetry?"

Harley watched as his friend went loping across the planks and up the shaky ramp. Out on the street, Red Legs slipped into a dark green car, one of three in his father's fleet of taxi cabs. Since high school graduation that's where he had been employed. Pugwash worked for his father, too, in the local bait and tackle shop. It was only Harley who'd gone away. Even Mairin was still in town, which showed you just how hard it was because Mairin was wild with wanderlust. She and Harley had had

13

a dream. He never knew why she gave it up and stopped believing in herself and the world of possibility.

From across the way, a burst of laughter nudged into his thoughts. He turned to look at the dancers again. They were all mixed in together now as they ambled past the chocolate shop back toward the edge of town. A couple of people walking along stopped and said hello to them. They were summer people naturally—no "year-round" person would ever do that—from one of the houses up the hill. The dancers smiled and clustered for a photograph.

Harley trailed them with his gaze as they neared the end of the promenade and the last of the fancy shops. The new girl lingered briefly, peering in the window, pointing something out to Moon. The sun on her dress turned the blue to radiance, and when she walked off around the bend, she left gold glitter in the air.

Harley knew that what he was thinking wasn't done. Even his dad, who liked to break the rules himself, told him to leave those girls alone. "It isn't worth it," Liam said. "You'd wish you hadn't in the end." And Liam would know. When he was a lost, young widower, he'd had a fling with one of the visiting teachers there. She was beautiful and crazy. Liam still bore the remnant scar, a fadeless crescent on his neck. And that was before—long years before—the thing that happened to Teddy Flynn.

Chapter 2

It was almost nine P.M. when Harley arrived at the old frame house. As he climbed the steps to the sagging porch, he could hear the rowdy sounds inside. Laughter and loud male voices. A girl's high squeal and the throb of a song that was hot and popular last year. He paused for a second at the door, and ran a hand over his WELCOME mat of hair. It was just that scruffy. Same color, like straw. He was wearing old jeans and a bleached-out shirt. Nothing that hinted at any change.

"Yo, Harley! Hey!" The minute he entered the living room, a barrage of voices greeted him. It was dark in the house—for "atmosphere"—but he knew each face even through the shadows and could put a name to every hello. Yet, it all felt kind of warp-y, as if he were stepping back in time.

"Hey, man," he said, smacking a couple of beefy arms. "How are you doing, Johnny? Hi there, Fitz. Hey, Davy. Holy shit, are you drinking beer?" That last he said to his friend John's younger brother. Davy thought Harley was the man. He wanted to *be* like Harley. Go to college. Get away. He'd sent a few e-mails during the year, asking Harley what it was like. What classes was he taking? Were the girls at college as hot as they said?

"How's school?" he said to Davy now. "Are you ready for the SATs?"

Davy beamed and said he was doing fine with math but working on his verbal skills. That cracked everybody up. For the next five minutes they teased the pants off Davy, goofing about his "verbal skills" and laughing so hard they spit their beer. Harley laughed, too; he sort of couldn't help it. Hearing the hilarity, a couple of girls came drifting in from the other room.

"Harley, hi!" Sue and Lacy, in the low-cut tank tops they always wore, came over to say hello to him. He kissed them both, and said they looked good.

"So do you, bro," said Lacy, eyes roving up his T-shirt and back to his face.

"Hey, guess what? Me and Sue are going to open a nail salon. We're getting licenses and stuff."

"Wow," said Harley. "That's really great."

"It's going to be more like a *spa*," said Sue, chomping on a pretzel stick.

"Here in town?"

"Well, of course, in town. Where else would we go? Winters might be a little slow, but we're going to clean up in summertime with those muckety-mucks from up the hill."

"Cool," said Harley, trying hard to picture that.

"Hey," said Lacy softly then, "Mairin's somewhere in the house. Have you seen her yet since you've been back?"

Harley said no, and Sue and Lacy exchanged a glance.

"I think she looks good." That was Sue.

"Yeah," said Lacy. "I think so, too."

Harley was glad when Red Legs came into the living room and pulled him from the girls. "Looks like you're the star tonight."

"Yeah," said Harley. "It's fun to be back." He glanced around the dimly lit space. "The house hasn't changed. It's kind of nice. Brings back a lot of memories."

"Yeah," said Red Legs. "High school was wild."

"Everybody's still around."

"Yeah, I know. But it's not the same. Everybody's working now. Too tired to do our crazy shit. Or party hardy like we did."

From another room, Pugwash suddenly appeared. The other mate in their wild, childhood pirate crew, he grabbed for Harley and slugged his back.

"Hey there, college boy. What goes?"

"Great to see you," Harley said. He took a step back and smiled at his friend. Pugwash's face was already deeply tanned from long, hot days on the fishing boat. "How's everything going? Your dad okay?"

Pugwash laughed. "My dad's an ox. How about yours? I bet he misses your sorry ass."

"Don't know about that. But he's doing okay."

"Hey, Becks, come here!" yelled Pugwash, and a short, plump girl broke from a group across the room. Her face was pink and impish with a scattering of freckles that matched her reddish hair.

"Harley, hi!" She kissed his cheek. "Is everything good? You look so great!"

"Things are fine. How about you? I heard that you're in college, too."

Becky latched on to Pugs's arm. They'd turned into something more than friends just before Christmastime last year. "The community college. No big deal."

"It is a big deal," said Harley. "That's really hard when you're working, too."

"It's harder on Pugwash," Red Legs joked. Then, "Hey, Captain Blood, you need a beer. The keg's outside on the porch in back." He motioned for Harley to move his ass.

Harley passed through the kitchen. The light was harsh, familiar, a pulsing glow from a ring-shaped fluorescent over the sink. There was stuff all over the green Formica counters, and bowls of chips and store-bought dips on a table against the wall. Above the door that led outside was a ship's wheel clock, still ticking away as it had since Harley and Red Legs were five, two flush-faced kids running in from the cold. He moved toward the door, and it suddenly opened in front of him. Mairin appeared, framed in the darkness of the yard. Deep in his chest, Harley's heart took an extra beat.

"Mairin."

"Harley."

For several seconds, they faced each other silently. Harley's first impression was the Mairin of his memory. A whip-thin girl with haywire curls and pale-green, wild-looking eyes. Eyes that belonged to something not quite human, like a fairy or sprite, or maybe an enchanted cat. But seconds passed, and he saw her again as she really was, her face a little fuller, and something tepid in her eyes. He found that he couldn't say a word.

Mairin stepped in and closed the door.

"When did you get here?" she asked him then. What did she mean? Here at the party? Here in town? Harley's head felt full of fog, and for several dragging seconds he still couldn't seem to speak. "You look good," she said without a smile.

"You, too," he finally murmured. His first half-sentence to her, a lie.

She moved from the door and crossed the room. Harley could see her better now. He could notice all the little things. The piece of string she'd tied around the rampant curls. The blue of her throat. The thin, gold cross. How the neckline of her shirt was frayed like a rim of poky hairs. Then he noticed the other thing. He already knew—Pugs had told him on the phone—but seeing it was different. And it left him so unbalanced he had to lean back on the solid wall.

"Don't worry," she said, meeting his gaze. "We're going to get married soon." Her rangy hands, with their long and slender fingers, spread like a net on the subtle rise beneath her shirt. "I think it's a boy. I hope it is. I'd be much better with a boy."

"You'd be good with anything," Harley said, his voice coming out in a long, slow wisp. A wisp he almost seemed to see, like a trail of smoke in the harsh glare.

"No, I wouldn't," Mairin said. "A girl might drive me crazy. Dolls and dresses and things like that. Stuff I never cared about."

"When?" asked Harley softly. "I mean, why?" he said when she didn't reply. "Why do you have to do this now?"

Mairin glanced away from him. "It's already done. The question's moot."

"Mairin."

"What?" What Harley was thinking he couldn't say. *How could you do this to yourself? How could you throw your life away when it hasn't even started yet?* Instead he asked, "But why do you have to marry him?"

"My mother says she can't be the grandma if I don't."

"Your mother. Great," snapped Harley. The same adoring mother who'd quashed Mairin's plans for college. Who'd told her she was selfish for even thinking of such a thing with five young siblings after her. Leave Harley to his harebrained dreams.

"You're eighteen years old," said Harley.

"My mom was that age when she had me."

"That's a real good reason to do the same." He hadn't meant to say that, but as he did, it all came clear. He saw it printed on Mairin's face. In the set of her jaw. In her altered eyes.

"The whole world's black and white with you." He stared across the space at her. "You either break out completely or bury yourself in this crappy town with the biggest asshole you can find. You'll show your mother, won't you, Mair?"

"Smits is not an asshole," Mairin said in a toneless voice. "He's a licensed tradesman, I'll have you know. Something you will never be."

Harley couldn't believe his ears. Couldn't believe that words like this were coming out of Mairin's mouth. He suddenly couldn't look at her. At her face, her hands, that bulge of body under her shirt. The worst part was that he knew he was right; she'd done the damage to herself. Had set her sights on the quickest route to the deepest fall. And it made him so mad he wanted to do some violence. Smash a table. Throw a chair. He wanted to shake her like a rag.

"I'm going to get a beer," he said. He grabbed for the door, and pushed outside. A moth-blurred bulb hung above the hefty keg, but the rest of the yard was steeped in the darkness Harley craved. He waded into the weedy grass, an image of Mairin in his head. A day last summer out on the boat. She was gripping the wooden steering wheel, racing to port as a squall rolled in. The sky was black, ripped with streaks of lightning, but Mairin was in her element, her hair flung out like streamers as she hooted at the wind. By that point she'd decided not to go away with him, but Harley knew she'd change her mind because no one like that would lose her courage for very long. Now he knew it wasn't courage that she'd lost. Turning, he headed back toward the house. He stopped at the keg and filled a cup until it hit the brim.

When Harley got back to the living room, the mood of the party was up a notch. More kids had arrived and a bottle of vodka was floating around. Most of the guests were people from his high school class. They all flocked over to say "hello" and ask how his freshman year had gone. A few of the guys were former stars of the football team. Somehow they seemed smaller now, their necks thinned out, their muscles less impressive in the sleeves of ordinary shirts. Harley talked to everyone, drinking maybe a little too fast, washing Mairin out of his head. Her face. Her eyes. The way she looked backed against the counter, her hands splayed out, all beautiful knobs and spider bones, over the small, white lump. Smits had come to take her home. Harley just caught a glimpse of him as they passed through the door and into the night.

"So you saw her, huh?" asked Lacy, coming over to talk again.

"It must've been kind of a shock," said Sue. "Did you hear they're getting married? Probably in a week or two." Harley said something he didn't mean. That he wished them luck, and that Smits, he guessed, was a decent guy.

"He's a total bastard," Lacy said.

Sue agreed. "He's an effing creep."

⁓

Harley was with Davy, filling him in on "college life," when Smits returned to the house alone. He bee-lined for the vodka and filled a plastic cup. Harley looked him over, not liking any part of him. He had really lousy posture, which gave him a kind of slinky look. His face was pretty weasely, too. Squinty eyes and a pointy nose. Red-brown hair all puffed with gel. He was wearing khakis instead of jeans, like he wanted to seem classier than everybody else. Hell, maybe he was since he had a fucking *license*, right? When Davy left, Harley got up for another beer. He hated Smits and decided this would be his last if that asshole planned to hang around.

⁓

As soon as Harley reached the docks, he noticed the lights in the port-holes of the *Alma*. His dad was back from Boston, where he'd gone for a couple of days to work. And to visit with Vanessa, an artist he saw a few times a month. Harley tested his walking skills. Assessed his steps on the line of a plank. Not that Liam would give a damn. Liam was for liberty. The minute Harley hit fifteen, he'd given him full rein. "You are who you are by now," he'd said. "Hope it's good 'cause there's nothing more that I can do." And Harley *was* good. He tried to be. He thought he must have his mother's genes, that angel-woman he'd heard about, because Liam Jamison wasn't that good. By the definition most people had.

As he slipped into the cabin, he realized how chilly he had been on the downhill walk from Red Legs's house. The air below was dry and warm. Amber lights played along the woodwork, the *bas-reliefs* and carvings, which Liam had fitted into the hull. Some of the sculptures Liam had done himself, and others were ornate fragments he'd bought on trips to Europe years ago when he used to be a well-known restorer of all things wood. Liam himself was stretched full out on the portside bunk, reading Harley's book of poems.

"Ahoy," he greeted, looking up.

"Hi," said Harley. "Welcome back."

"Been hitting the schnapps?" asked Liam, a smile creasing his already craggy, deep-lined face. He was forty-nine but looked like sixty, Harley thought. Strangely enough, women liked his rugged mug.

"Red Legs had a little gathering," Harley said, as he flopped on the bunk across the way.

"Good time?"

"All right. A little bit weird."

"Parties in themselves are weird. I went to one in Boston. Stood around on a terrace with a goldfish pond, talking about the downfall of the Eurozone."

"We talked about licenses," Harley said.

"Licenses?"

"Yeah. Did you know you need a license to paint somebody's fingernails?"

"News to me," said Liam. "One of your friends get a license like that?"

"Lacy Mullen and Sue Malone are apparently working on getting one. They're opening a spa."

Liam chuckled. "Town needs one of them for sure. Hey, listen to this—" He deepened his voice and read from the page: *"Full fathom five thy father lies; Of his bones are coral made; Those are the pearls that were his eyes."* He looked up from the book. "That's pretty good shit."

"Mairin's going to marry Smits," Harley announced, staring at Liam across the space.

"Who told you that?"

"*She* told me. I saw her at the party tonight."

"That's totally crazy. Makes no sense. Why doesn't she just get rid of it?"

"Get rid of what?"

"You know what. It's not illegal nowadays."

"She's Catholic," said Harley, a fog of confusion swamping his head. "Plus, I think it's too late. You can see it there. This tiny lump under her shirt."

"Fuck," said Liam solemnly, and he rose from the bunk and fetched the scotch. He poured a glass for each of them. "Must have been hell for you tonight."

"It's like she's dead," said Harley. "Like she's gone forever and can't come back."

The fiery drink went down his throat, burning a passage through his chest.

"I was worried for you," Liam said when some time had passed. "Back last year when Mairin decided not to go to college, I thought she might try to keep you here."

"She'd never do that."

"Just the same. I thought you might decide yourself. Mairin's a little witchy thing. Hard to walk away from her."

Harley uttered a bitter laugh. She'd actually made it easy—or if not easy, painfully clear—by taking up with Smits before he'd even packed his bags. Told him it was over. That they'd reached a fork in the road of their lives. So he'd gone to Colby up in Maine, hoping all semester that she'd realize she'd made a big mistake and get her plans on track again. She'd gotten a partial scholarship. Financial aid was all lined up. There was just the question of the loans, and that's when everything fell apart. Harley came home for Christmas. At some party in town, he saw her making out with Smits. All heavy and hot—she knew that he was watching her—which told him her choice was sealed.

"I'm sorry," said Liam to Harley now. "I thought you two—ah, what the hell. It's a big cliché, but you've got to move on. Have another scotch, my boy."

◈

Harley lay, still half-awake, in his narrow bunk at the bow of the boat. Water skidded along the hull, and the *Alma* rocked with a mesmerizing motion that usually put him right to sleep. He kept picturing Mairin the way she'd looked. That piece of string in her crazy hair. The renegade curls. The fraying cloth. And in the hollow of her throat, that tiny cross her mother gave her when she was ten, glinting in the light. He hated Mairin's mother. Holy and dumb, lost in another century.

As he drifted in and out of sleep, other memories floated back. Mairin in her nubby cap. In her tattered, dark-blue bathing suit. Goosebumped legs and school-plaid skirt. An axe through her head on Halloween when all the girls were fairy queens. Her rumpled scarf. Her dirty shoes. The tidbit buttons on her shirt, hopeless in his fingertips. Pictures blurred and merged with dream; three stars spun, all dizzy, in the circle of the porthole's rim.

Chapter 3

"Hey, get up! I need your help." Liam's voice broke into the fuzz of Harley's sleep. His eyes eased open slowly, and the yellow ooze of sun leaked in.

"What the hell time is it?" he groaned, rolling over to face the wall. A heavy weight seemed pressed to the bone above his eyes.

"It's nine o'clock, you lazy ass. Hannah just called me from the school. They got a leak and they need us to come."

"Us?"

"Yeah, us. A broken pipe. I need a lackey for something like this."

Harley tried to lift his head, and the sun shot through to the back of his eyes.

"Come on," groused Liam, yanking the sheets.

"Yeah, all right. But, I'm not any good."

Ten minutes later, Harley was at the wheel of the Jeep, lurching up the twisty hill. Pebbles shot out from under the wheels, every *ping* hitting a nerve in his aching head. Off to the right on the ocean side, the mansions rolled by in a gray parade. Solid and implacable, they perched on the edge of the seaside cliff as if daring the wind to blow them off. Driving on, they clattered past the Black estate and the rolling meadow next to it. A little farther up the hill, they swerved around the tree-lined bend and the tall, stone hulk of Ocean Watch swept suddenly into view.

The sight of the house startled Harley every time, appearing abruptly as it did, solid and imposing, a stern, gray shape in the fleecy sky. Even the narrow tower that rose above the slated roofs seemed rooted to the ground. From the boat at night, the light in its high-up window looked like an ancient, dimming eye that followed you down the coast.

The estate had no gate, but two stone posts marked the entrance to the drive. Harley turned in and parked the Jeep. Unloading their tools, Harley and Liam trekked across the front of the house, where marble steps ascended to a massive door. A scrollwork fence surrounded Hannah's garden tucked away at the far left side. They followed a path through vegetables and roses to the kitchen door where Hannah stood. With her thick red braids and granny dress, she looked like an enormous doll.

"Thanks for coming, boys," she said, ushering them in. She studied Harley, nodding her head. "Good to see you. You're looking fine. Glad you're still willing to do real work."

"Hi," said Harley, smiling back. Though he'd known her since he was two years old, she was not the kind of woman you kissed.

"Flooded," she said, "before I could get the water off. It's not like there's anyone here to help."

Harley pulled his sneakers off. Then, rolling the bottom of his jeans, he waded into the shallow lake that spread across the floor.

"You start to mop," said Liam. "I'll go take a look at things." He removed his beat-up deck shoes and headed for the sink.

Mopping wasn't all that bad. The bucket had wheels and a wringer on top, so you didn't have to wet your hands. Plus, Hannah had made coffee, dark and hot, soothing as a medicine. Harley established a rhythm, swabbing back and forth across the length of the checkerboard floor. He only paused to dump the bucket now and then in Hannah's designated spot in the garden near the fence. The chore was dull and mindless, and he settled into a lazy pace. On one of his dumping trips outside, he stopped for a moment to take a rest. The air was thick and yellow, hazy with a scrim of gnats. At first he wasn't certain that he'd seen the flash at the garden's edge. He lingered at the doorway, peering down the fuzzy path. Probably just a bird, he guessed. But just as he heaved the bucket up, he saw it again—and it wasn't a bird. It was a guy.

"Hey!" he called. He took a step forward, craning his neck. The quiet of the garden was cut with a sudden thrashing sound. Down behind the hollyhocks, Harley could see a frantic trembling in the leaves. Then, he saw the guy again. He was tall and blond, and with him was a tiny girl with long, red hair like a trailing flare. Harley ducked into a row of corn and watched them through the eye-high stalks. From here, he could see them fling open the garden gate and make a run toward the front of the house. He knew who they were. The boy was the blond, that hotshot guy with the chiseled face. The tiny girl, with the fiery hair, so long it reached the back of her knees— she was Moon!

Harley felt a wave of feeling he couldn't quite name. He felt like chasing down the guy and bashing in his face. What the hell was he doing with Moon? He could have any girl at school. Girls his age, not little kids, which was what Moon was. Harley edged out of the quivering corn. The bucket stood waiting near the door, and as he rolled it back inside, he thought about mentioning what he'd seen. Hannah, he knew, wouldn't be too pleased.

But when he went back, Hannah and Liam were not in the room. Faintly, he heard his father's voice talking on a telephone somewhere down a hall. He was probably ordering a part. Harley started to swab again, sloshing the water back and forth. As the bucket rolled on its cranky wheels, he turned with a clumsy motion, coming face to face with someone at the kitchen door. He caught his breath. Froze in place. His fingers stuck to the wooden handle of the mop.

It was totally crazy. But it was the girl—the new one—in a skimpy leotard and tights. His eyes dropped down and he found himself staring at her feet. She was wearing those ballerina shoes, shiny and pink, with crisscrossed satin ribbons that wound and tucked on her small, exquisite anklebones.

With a jab that felt like actual pain, Harley realized how *he* must look. Pants rolled up, inches deep in water, hugging a mop as if he were in love with it.

"There was a leak," he lamely explained. Like she wouldn't be able to figure that out.

"Listen," she said as if he hadn't spoken, "did you see anyone around? A girl. Really small. Kind of carrot-y hair?" She fixed him with her huge, blue eyes.

Harley swallowed. "Yeah," he said. "She was out in the garden a minute ago."

It was hard for him to look at her. She was even more beautiful than he'd thought. More perfect up close than any girl he'd ever seen. It stunned him how delicate she was, like some hybrid form of human being. She had thin yet sculpted arms and legs. Branch-like bones. A willowy neck. Skin like a petal, Harley thought, blinking from her face.

"You really saw her?" she asked him then.

"Yeah," said Harley. "With some guy."

"A guy?"

"A blond. Much older than her."

"I'm going to kill him," whispered the girl. Harley didn't answer. She rushed ahead in a quiet voice, "He's not supposed to be here. We don't have class on Sunday, so he shouldn't even be on the grounds." Harley nodded. He knew the boys didn't board here, that summer people put them up in their extra rooms.

"Anyway, thank you," murmured the girl. She took a step back, pausing for a moment, her weight transferred to one pink foot. Her wide, blue eyes, which Harley decided were sky not sea, lingered briefly on the floor, then floated to his face again. "Do you work here?" she asked him suddenly.

"Only when something breaks," he said.

"So you must be that father and son." Weird description, Harley thought, but he answered with a wordless nod. "People say you're the only ones that Hannah can call. That no one in town wants to come to the school."

"There are reasons for that," said Harley, wondering just how much she knew.

"So what's your name?"

"I'm Harley."

"I'm Cassandra. Good luck with the floor." She spun around before he had time to answer her. In a second, she was gone. She left in the air an after-image of her back, bare and smooth in the V of the deep-cut leotard. In his ears, he heard the clatter of those strange, stiff shoes. When Liam returned with Hannah, Harley was still at the doorway, dazed.

"I think we need breakfast," Hannah remarked. Hiking up her dress again, she sloshed to the old-fashioned stove, lighting it with a match.

They sat outside at the table in the garden, the morning air spiked with the smell of roses and herbs. Hannah's grapes, a luminous green, hung from the arbor overhead like a string of tinted Christmas lights, and through the leaves sunlight played on her ruddy face.

"Great breakfast, as usual," Liam said. "No one makes omelets as good as you."

"It's the *fines herbes,*" said Hannah. "I always use them in the eggs." She glanced at Harley, smiling. "This one used to weed them out."

"*Weed* is right," said Harley. "I thought that's what they were." Hannah laughed, and Harley noticed her straight, white teeth. She was probably close to Liam's age, but she looked the same as she had when he was a little kid and she'd come to the boat to cook for them. She was one of those people who never changed, who never looked either old or young. Again, Harley considered telling her about the boy. But in the end, he didn't. Maybe it was stupid, but the silence he chose made him feel that he had a secret with the girl. *Cassandra.* God. What a beautiful name.

After breakfast, Harley went back to mopping the floor, and Liam determined grimly that he'd have to take a trip to town to purchase some replacement pipe. It made him mad that he'd have to buy it from the Smits's, the only plumbing store around.

"He's a goddamn crook. And everybody knows it," Liam growled as Hannah passed him the worn-out pipe, wrapped in a kitchen towel. "And now we've got Crook Junior, too. He's a smirker, you know. Like the whole world's funny. A great big joke."

"Don't worry about the money," Hannah said, as Liam pulled on his shoes. "The school is paying, not you or me."

"You heard about Mairin?" he suddenly asked. "I know you did. You always hear." Harley turned to Hannah in time to see her tight-lipped nod.

"There's something else you ought to know," she said to Liam, grimly. "That woman's back. That friend of yours."

Liam half-smiled. "What friend of—"

"The one who almost slit your throat."

"Theodosia Ravenska?"

"None other than. She's staging the performance, the one they put on at the end of the term. Everyone's excited. Nabbing her was quite the coup."

"Do me a favor, Hannah. Don't call me up here anymore." Liam's fingers roamed to his neck, grazing the half-moon scar.

"You should have had her put away," Hannah commented under her breath.

"Did she really try to off you, Dad?" Harley asked with a skeptical grin. "I thought it was just some crazy spat."

Hannah scowled. "A crazy spat with a pair of sharpened scissors."

"She was overwrought," said Liam. "I didn't handle the whole thing right."

"What did you do to her?" Harley asked. "I never really heard the dirt. How'd you get her so pissed off?"

"I told her I wanted to break things off."

"That's it?"

"That's it."

"And for that she stabbed you in the neck?" The story wasn't funny, but the melodrama of it all made Harley want to laugh.

"She was very high-strung. Artistic. And she'd recently lost her fiancé. We were both messed up. I never should have—"

"Damn right about that," growled Hannah.

"I was lonely back then. And out of the blue, this famous ballerina, this gorgeous babe, has the hots for me."

"Yeah, go figure," Harley agreed. He turned to Hannah. "That was quite a while ago. What does she look like nowadays?"

"She's ugly," Hannah answered. "She was ugly then, and she's ugly now. The kind of ugly that comes from the soul."

"She was anything but ugly," Liam said with a little wince. "But whenever I try to picture her, all I can see is her twisted face and scissors aiming for my neck."

"Jeez," said Harley, his smirk gone flat.

Liam took the car keys, and Harley returned to the bucket and mop. In half an hour he'd finished his chore. Hannah was bustling back and forth, preparing for the students' lunch, and he drifted slowly out the door. The summer day was heating up, and the drone of bees weighted the air. He walked through the rows of peppers and the green tomatoes on their vines, down beyond the hollyhocks where he'd glimpsed the boy and Moon. There were trampled stems and flowers, and it made him mad how careless they'd been. As if it didn't matter what kind of ruin they'd left behind. He followed their trail through the banks of wild roses and over to the gate. Then, exiting the garden, he made his way toward the front of the massive house.

On the right side of the property a vast green field slanted upward toward the cliff. Queen Anne's lace grew among the dry, tough grass, and its airy blooms gave an impression of low-hung mist. When Harley was a little kid, he and his friends used to sled there in wintertime. They'd start near the cliff and ride the slope down into the road. There were never any cars back then. Not in the winter. Not up here.

Harley walked at the edge of the field along the great stone house. He could see inside through some of the downstairs windows—sprawling rooms with chandeliers and archways leading to vaulted halls. Walking on, he approached the mansion's eastward wing, the widest section of the house that overlooked the sea. A cellar door jutted out where the sections met. He and his friends had always talked about breaking into that bolted door. There was secret treasure hidden there; Captain Greywood, who built the place, had buried it himself.

Harley arrived at the back of the house, or the front, he supposed, if you loved the sea. A stone veranda extended from the lower floor, and just past that a line of rocks formed a sharp-toothed fence. Harley pushed through an opening and descended a narrow path. A jumble of stones led downward to a rocky ledge. At the end of the ledge, maybe twelve feet out, the earth abruptly dropped away. Harley paused at the bottom of the rough-hewn steps. The view was panoramic, the ocean blue and limitless, sparkling in the sun. The last time he'd been here, five years ago, he was trespassing with his friends. Early September. A moonless night. They'd brought their flashlights along with them to look for signs of blood. Pugs had actually found some rocks still splattered with reddish stains. He'd taken them with him in a bag, and brought to them to the pirate cave. They were probably still in their hiding place in one of the hollows in the wall. The rocks that Harley stood on now were white with sun, cleansed and bleached with wind and snow and a thousand rains.

∽∽∽

The administration at Ocean Watch Academy claimed that Teddy, who had no business being in the tower, fell out of the window that August night. He must have been drinking, they maintained, and the autopsy proved that this was true. Yet no one in town believed he could have fallen, alcohol or not. He jumped was the theory they floated next. But why would he do a thing like that? Teddy was happy, everyone said. Happier, in fact, than he'd been in months. He'd just had a birthday. Had turned eighteen.

The school brought in their bigwig lawyers. In the end, no one was held responsible, and Teddy was declared a drunk. The people in town could never explain what he was doing up at the school.

Harley trekked back, keeping some distance from the house. He knew that it was possible. People could seem happy, could walk around like everything was normal, like the girl at school who was in his class one morning and in the hospital that night after downing a bunch of pills. He never really knew Teddy Flynn. He was four years older than Harley. But he seemed okay. A normal guy. Harley had never liked the idea of taking the bloody stones.

It was warm on the grounds after the cool of the seaside ledge. Nothing stirred, and heat seemed to rise from the hazy field. Over the hum of insects whining in the Queen Anne's lace, the sounds of a piano drifted faintly in the air. When Harley looked up at the open window from which the music seemed to come, he felt he could almost see the notes, floating out in lacy shapes over the sun-dazed grass.

As he watched the window, a figure suddenly came into view. It was a woman, not a girl. She had jet-black hair and a slender frame, and even from his distance, Harley sensed a dark, alluring glamour. She must have been a teacher, one of those ballerinas who came to coach at Ocean Watch when her stage career had reached its end. Or could it be *her*—the crazy one, who'd signed her name in Liam's neck? Her face didn't move as he passed the window, retracing his steps. But he knew that she was watching him, and he felt her gaze like a cold, blue beam following him down the drive until he dipped from sight at the front of the house. There were rules about boys at Ocean Watch.

Chapter 4

The following week Harley started his summer job, fishing with Pugs for his father's bait and tackle shop. It was tough to get up in the chilly dark, but as he and Pugwash left the port, the sun would rise in front of them, a daily show which almost made the pain worthwhile. The sky would flood with tender pink and a yellow so pale and radiant it turned to silver in his eyes. Harley decided that this was the "light" God created on the morning of Day One. He decided, too, that this blinding color, which had no name, was the color of Cassandra's hair.

Monday and Tuesday they trawled for killies along the shore. On Wednesday, they also dug for worms, ankles deep in pungent mud, piss clams squirting up their legs. Thursday was cold and drizzly with a gusty wind, predicting a storm. By Friday they could smell it and taste it on their tongues. They hauled in early and headed for port, bucking whitecaps on the way.

The storm rolled in on Friday night. By the early hours of Saturday it was socked in tight, a wet nor'easter with howling wind. If Liam were here, Harley and he would have taken the *Alma* out to port and put her on a mooring so she wouldn't get jostled at the dock. But Liam was back in Boston. He'd gone on Wednesday to finish some work. Harley didn't trust himself, even with help, to move the boat. So he just kept watch on the fenders and lines and battened down everything in sight. The truth of it was that he was more pissed off than worried. This storm was messing up his plan, the one in which he'd bump into Cassandra on her Saturday walk to town. The girls wouldn't come in weather like this, which meant he'd have to wait a week just to see her face again.

In the afternoon, a lull set in. Harley knew it wouldn't last. Its silence was thick and ominous, the streak of sun unnatural as it slanted through the clouds. At four o'clock all hell broke loose. The low sky split and the rain poured down in tilted sheets. The wind kicked up with vengeance, shoving the oily waves toward shore. Pugwash called and asked for help with the fishing boats. One had come loose already, and they needed to secure more lines. Harley donned foul-weather gear, and fought his way against the gusts. Out beyond the harbor, the water reflected the low-hung sky—cold, slate-gray with a bruise-like edge. In at the docks, it was all white chop.

Pugs and his father were each on a boat, two hunched figures in the rain. It was hard to hear through the din of wind and the pellets of water drilling the dock. But Harley knew what they needed to do. He crouched on the planks, catching the ropes they hurled to him, winding them tight around the chocks. Then Pugs and his father climbed back to the dock, the sturdy boats bobbing, weightless, under their boots. A groan of thunder sounded. All three of them turned and ran, heads bent, toward the small frame hut at the end of the wharf. Once inside, they stood for a moment, catching their breath. Their yellow raingear glistened, pooling water on the floor.

"Wow," said Harley. "I didn't realize how bad it was."

"A stink," said Pugs, "and it's getting worse."

"Harley," said his father, "Billy told me your dad's away. Why don't you come home with us?"

"Thanks, but no. I think I ought to stay on the boat. Just to keep an eye on things."

"You'll call if need us?"

"You know I will."

They plunged out into the storm again. Pugs and his father took off toward town. Harley turned, and fighting the wind, began the trek back along the waterfront.

Across the way, the town looked eerie. Desolate. The shops were closed, and the air had the gloom of winter dusk. Reflected in the windows, Harley could see the dismal sky. Thunder boomed, and a day-bright streak of lightning cracked the plates of glass. In the brilliant flash, Harley saw a small and cowering figure hunched at the door of one of the shops. He squinted through the darkness that followed the snap of light. Yes, someone was there. Someone who clearly needed help. Harley rushed across the street.

"Hey!" he called as he approached. The figure turned, and what he saw did not make sense. It looked like Cassandra, huge blue eyes peering from under a dripping shawl. But even as he stared at her, at that face he'd seen in a dozen drawn-out daydreams, he knew it was impossible. Why would she be here, after all? And how could she have gotten here in weather as wild as this?

"Oh God, is it you? Harley, right?" The trembling voice astonished him almost as much as the first, unlikely glimpse of her. "It's me. Cassandra. What on earth are you doing here?"

"Me?" Harley had to stop for air. He couldn't believe she remembered his name. "What are *you* doing out in this?"

"I'm looking for Pia and Julian."

"What?"

"That guy you saw the other day. Pia's gone off with him again."

"It's pouring rain. That's crazy."

"Well, Julian's crazy. He—" Her voice broke into a terrified squeal as another chord of thunder crashed and a snap of lightning zapped the air.

"This is dangerous," Harley said. He wasn't kidding, either. He could feel the static in his hair. "Here," he ordered. "Put this on." He yanked off his jacket and held it out. She seemed about to argue, then changed her mind and slipped her arms through the giant sleeves.

Harley reached to grab her hand. It wasn't a tender gesture, but the instant he felt her tiny wrist, something inside him melted. He couldn't believe how the whole, soft, trembling entity—silk and bone and fingers—was swallowed whole in his big, rough palm. He pulled her from the doorway and into the teeming street.

"Where are we going?" she called to him, her voice barely audible over the wind.

"To my boat," he said. "It's safer there." She didn't say anything after that. Or if she did, Harley didn't hear it as they sloshed through the puddles and pushed toward the docks. The wind was like a huge, flat hand, trying to shove them back again. Harley felt she might blow away if he didn't keep a grip on her. He clamped her shoulder under his arm as they struggled down the tilted ramp that led to the *Alma*'s slip. He could feel her shivering under the coat, like something rattling in a bag. There was one advantage: The tide was high. Though the water was rough, there was not a big drop from the dock to the boat. Harley gave instructions, then swung down first ahead of her. For a couple of seconds, he balanced there, gauging the motion of the waves before shouting the order "Jump!"

With an ease and speed that startled him, Cassandra leapt across the rails and landed against his chest. For a couple of seconds, she held him tight. Those same small fingers, which moments ago had seemed so fragile in his hand, clutched him with a steely grip. Harley felt his arms fold in—they seemed to be thinking for themselves—enclosing her trembling body in his own unsteady clasp.

It all felt weird. Dramatic. Like a scene in a movie he'd never watch.

⁓

Harley shut the door to the boat, muting the noise of the howling storm. He flicked on a light and Cassandra stood there, shivering.

"Thank you," she murmured, the shawl clutched tight against her throat. "I really thought I was going to die."

"I don't get it," Harley said. "How could you go out the door, with no raincoat, nothing? It's wild out there."

"It wasn't like this when I left the house. I thought that it was over. The sun was—" Her words broke off as her drifting gaze fell on the carvings along the hull. "Oh my God, what *is* this place? Am I on some kind of *magic* boat?" She stared at a scene of mermaids that ran along the starboard wall.

Harley smiled. "No magic. Just some woodwork by my dad."

"Your father did *this*?" Cassandra's eyes roamed across the bulkhead and down the facing wall. "I thought he was a plumber. That's what everybody—"

"He does that, too. He's a talented guy."

A gust of wind slammed against the *Alma*'s side, and Cassandra breathed, "Are we going to sink?"

Harley almost laughed at that, but swallowed his grin when he looked at her face. "No. Don't worry. We're totally safe." A second ticked. "Want to get that raingear off?"

"What?"

"The raincoat. It's dripping wet."

"You're a whole lot wetter than me," she said. Her eyes roved over Harley's shirt, sending slow, hot shivers up his neck. He took the raincoat as she pulled it off. Underneath, her clothes were soaked. The scrolled designs in her clinging top looked like an etching on her skin, which showed with a tinge of pinkness through the thin, transparent cloth. The line of her jeans was dark and low.

"I still can't believe you found me," she said. "It's like some crazy miracle."

Harley's gaze caught in one of the swirls on her shirt. He agreed about the crazy part, but it took his breath that she thought it was a *miracle*.

"Hey," she said, "any chance you'd have a towel?" The question snapped him out of his fog.

"Sure, of course. I've also got some extra clothes. I mean, just for now. If you want to change?"

"I *am* kind of cold. That'd be nice."

"Okay. Wait here. I'll be right back." Harley rushed off to the forward quarters where he slept, and dug in his drawers for something half-decent that she could wear. Thank God they'd done laundry the other day.

"These okay?" he asked her, returning with some dark blue sweats.

"Perfect," she said. "They look so warm."

"You can change up forward. I'll close the door."

"But please don't go away," she begged. "I mean, stay right here. Don't move an inch. I'm really scared to be alone."

He waited in the galleyway as Cassandra fumbled behind the door. Every few seconds, she called to check that he was there. With each bright flash of lightning, she let out a little squeal. Finally, he heard the doorknob click, and she tumbled out in front of him. She looked even tinier in Harley's sweats. Her face was pale and luminous in the oval of the dark blue hood.

"I'm sorry, Harley. I'm usually not such a wimp."

"There's nothing to be sorry for." He reached for her arm, which seemed to float in the dangling sleeve, and guided her toward the cabin and onto a cushioned bunk.

"You need to change, too," she told him, her eyes taking in his clothes again. "You'll catch a cold if you stay like that."

"It can wait."

"No. Go and change."

"Are you sure?"

"I'm sure—but *hurry up*."

In all his life Harley had never moved so fast. In less than thirty seconds, he had ripped off his clothes, yanked out dry ones, and pulled them on. Still zipping his jeans, he pushed through the door. As he entered the cabin, his heart went *thump*.

Chapter 5

Cassandra had unwound her hair and was combing it out to let it dry. Silky and white, it fell down one shoulder right to her waist, shimmering like a stream. She had curled up her legs, and was leaning back against the wall under a carving of ocean waves. She looked like a mermaid, Harley thought. He could almost see the pulsing tail in the S-shaped curve of the dark blue sweats. He grabbed for a rail as the boat rose up on a sudden wave, wobbling as it sank back down. He steadied himself against the wall.

"That's better," she said, looking up at him. "Now both of us are nice and dry."

Harley felt his face grow hot. "Maybe I should make some tea."

"And I should probably call the school." From the elephant trunk of a long, dark sleeve, Cassandra pulled out her phone. "They might be wondering where I am."

As Harley turned to light the stove, she punched the numbers and started to talk. He caught a few words every now and then. *Pia*. And *town*. And *Julian*. Then, he heard her say his name. He spun around and she held out the phone. "Hannah wants to talk to you."

The reception wasn't very good, but Hannah's annoyance was loud and clear.

"I want that girl back up at the school."

"As soon as the rain—"

"Where's your father?"

"Boston."

A gust of wind whined in Harley's other ear. "Don't you Jamisons ever learn?"

43

Harley didn't answer that. Cassandra would hear whatever he said, and any response would have sounded weird. Plus, he hated when Hannah talked like this, like he and Liam were one and the same. "I suppose," she growled, "that he took the car." Harley said yeah, then told her she was breaking up. Tapping a finger, he clicked her off.

"I guess you heard," Cassandra said in a sheepish voice as he passed the cell phone back to her.

"Heard what?"

"About Pia. She's up at school. She wasn't with Julian after all."

"But I thought you said—"

"A few of the girls told me that they saw them. Maybe it got too stormy and Julian changed his mind." Cassandra shifted on the bunk, drawing her knees against her chest. "You must think I'm a total idiot."

"No, I don't. It's nice that you look out for her."

"She's my roommate, you know. We picked from a hat and that's who I got. She's really sweet. Like the little sister I never had." Lightning flashed, and she ducked her face behind her knees. "Do you have a little sister?" she asked, peeking out when a second had passed.

"No sister. No brother. Just me and my dad."

"An only child, just like me. I always wished I had someone else." She paused for a second. "Where's your mom?"

"My mother died when I was two."

"Oh, God. How sad."

"I really don't remember her, so it isn't sad in the usual way."

"But still, you know, a little boy should have a mom." Her wondering gaze drifted through the cabin. "Do you really and truly live on this boat?"

"Yeah," said Harley. "When I'm not at college up in Maine."

"Maine. Oh wow. I heard it's really cold in Maine."

"I've always kind of liked the cold. How about you? Where do you live?"

"New York. Where else? Like everyone at Ocean Watch."

"New York is cool," said Harley. "I've visited with my dad."

"I couldn't wait to get away."

Harley smiled. "Guess it can be crazy, too."

"It isn't that," Cassandra said. "Something happened. Something bad. I just couldn't be there anymore." Her eyes slid up as a splash of water smacked against the windowpane. "It had to do with a guy, of course. It always has to do with a guy."

Harley nodded but didn't speak. He tried to look sympathetic, but his stomach had dropped like a sinker on a fishing line. He should have known there'd be a "guy." How could this gorgeous mermaid girl *not* have a story about a guy?

"Boys can be such bastards," Cassandra went on in a quiet voice. "Sorry, Harley, but it's true. And I don't want Pia getting hurt. She's just so sweet and innocent—and Julian's a creep. I know him from ballet school back home. He's always playing games with girls."

"What kind of games?"

"Stupid stuff. Like, he has these contests with his friends. Who can get the youngest girl? Or the oldest one? Or the most within a certain time?"

Is that what your boyfriend used to do? Harley wondered, watching the tiny frown line in the space above her nose. But, of course, he couldn't ask her that. Instead, he said in an earnest voice, "Not all guys are bastards. But the bastards give us a lousy rap."

"Yeah," said Cassandra. "It isn't right. Something should be done about them."

"Done?"

"Yes, *done*. Karma never happens, or if it does, it takes too long. And in the meantime, innocent girls get used and hurt. Guys like Julian have to be stopped."

"Yeah, okay," said Harley. "But can't you talk to Pia, too? Fill her in on the facts of life?"

"I have. I've tried. I've told her how cute and pretty she is and how careful she has to be with boys. *All* the girls have talked to her." A soft, slow smile tipped her lips. "That's what's so strange about Ocean Watch. Most of the girls know each other from back in New York. Back there, we don't care about anyone else. We're horrid and competitive. This is my first summer here, and I can't believe how different everybody acts. Girls who were mean are suddenly so nice and sweet. Maybe it's the salty air."

Harley nodded but didn't speak. He couldn't stop thinking about the guy. The *boyfriend*. He was probably a dancer, too. Tall and lean, like Julian. Marble cheekbones. Chiseled face. He hated him already. Whoever he was, whatever he'd done. Leaning forward, he nudged Cassandra's mug of tea. She smiled and reached to take it, her small, pale hand wriggling from the length of sleeve. That was when the thunder struck.

The flash that followed blanched the air. Mermaids, monsters, gleaming Tritons on the wall sprang to life in the stark, white snap. Cassandra screamed and Harley jumped. It happened so fast and was just so bright and deafening that for one uncertain second Harley thought a bolt might have actually struck the mast. Relief sank in like a second shock, and he dropped beside her on the bunk.

"Yikes!" she uttered. "That was really horrible. I hope we didn't spring a leak."

"We're okay," he promised her. "It was close enough, but we weren't hit. Plus the *Alma*'s grounded. We've got a lightning rod hooked up."

She turned and stared straight into his eyes, and the trust he saw in that open gaze totally dismantled him. He would have to find, he realized, in places still unknown to him, those things that she seemed to think were there.

"Can you stay with me?" Her voice was airy as a breath.

"Of course I can."

"I mean here, right here. Right next to me."

"I'm not going anywhere."

She settled back against the bunk and gathered her scattered hair. Winding it into a pale, thick coil, she tossed it down her back. For a moment she was quiet, and then she asked, "So what kind of poetry do you like?"

"What?"

"I see some books of poetry."

He followed her eyes to the messy ledge where he and his dad stored their dog-eared library. Of all the choices on the shelf . . .

His cheeks inflamed. "They aren't mine."

"I've always loved poems. Don't you?"

"Yeah, I guess." What an idiot he was; she wasn't his buddy Red Legs, who equated reading poetry with losing your grip on life. "Sometimes I get in the mood."

"Oh, Harley, can you read me one?"

"I wouldn't do that to a poem," Harley answered, not kidding around.

"Oh, please," said Cassandra softly. She slid from the bunk and onto her feet. The mane of hair fell like water down her back as she reached to take a book. She brought it back and settled at his side again. "It would make me feel calm. Just one little poem."

"What do you want me to read?" he asked.

"It doesn't matter. Whatever you like." She curled up her legs, making her graceful body small. Harley thought of mermaids again, and sailors who'd been gone too long and had lost their bearings with the earth. His fingers riffled pages. His hand shook slightly holding the book.

"Searching my heart for its true sorrow,
This is the thing I find to be:
That I am weary of words and people.
Sick of the city, wanting the sea."

His voice sounded foreign, as if it belonged to someone else. Someone he didn't think he'd like. He'd never read a poem aloud. Cassandra, however, was rapt and still. Harley thought he could hear her blink in the space between his words.

When he was finished, she clapped her hands in a way that hardly made a sound. "That was beautiful," she said. "'Sick of the city'—just like me." Harley smiled and passed her the book.

"It's your turn now. You read to me."

"Okay," she said. "But you have to relax." She unfolded her legs and stretched them out along the bunk. "Come on, Harley. Sit with me." She patted the space beside herself, and Harley shifted over, his back against the bulkhead wall. Side by side, they barely fit on the narrow bunk. But it was nice, and as she leaned above the page Harley could smell the fragrance of her still-damp hair.

She read "The Road Not Taken" by Robert Frost. "That's me, too," she murmured when she finished. "The part about the forking roads and how you want to try them both. But when you dance, there's only one."

"'The road less traveled?'"

"Something like that." She read two Emily Dickinson poems and shifted the book toward him again.

Harley chose "In Memorium A.H.H." by Alfred, Lord Tennyson and then "The White Birds" by William Butler Yeats. *"I would that we were, my beloved, white birds on the foam of the sea!"* As Cassandra searched for another poem, he circled his arm around her neck. Her voice was soft and sing-song, stumbling through William Wordsworth's "Daffodils." She settled back against his chest. She was weightless against his body, and the lightness was strange, something that took him past desire. Everything about her seemed so fine and delicate, and he couldn't imagine touching her in other ways beyond this soft protectiveness. This touch that was hardly touch at all.

Outside, the wind continued to wail. Harley and Cassandra nestled on the rocking bunk. The *Alma*'s lines groaned in their chocks on the swelling waves, and from over the docks, the riggings of the sailboats clattered like a million bells. When thunder groaned, he told her not to worry. When lightning flashed, he made a mask of fingers and covered her wide, blue eyes.

Chapter 6

Red Legs wasn't exactly rude. But he certainly wasn't friendly as he handed Harley the keys to one of his father's cabs.

"It's great to meet you," Cassandra said. "Harley told me what an amazing guy you are." She was still in Harley's navy sweats, her mane of hair tumbling down the hoodie's front. In her hand was a dog-eared plastic bag full of her own wet clothes.

"Amazing, huh?" Red Legs looked into Harley's eyes. It was clear what he was thinking. *When did all this happen? And what do you want with one of those girls?*

Hannah had phoned when the storm went into its second lull. She wanted Cassandra back at the house for dinnertime. Harley had made a call to Red Legs and, without an explanation, had asked to borrow one of the cars. Red Legs, of course, had told him yes. He was standing on the sidewalk now, watching as Harley pulled from the curb. He looked pissed off. As if Harley had betrayed a trust.

It was less than five minutes up to the school, but Harley drove slowly to stretch the time. Over the bluffs, the ocean was a leaden gray, its lumpy swells rolling sluggishly toward the shore. The wind had swept some of the clouds away, but off on the horizon, heavy billows were drifting in. They looked to Harley like miles and miles of weighted cloth. A pinprick in the fabric would split the straining seam.

Cassandra gazed out at the brooding scene. "Thanks for taking care of me. I don't know what I would have done if you hadn't come along like that." She turned her face to look at him. "I don't think I've ever felt as safe as I did with you on the boat today."

Harley smiled. "You could have fooled me."

"I mean, you know . . . when you sat with me."

"Yeah," said Harley. "I liked that, too."

"You're different from the guys I know."

"Yeah, I bet." Harley pictured Julian and the other boys from the ballet school with their sleek physiques and well-cut hair.

"That's a *good* thing," Cassandra said. "They're snobby and vain. And they always lie." On her silky forehead a frown appeared, the way it had when she'd spoken of her old boyfriend, and for one split second her face looked hard. In a lighter voice she added, "You're—I don't know . . . real. Like the true-blue guy I've heard about but never actually met—'til now."

"I could say the same for you. I've never met anyone like *you*."

"I'm nothing special," Cassandra said. "Yeah, I dance. But so do a million other girls."

"All the same, you come from a different world than here."

"That doesn't mean it's a better world. I love to dance, but sometimes I want to just break loose. I feel like it's the time for me. This summer, I want to have some fun." She stopped for a moment and widened her eyes. "You know what I'd really love to do? I'd love to go out on your boat again. I mean, out for a ride when the weather's nice."

"You mean it?"

"Yes. In pictures it looks so beautiful. The wavy water, those big white sails."

"We could go next weekend," Harley said.

"Really?"

"Yeah. I just have to find someone to come with us. You need two guys to handle that boat." As Harley said the words out loud, he realized the problem this might entail. One of the guys shouldn't be his father and he already sensed what Red Legs would say. "I'll ask around and let you know."

"Oh, Harley, that's great! I can put my number into your phone." Harley passed his cell phone. He could hardly believe that this was really happening. That this beautiful ballerina was clicking her presence into his life.

⚬⚭⚬

Beyond the jut of branches, the massive shape of Ocean Watch cast its darkness on the sky. Lights in the downstairs windows glowed warm as fire in the gray and drizzly atmosphere.

"Park on the side," Cassandra said as Harley turned into the gravel drive. "There's a door over there. I can sneak right in."

"Why do you have to sneak?"

"I don't feel like meeting Hannah. Plus, I want to find Pia and strangle her."

Harley walked her toward the door. The path was strewn with branches, and off to the side the whole green meadow seemed to hunch. Gusts from the sea whistled through the pointy rocks with a weepy, almost human moan. Suddenly Harley stopped in place. He spun around, peering back from where they'd come. There was no one there. Nothing to see. Yet the sound was unmistakable. There *was* a plaintive human cry at the bottom of the wind's low howl.

The cries seemed to come from somewhere close, yet they also seemed strangely faraway, muted and dim, as if finding their way from under the ground. Cassandra gasped at a sudden thump. Harley reached to take her hand. More thuds sounded, weaker and yet more urgent, and led them to the cellar door, which slanted, ramp-like, against the house. The thumps and cries were coming from there.

"Don't open it!" Cassandra cried as Harley reached down to slip the latch.

"Find out who it is!"

"Help me! Help!" The person inside had heard their voices through the door.

"Someone, help! Before I die!"

Harley shook off Cassandra's hand and knocked the sliver of soggy wood out the metal latch. He flung open the set of double doors, and a figure tumbled out of the dark, falling face down onto the rain-soaked ground. The body shook with tremors, and as Harley turned it over, Cassandra let out a scream.

"Oh my God. It's Julian!"

"Call an ambulance," Harley said.

"No!" rasped Julian violently. "My inhaler—it fell! Just get—"

"It's in the cellar?"

"Yes."

"Stay here, Cassandra," Harley said. "I'll see if I can find it there."

"No! *Don't go!*" Julian's fingers latched like claws to Harley's arms. "Don't leave me with her! Don't—" His breath ran out, but the iron grip on Harley's arm threatened to break his bones.

"I'll go down," Cassandra said. She sprang to her feet and slipped through the doors. She found the inhaler right away. She also brought out a cell phone, which in his panic Julian must have dropped, as well. She passed the inhaler to Harley, and Julian grabbed it from his hand. For several seconds, he pumped away, drinking in the healing mist, his body heaving with each pained gulp. At last, he stopped and lifted his head.

He gazed at Harley dimly, seeming to realize only now that he didn't know who he was. Harley could almost have said the same. The beautiful hotshot Julian was barely recognizable. His fine-boned face was blotchy, smeared with a mix of dirt and tears. He was sopping wet, the filth on his clothes congealed to mud. Streaks of it dripped from his gorgeous curls and squiggled down his neck. Harley might have been amused, if it hadn't been for the asthma part. The guy was really traumatized. He'd thought he was going to die down there.

"Should I call the people you're staying with?" Cassandra asked in a gentle voice.

"Just give me my phone," snapped Julian. He was shaking so hard, he could barely hold it in his hand, let alone punch the numbers in.

A slant of light fell across the driveway as a door opened up on the side of the house. Hannah appeared in the yellow glare, a hulking silhouette. Julian started to gasp again as she stomped across the driveway, her fisherman's galoshes splashing the squares of light.

"What on earth is going on?" She towered over the three of them, hands on her massive hips. Julian wheezed dramatically.

"They attacked me!" he rasped. "The . . . bunch of them."

"The bunch of who?"

"Those bitches! Those girls. Those—"

"Don't say 'bitches,'" Hannah growled.

"*Witches* then! Those *witches*. They locked me in the cellar! I lost my inhaler! I couldn't breathe."

"You seem to be breathing all right to me."

Julian choked in reply to that. "They pushed me in!" he sputtered. "It was dark down there! They locked the door!"

Hannah drew in closer, peering down at his mud-streaked face. "You couldn't fight off a couple of girls?"

"It wasn't just a couple of girls! It was a pack! And they were as strong as Amazons!"

"Which girls?" demanded Hannah. "I want a list of names."

"How would I *know*? They came up from behind like a—"

"You didn't actually see them then." Hannah waited for him to speak, and when he didn't answer: "What were you doing here today? Classes were canceled for the boys."

"I wasn't doing anything. I—why are you putting this on *me*? They locked me in a cellar. I could have *died*! Do you *understand*?"

"He's lying!" cried Cassandra. "No one would do a thing like that."

"Am I Houdini?" Julian shrilled. "Do you think I locked *myself* down there?"

"I don't know what happened, but—"

"Don't lie! You know. *All* of you know!"

"Here's what *I* know," said Hannah, looming over Julian. "You were trespassing on the property. I'll talk to the girls; you can count on that. I don't approve of pranks like this. But I'm going to tell you one more time: Stay away from Ocean Watch when you don't have any business here." Hannah turned to Harley then. "I'll give the same advice to you."

"He drove me home!" Cassandra cried. "If it wasn't for him, I'd—"

"You'd what? Learn to have a little sense? You went off on a silly goose chase. For no good reason on this earth."

"Oh, there was a reason," Cassandra said, fixing Julian with a glare. He opened his mouth to answer her, but Hannah cut him off.

"All of you, I've had enough. Harley, you get out of here. And you, Cassandra, go up and change. Dinner's in a half an hour." She saved her last for Julian. "Can you stand up on your own two feet or do I need to carry you?"

"Don't touch me," he snarled as he pulled to his knees.

Harley met Cassandra's eyes. She shook her head as if to say that Julian was crazy. *Call me,* she mouthed, holding her cell phone near her face. Then, blowing a kiss, she turned and ran toward the door of the house. The last thing he saw was her long, pale hair, like a ribbon of streaming light.

Julian was limping as they walked up the drive toward the front of the house. An act, suspected Harley, so Hannah would feel bad for him. He stopped at Red Legs's car and peered into her angry face. "Does he need a ride? I could take him home."

"No," said Hannah sharply. "Mr. J and I are going to have a little chat."

"I can wait if you want," said Harley. He wanted like hell to stick around and find out what was going on.

Hannah scowled. "Get back to the boat where you belong."

"Yeah, all right. So long," he said to Julian.

The dancer answered with shrug, a muddy curl falling over one eye. *You're welcome, jerk. It was a pleasure to save your life.*

The storm swooped back in a fury that night. One of the yachts in the harbor broke loose, and some men from town went out in a scow to rescue her. Harley watched the spectacle as bobbing lights jittered on the water, and the tall, white boats circled on the ends of thread. He found it hard to get to sleep. He'd called Cassandra several times, but she'd turned off her phone apparently. He wanted to know if she'd talked to her friends and had found out what had happened. And more than that, he wanted to hear voice again. He wanted to say goodnight to her.

Liam called from Boston, and Harley told him the *Alma* was fine and everything was battened down. "Are *you* battened down?" Liam asked. Harley said yeah, but that was a lie. He wasn't battened down at all. He was floating away, his anchor loose. Already he could feel the knots slipping from their safe, tight hold.

Chapter 7

Harley slid onto a twirling stool at the counter of Nellie's Luncheonette. He smiled and waved at Becky, who was setting down a plate of eggs in front of Wally Callister. The place was crowded, everyone buzzing about the storm.

"Hey, Harley," Becky greeted him, heading over to where he sat. "Some crazy night. You weather through?"

"Yeah, no problem. The *Alma*'s fine."

"I heard one of the boats in the fleet broke loose."

"They got her in."

"Thank God for that," Becky smiled. "I bet you're pretty hungry. Everyone's got an appetite."

"I actually didn't come to eat. I came to ask a favor of you."

"Sure. What's up?"

"The thing is this—" Harley paused. "Maybe some coffee would be good."

Becky was back in seconds with a steaming cup and a pitcher of cream. "You've got me really curious."

Harley dumped in his usual load of sugar and churned it with a spoon.

"I wanted to tell you . . . I met a girl."

Becky blinked. She leaned against the counter, waiting for Harley to tell her more. "It's okay," she coaxed him. "What else were you supposed to do with Mairin hooking up with Smits? So, who is she? A Colby girl?"

"No," said Harley, bracing himself. "She's someone from here. Well, not from here exactly. She's someone from the ballet school." Becky's body straightened up. On her soft, pink face, her freckles looked suddenly dark and hard.

Harley raced on. "I met her last week when my dad and I did some work up there. And, yesterday, she somehow got stranded in the storm and I brought her to the boat."

"I heard that from Billy," Becky said, using Pugs's real-life name. "Red told him he let you use a car. I didn't think it was more than that. More than you just being nice."

"You're going to like her," Harley said. "And she'll like you. I know she will. I just need you to have an open mind."

"Don't put it like that."

"Oh, come on, Becks, you're not like the dummies in this town. Everyone at Ocean Watch isn't some fiend from hell."

"Of course, they're not. It's just, you know . . . I guess you'd call it loyalty."

"To what?"

"To the town. To Mrs. Flynn."

"I understand that," said Harley. "I mean, feeling bad for Teddy's mom—"

"And what about your father? Have you forgotten what happened to him?"

"That's all ancient history now. And hating an entire place because of a few bad incidents just doesn't make any sense."

"It's not all ancient history. That school is always screwing the town. Buying up all the hillside land. Kicking out people when they do. They get all kinds of tax breaks we don't get, and they never do anything for us."

"Yeah, okay. The powers-that-be are greedy bums. But it's not the fault of the students there."

"Maybe not. But you don't see *them* being very nice. They come here every summer and all they do is walk around with their noses up."

"She isn't like that, I promise, Becks."

From across the shop, a customer called for Becky and she slid away from Harley, stopping to fetch the coffee pot. He watched as she refilled the cups and chatted with Wally and some of the guys. A few minutes later, she shuffled back. She stood in front of Harley's seat.

"So what are you asking me to do?"

Harley's heart popped up to his throat. He swallowed hard before he spoke. "She wants to go for a sail sometime. I told her that I'd take her. But I need for you and Pugs to come."

Becky frowned. She took forever to answer him. "I don't know," she finally said. "I just can't imagine doing that."

"Doing what? You love to sail."

"I mean, hanging out with one of those girls. Finding something to say to her."

"Don't be crazy, Becky. She's a regular person, just like you."

"She's not like me. And let's not pretend she is, all right?"

"Really, I swear, she's not what you think. She's sweet and not a snob at all. She wants to have fun this summer. Can't you give her half a chance?"

"I want to, but I—"

"What?"

"You know what." Becky's eyes dropped down to the apron around her waist. Her fingers toyed with the frayed, red strings. "I'd feel so self-conscious being with her. Some fancy ballerina. She's probably rich and lives in New York. Look at me. What on earth would we talk about?"

"You could talk about a million things! Like how you go to college. How your dream is to work with special-needs kids. You could talk about the weather, and if worse comes to worst, you could talk about me. How great I am. What a fabulous friend I've been to you and how happy you are that I finally found someone new."

Becky cracked a slow, faint smile. For a moment, she chewed on her bottom lip. "Yeah, all right. I guess I could go on your stupid sail."

"Really? You will!" Harley popped up and bent across the counter to kiss her on the cheek. "You're an angel," he said. "Now, see if you can work on Pugs."

"What? Are you kidding? You haven't talked to Billy yet?"

"I know what he'll say."

"And what makes you think he'll listen to me?"

"He's crazy about you, Becky. Just turn on the charm. He'll do whatever you want him to."

"You're full of it, Harley Jamison. I think you get it from your dad."

Under the saucer, Harley stuck a couple of bills. "The coffee was great. And thanks a mil. I owe you big."

He was halfway across the luncheonette when Becky called out, "So, what's her name?"

Harley turned and stopped in place. He'd never said it to anyone yet and it felt momentous to do so now.

"Cassandra," he said, his voice caressing every inch of syllable. He loved the way it sounded. He said it again a hundred times as he walked down toward the waterfront and then up the winding hill.

❦

He waited in the spotty shade across the way from the Black estate. Cassandra was already ten minutes late. He kept checking his watch and peering around the pine tree that marked the turning of the road and the final stretch toward Ocean Watch. Finally he caught sight of her. She was walking quickly down the hill, clinging to the wooded side. Even in the shadows her hair seemed silvery with sun. She was wearing a tiny pair of shorts and underneath, pale-pink tights with the feet cut off. Harley noticed everything—her gold, metallic sandals, a Band-Aid on her middle toe, complicated crisscrossed straps—as she neared his shaded hiding place. He could hear his heart, a crazy thumping in his ears.

"There you are!" Her voice was high, excited, as Harley stepped out from behind the tree. She ran into his arms, and he held her tight, feeling again those fine, impossibly slender bones. She made him feel enormous, like some great and solid rock.

Drawing away, she looked at him. In her large, blue eyes, he could see the sky—the actual sky behind him, white clouds sailing across the gleam. Her hair was pulled into in a knobby bun with two white flowers at the side. Harley leaned down, unthinking, and pressed his lips to her upturned mouth. He lingered, and she let him, and he was the one who finally, slowly, drew away.

Her face was flushed. "I'm sorry I'm late."

"It's okay."

"It was really hard to get away." She tucked a couple of loosened strands of hair in the curve behind her ear. "Everyone's so crazy now. And classes are going overtime because of auditions coming up."

"Auditions?"

"Yes. For the final performance we do each year. I'm sure you must have been to one."

"Sorry, no," said Harley. He knew what she meant. The show that Ocean Watch put on at the end of every August in a theatre out in Sandy Bluff. Hannah had said, he dimly recalled, that Liam's old flame, the Russian, had come to the school to stage it this year. None of the locals ever went. Another demonstration of what the town called "loyalty."

"Well, I hope you're going to go this time," Cassandra said with a beaming smile. "We're doing my favorite ballet, *Giselle*."

"That's great," said Harley. He smiled then. "Not that I ever heard of it."

"It's the saddest, most beautiful story on earth. I'll tell you about it when we have time." She paused for a beat. "Are we going sailing on Saturday?"

"It looks pretty sure," said Harley. "I'll try to let you know tonight."

"I won't turn off my phone this time. No matter what anybody says."

Harley glanced up at her last few words, but Cassandra rushed on in a secretive voice, "By the way, I found out what happened with Julian."

"Is he okay?"

"Yeah, he'll be fine. He twisted his foot or something, but he'll be back in a day or two."

"Good. I'm glad. Things could have ended up much worse."

"They didn't mean to hurt him. They only did it to scare him off."

"Who?" asked Harley.

"A few of the girls. No one thought he'd freak like that and drop his inhaler on the floor."

"All the same, that was a dangerous thing to do. If you and I hadn't come along, Julian might have—"

"Do you know what he did?" Cassandra cried. "The day of the storm he kidnapped Pia from the house—"

"Kidnapped?"

"Well, he *took* her. Christina and Dagmar found them in an empty barn on one of the estates. They were lying on a pile of hay! She has three huge hickeys on her neck."

"The guy's a creep. But it still wasn't cool to lock him in the cellar. How long were they planning to leave him there?"

"I don't know. A couple of hours. Just to give him time to think."

"I get what they were doing, but it really could have turned out bad."

Cassandra looked down. "You're right. I know." Her long, white fingers fidgeted. "But nothing happened in the end. And maybe Julian got the point and won't be doing his stupid stuff. Not with Pia anyway."

"And your friends, those girls, did they get the point?"

"Harley, please. They just wanted to send a message. We want him to stay away from her." She crinkled her eyes as she looked at him. "I told you how it is up there. We look out for each other, like sisters would. Is that really so different from you and your friends?"

Harley mulled it over. He remembered fights with the lame-ass guys on Baxter Street when one of them insulted Pugs. He remembered, too, doing something just as stupid as what Cassandra's friends had done, burying Richy Hartigan up to his neck in sand. But they were a whole lot younger then. Probably only twelve or so. And something else seemed different, too. It was sexist, he knew, but it seemed sort of odd and creepy for girls to do violent stuff like this. Especially such lovely girls, who looked so sweet and delicate with little, pink flowers in their hair.

To Cassandra, he said, "I understand. Friends do crazy things for friends."

Cassandra smiled. "Speaking of friends, is Red Legs the guy who's coming on the boat with us?"

"No, this one's name is Pugwash. His girlfriend's Becky. She's super nice."

"Your friends have really funny names."

"They're pirate names from when we were kids. They just kind of stuck, except for mine."

"What was yours?"

"I was Captain Blood."

"I love it," said Cassandra. "And I really can't wait to meet your friends. I can't believe you've known them your entire life."

"That tends to happen in little towns."

"I think it's nice. And I like this town. I don't understand why there's such bad feeling up at the school." From around the bend, a crunch of wheels sounded on the gravel road. Harley drew Cassandra back as

Wally Callister's truck lurched by, the logo of a dancing clam on its battered silver side. He was pretty sure Wally hadn't seen them there.

"You haven't heard the story then?"

Cassandra looked back at Harley. "You mean the one about that boy?"

Harley nodded. "Teddy Flynn."

"Yes, I heard. It's really sad."

"His mom has never been the same."

"Did you know him?"

"Sort of. He lived in town. He was older than me, so we never hung out."

"It's horrid that he was so depressed. I mean, sad enough to take his life—"

"Teddy didn't—"

"I've felt like that, so I understand."

"You've felt like you wanted to—" The conversation was switching gears, and Harley wasn't certain in which direction he ought to go. He drew a breath. "What on earth could ever have made you feel that bad? If it's okay to ask, I mean."

"I told you, Harley, that day on the boat."

"That guy?"

She nodded. "I don't want to talk about it now. I'm only saying that when people have their hearts destroyed . . . well, sometimes they do crazy things."

"I hate that guy," he muttered. "Really, I mean it. Whoever he is."

"I love that you hate him." Cassandra smiled. "I hate him, too, but it's over now. I'm trying to forget the past."

"Some people can't," said Harley. "Like my buddy, Pugs, for instance. That's why I have to ask you not to mention Teddy Flynn while we're on the boat next Saturday."

"Were Pugs and him close?"

"Not really. But his godfather, Mike, was one of the cops who first came on the scene that night. Mike believed—" Harley broke off. "Never mind. The whole thing happened so long ago. Let's just say the town and the school don't agree on the how and why of Teddy's death."

"But it's all been proven, hasn't it? That's what everybody says."

"You mean everyone at Ocean Watch."

"I know the girls who found him that night."

"What do you mean?"

"They told me all about it. It was toward the end of August, a week before they were going home. They got this idea to go down to the bluff behind the school. There's a ledge of rocks, they told me, high above the water, and you can walk out to the very edge. It makes you dizzy, Dagmar said, so you almost feel like you want to jump. Anyway, they were close to the edge when they saw this person lying there. He looked like he was sleeping. But when they got close, something about his neck seemed wrong. Like it wasn't on his body right." Cassandra paused and shivered. "Then they saw the pool of blood, and they realized he was dead."

Harley's breath felt caught in his throat. In all the years of hearing the story again and again, a hundred different versions of it, he'd never heard this—that the body was found by a group of girls.

"I thought he was seen by someone out a window. One of the teachers, who called the police."

"The teacher may have called the police. But my friends were the ones who found him there. They were only thirteen; they were traumatized. He was on his back, Christina said, and the look on his face was horrible. His eyes were open really wide, as if he had been *scared* to death." Harley stared into her cloud-filled gaze. He struggled to pick his words with care, but there wasn't a way to speak about Teddy's death with grace.

"Cassandra," he said when some seconds had passed, "the people who knew Teddy best don't believe he jumped. They think that something happened up there."

"Something like what?" Cassandra's eyes grew rounder.

"That's the problem. We don't know. They had some kind of inquest, but it all seemed biased toward the school. In the end, some judge declared that he jumped or accidentally fell."

"And why don't you believe that?"

"Teddy was happy. He wasn't depressed. His friends and family swear to that."

"Whatever happened, it's all so sad. It's hard to even think of it."

"Yeah, I know. I'm sorry." Harley reached out and took her hands, squeezing them in his own. He didn't mention Teddy's hands. How Mike had said they were all torn up, as if he'd been clinging desperately, probably to a window frame. "You asked me why the town and the school have problems. Teddy's one of the reasons why. There are others, too, but—" Harley broke off. He was not in the mood to tell her the sordid story about Ravenska and his dad. Nor could he begin to explain the list of grievances.

It would touch on just too many things, including their relationship— if that's what they were starting to have—and all the reasons it might not work. You'd have to live here to understand. The old, old story, as Pugs would say: money and power always win out. After the "Teddy incident," the school with its bigwig lawyers had stomped all over the local police. Facts and details were covered up and Teddy was portrayed as someone he had never been. Harley knew now, if what Cassandra had told him was true, that the school had hidden even the most essential facts, like who'd found Teddy's body first. This shouldn't have surprised him, but somehow it still did.

For a few long moments, neither spoke. Cassandra pulled her cell phone out, glancing at the time.

"I'm sorry, Harley. I have to get back before Madame notices I'm gone. Thanks so much for meeting me."

"Thanks for sneaking away like this."

"I won't have to sneak on Saturday. I have permission from my mom and she's already called the school." Cassandra smiled up at him. "I told her all about you. How you saved me in the thunderstorm. How you live on a boat and go to college up in Maine. She already thinks you're wonderful. She's so happy I'm having fun again."

"Yeah, me, too," said Harley, not totally sure what he meant by that. The whole conversation had rattled him. Plus, it made him feel weird to know she'd discussed him with her mom. "I'll let you know when I hear from Pugs. Oh, one last thing—on Saturday, don't wear a dress. And sneakers are best for sailing. Bring a sweater; it might get cold."

"Aye, aye, captain," Cassandra said. She stuck her phone back into her shorts. Then, blowing a kiss, she drew away and swung around the bend of pine. Harley stepped onto the empty road and watched as she ran up the hill, easily and quickly as if it were nothing at all to her. The late-day sun struck her hair and shimmered on the shade's rough edge.

Chapter 8

Harley spotted them right away. Like clockwork, they came around the bend, heading for the chocolate shop. Six of them, as always. Sun on their dresses. Flowers fluttering in their hair. He zoomed in on Cassandra, and felt a pinching in his heart. She was wearing white, pants and top, and her hair was wound in a long, thick braid. She looked even more beautiful, he thought, than the first time he laid eyes on her, a blot of light in the orb of his binoculars. He climbed from the *Alma* and sprinted up the tilting ramp. At the entrance to the docks he paused, wiping his hands against his jeans. His palms were wet. He was sweating like a twelve-year-old.

From across the street, Cassandra spotted him and waved. The other girls turned in unison, heads inclined on those long, thin necks. Harley waved back, and Cassandra motioned for him to come. Holy shit. She wanted him to meet her friends. His eyes ran down his faded jeans to the ratty deck shoes on his feet. At least he'd worn his hole-less shirt.

As he crossed the street, he could feel the whole group watching him. They blurred in his vision as he approached, a mash of colors that made him think of candy. Soft, pale mints and Easter-colored M&M's. Up close they came into focus, and now they suddenly looked like birds. Thin, exotic, spindly birds who might, he thought, decide to peck his eyeballs out.

"Harley!" called Cassandra. She reached for his hand, all smiles, and pulled him toward the group. "This is Harley, everyone!"

His cheeks inflamed as their eyes homed in, and a quiet chorus mumbled, "Hi."

Then Cassandra went around the group, introducing each of them. First: Christina Whitley, the tall, thin blonde whom Harley and his buddies had nicknamed Princess Ice. She nodded and gave him half a smile. They'd named her right. With those cool and glinting sapphire eyes, she looked like something made of glass.

"I think I've seen you up at school." Her voice was flat and chilly, too. "You and your father fix things, right?"

Harley nodded. "From time to time." Just call me Mr. Fix-It Guy.

"And here are Blanca. And Varya." (Conchita and Vampire Sally). Harley said hello to them. Blanca was dark, exotic. She gazed at him as if from some enormous height. Harley found himself staring at her nostrils, two beautiful holes that flared at the edges, as if she were smelling something bad. Varya's eyes were velvety, the brown so deep it blended with the pupil's black. Her nickname also fit just right. Bloodless skin and crimson lips. When she said "hello," the *o* dropped down an octave so it felt more like "goodbye."

"This is Dagmar," Cassandra went on, and Spy, in her big, black glasses, flashed a smile and murmured "Hi." She was looking Harley over. He could sense her gaze behind the shades slipping southward from his waist. He felt like he was being peeled.

"And finally, my roommate, Pia," Cassandra announced as she turned to Moon.

"Hi, Harley," the tiny redhead said. She took a step forward, extending a hand. Her fingers were as small as matchsticks, yet Harley could feel, like current, a pulsing strength in each slim bone.

"Well," said Cassandra. "We'd better go. Wish us all a *bon voyage!*"

No one did. But Pia waved as they drew away. "Don't fall overboard!" she called. Harley waved back. At least little Moon was on his side. Lovesick Moon with the three fat hickeys on her neck. Cassandra blew a kiss to her and latched on to Harley's arm.

"Wow," he murmured. "That was weird." He could still feel them staring at his back. Later, he knew, he'd find the marks, little, pinkish almond shapes seared into his skin.

"What do you mean?" Cassandra asked, slowing her steps to look at him.

"Are you kidding me?"

"No. What happened?"

Harley gazed back at her innocent eyes. "They just weren't exactly friendly, is all."

"Don't be silly, Harley. I could tell by their faces they thought you were cute. They just want to make sure you're nice. And good."

"Good?"

"They know about my boyfriend—my old one, last year—and they don't want me getting hurt again."

"Well, they don't have to worry," Harley said. "And neither do you, I hope you know." He squeezed her hand and pulled her forward toward the docks. "One of these days you're going to have to tell me what the hell that bastard did."

"He stole from me. Something that you can't get back."

Harley opened his mouth to speak, but Cassandra suddenly pulled from his clasp. "Come on!" she called. Smiling, she began to run. Harley sprinted after her, catching her by the swinging braid just as she reached the dock. He pulled her close and kissed her, which he'd wanted to do from minute one.

⚮

When they reached the boat, Pugs and Becky were already there. One glance at Cassandra, and Becky went green. Even in her sailing clothes, Cassandra looked like a picture in a magazine. Her thin, white top fluttered slightly in the breeze as she lifted each graceful dancer's leg

73

over the rail and onto the boat. Pugwash stared as if at something from outer space.

"Hey there, Becky," Harley said in a high and way-too-cheerful voice. "Cassandra, this is Becky. And this is my buddy, Pugs."

"Hi," said Cassandra, reaching a hand toward Becky. "It's great to meet you. Hello, Pugs."

"Hi," said Becky. "His name is Billy. Actually." Pugs responded with a grunt.

"Sorry. *Billy*." Cassandra giggled, glancing around. "I'm so excited. I've never been out on a boat before."

"You'll like it, I'm sure," said Becky. Then filling the silence that followed that: "I brought some food. And I made a bunch of brownies, too."

"Great," said Harley. "Thanks a lot." He moved toward the stern where Pugwash stood. "And thanks for coming. Really, man."

"I'm here against my will," said Pugs, growling the words in Harley's ear.

Becky grimaced. So was she. She climbed into the cabin to put away the food she'd brought. "Can I stow your bag?" she asked Cassandra, peeking out. She took the silver pocketbook. After several minutes, Becky came back up to the cockpit, where Harley and Pugs were undoing the ropes. "I can take care of the forward lines."

"What should I do?" Cassandra asked as everyone scrambled to a post.

Harley smiled. "Just relax. Next time out, we'll put you to work."

In less than a minute the lines had been freed and the *Alma* was motoring through the fleet. Once they cleared the harbor, Harley pulled the mainsail up and killed the engine with a flick. Cassandra watched in wonder as the huge, white handkerchief filled with wind. Pugwash worked the jib up front, hauling in lines, winding the winch. There was noisy chaos of flapping rope, and then, suddenly, perfect calm.

"Oh my God. How beautiful!" Cassandra exhaled as the *Alma* glided forward, flying on the full, white wings. For several moments no one spoke, and the only sound was the steady whooshing of the waves.

❧

They sailed straight east away from the shore. The wind was perfect. Not too strong, but good enough to keep them moving briskly, heeling gently to the side. Harley and Pugs took turns at the helm, while the girls worked hard at keeping the conversation up. At first they'd talked about practical stuff—the sails, the ropes, the weather—but once they wore those subjects out, the silences grew longer and Pugs's one-word comments hovered in the air like blimps. It was only after they'd broken out the Heineken that the scowl on his face began to melt. He laughed aloud when Cassandra said she'd never had a beer before.

"I've been drinking the stuff since I was twelve," he told her in a crowing voice. As if that was something to brag about.

"There are lots of things I've never done that people do when they're twelve years old," Cassandra admitting, smiling.

"Really? Like what?" asked Becky. She was inching closer to Pugwash now, relieved that he'd finally started to talk. Harley shared the sentiment.

"Like riding a bike. Or camping. All I've ever done is dance."

"Wow," said Becky. "When did you start?"

"I was six years old when I took my first class. I liked it a lot, and pretty soon I was taking classes every day. Then two a day. Then three and four—"

"Four classes a *day?*" squealed Becky. "When do you get to live your life?"

"That's the thing. It *is* my life."

"But what about school and friends and stuff?"

"All my friends are dancers, too. And I actually don't go to school."

"I should've been a ballet boy," Pugs remarked through a sip of beer. He'd never been too big on school.

"It's not like that," Cassandra explained. "I have tutors at home three times a week. I still have to study every night."

"It doesn't sound fun," said Becky. "I guess you must really love ballet."

"It's like being a nun," Cassandra said. She giggled and took a sip of beer. "At least, that's what one of our teachers says."

"Hear that, Harley?" Pugwash grinned.

Becky punched him in the arm. To Cassandra, she said, "I hope it's not as bad as that."

"Being a ballerina is a sacred dedication. That's what Madame Ravenska says. We have to stay pure and focused. And the worst distraction of all is boys." She made a face, and everyone laughed. Everyone but Harley. Alarms had gone off at the mention of the woman's name. "She, of course, had hundreds of lovers when she was young. But she says that she regrets it now. Men, she says, devour your soul, and it's best to stay away from them."

"She sounds all warm and fuzzy," said Pugs. Harley forced himself to smile. He could only imagine what they'd say if they knew that this Ravenska was the one with whom Liam had had his short-lived fling. That his scruffy dad was one of those soul-devouring men.

Becky's voice broke into his thoughts. She was talking to Cassandra, a playful glimmer in her eyes. "Did you know," she said, "that Ocean Watch actually *was* a convent before it became a ballet school?"

"Yes, I heard," Cassandra replied. "Ravenska lives in what used to be the chapel. It has stained-glass windows and marble floors, and it still has the Stations of the Cross."

"Weird," said Pugwash, under his breath.

"There's a spooky story about those nuns," Becky went on, making her voice mysterious. "There were twelve of them, and every week they'd walk to town. The people used to call them Air because when they came out on foggy days, their long, gray veils blended with the atmosphere."

"Oooh," said Cassandra. "Just like ghosts."

"My grandmother said the kids were all afraid of them. The story was that if one of the Air should meet your eye, something bad would happen to you."

"Something bad *did* happen," Pugwash said above his beer. A gust of wind ran through his hair, and some reddish frizz fell over one eye. "It was back in 1970. Some family friend was visiting the Mortimers. The Mortimers owned that mansion that they turned into the Breeze Hotel. He played the organ like a pro, and he started to play for the nuns at mass. Then one day—"

"An *organist*?" croaked Harley. "The last time I heard this story the guy was a photographer."

"I heard he was a gardener," Becky said with a little laugh.

"An *organist*," insisted Pugs, "who had an 'accident' up there. The next time people saw him, he was missing three fingers from his hand."

Cassandra squealed. "That's horrible!"

"And that's not the end of it," Pugs went on. "A few weeks later when the nuns were walking through the town, this bad little kid threw a rock at one of them. The nun turned around. She pulled her hand from under her sleeve and wagged it at the little kid. She was missing three fingers, too."

Pugs nodded grimly for emphasis. "Soon after that, news got out that one of the nuns was pregnant. Overnight, the convent closed and all the sisters went away, never to be seen again."

"I don't get it," Cassandra said. "What happened to their fingers?"

"Punishment for their sin," said Pugs.

"The 'Air' nuns cut their *fingers* off?"

Pugs gazed past her and toward the bow. "Nasty things involving men are kind of a tradition there."

"Oh, hush up, Billy," Becky said.

"Yeah, hush up," said Harley. He knew where Pugs was going with this, and he wasn't in the mood for it. "Hey, heads up. Let's come about." He nosed the boat straight into the wind.

There was brief and noisy confusion again as lines went loose and the flapping sails crossed over the decks. When everything settled down again, they were at an angle sailing north, heading up the coast. The sky was still blue in the glowing west, but the sun was starting its slow descent. It hung in the air like a great, round lantern on a string. For a while, conversation stopped as the lantern lowered slowly, turning the water to liquid light. The whole horizon simmered like flame, and bit by bit the orb descended toward the sea. There was one last glimpse, like the top of a dome, and the punctured lantern dropped from sight. For long, exquisite minutes, the shreds of fire lingered in the atmosphere. Then the fire cooled to dusky pink, and violet clouds streaked across the dimming blue.

"How beautiful!" Cassandra cried. She inched toward Harley at the helm. He could feel the trembling in her hand as he reached to take it in his own.

Twilight fell, and they all sat in the cockpit, eating the food that Becky had brought. Harley and Pugs took turns at the wheel, and the girls sat side by side. Harley could not stop watching them. It was clear that they were getting along. He could hear Cassandra asking Becky about herself. What was she studying at school? Did she find the courses very hard? Sometimes they'd laugh. At other times, their heads would lean together and their voices would dip into the whisper zone, so Harley imagined that he was being talked about. It made him self-conscious to think of this. Becky had known him all his life. Every stupid thing he'd done.

To Pugwash, he whispered, "I told you so. I told you they would hit it off."

"Becky's just being nice," said Pugs. But Harley knew this wasn't true. Becky was really talking, telling Cassandra about herself. How all her life she'd wanted to be a teacher. How she wanted to work in a nursery school with kids with special needs. Cassandra was asking questions; she was genuinely interested.

Harley said, "They like each other. You can tell."

"I don't see it," Pugwash scowled.

"What the hell is wrong with you?"

"I'll tell you what's wrong," said Pugwash. "I've been thinking all night of Mairin. The way it used to be with us. Those sails we'd take when—"

Harley moved abruptly, shielding Pugwash from the girls. "Why in hell are you bringing that up?"

"She knew how to sail. She was one of us. Becky and her are still real tight, and no one's going to take her place."

"No one's taking anyone's place."

"Don't be a goddamn traitor, Blood. They're all the same, those people up there."

"Are you back on that?"

"Yeah, I'm back, and I'll never forget. Teddy didn't kill himself. And he wasn't a spaz. He didn't fall out the window."

"It's over, Pugs. Can't you give it a rest?"

"Over, huh? Have you seen his mom? She's cross-eyed, crazy, crackers, and it happened all because of that. And Teddy's dad, he never came back. Couldn't stand to live in a town where the rich guys have the power and the regular people just get shit."

"Okay, okay," said Harley, his voice just barely audible, "but Cassandra has nothing to do with that. It's her first damn summer at the school. She just found out who Teddy *is*."

"Doesn't matter. They're all the same."

"Can you just shut up?" said Harley. "One small favor. That's all I ask. Don't mess up this night for me."

"Yeah, I'll shut up," growled Pugwash. "You won't hear another word from me." He shook back his hair and yelled across the cockpit. "Yo, Becky, hey. Grab some beers. Let's go up on the forward deck."

Becky grinned. "Are you trying to tell me you want to make out?"

"Yeah. Whatever." Pugs moved off.

Harley watched until they disappeared, their shadows lost behind the mast. He turned to Cassandra. "You want to steer?"

"Me? Are you kidding?"

"Just give it a try." He took a step back, carving a space between his body and the wheel, and Cassandra slid in with room to spare. He placed her hands on the wooden spokes and set his own on top of them. He fought off thoughts of Mairin, pissed at Pugs for stirring them up. With her, it would never have been like this. She'd have shoved him off if he ever tried to steer for her. Harley would have a bloody shin if he hemmed her in, if he pressed her like so against the wheel. He lowered his head and breathed in the girl who was really there. Soft and sweet and pliable. Her hair smelled like soap and nighttime breeze, and it felt like silk on the scruff of his jaw.

"I like your friends," she murmured. "Becky's so nice. I feel like I've known her all my life."

"Yeah," said Harley. "She has that effect."

"Billy doesn't care for me. But that's all right. I like him because he's your good friend."

"Your friends don't like me either," Harley said, smiling against her hair.

"They will. I promise. They'll come around."

"Next time," Harley whispered, "let's go somewhere by ourselves. We could take a drive to Green Banks. Have dinner in a place out there."

"I'd love that more than anything."

"How about next Saturday? My dad will be back and I'll have the car, if you don't mind driving in a Jeep."

"I wouldn't care if we drove in a yellow school bus. I'm just not sure if I'll be free. Auditions are on Thursday, and right after that rehearsals start. Remember I told you about *Giselle*?"

"I remember, sure. But they can't hold rehearsals on Saturday night."

"They can hold them any time they want. But let's just hope they don't." Cassandra leaned back against his chest, nuzzling slightly into him. Harley bent over and kissed her cheek. The sensitive *Alma* nosed off course, and he eased her back, gently guiding Cassandra's hands.

"Do you feel it?" he whispered against her hair. "Can you tell when the wind goes out of the sails?"

His mouth was just above her ear. Right at the edge of its curving rim. He didn't plan to kiss it, to close his lips on the soft, cool shape. But once he started, he couldn't stop, and he found himself lost in the delicate swirls, the tender, salty seashell that traveled round and round. He could feel her trembling in his arms, so weightless and small, so hurtable, and it stirred the strangest longing to crush and protect her both at once. Yet when he leaned down to kiss her mouth, his own limbs seemed to lose their strength. The touch of her lips made bone and muscle melt away. And when he raised his head again, he had to clasp the sturdy wheel to center himself in place.

He didn't trust his voice to talk, and they stood pressed close, in silence, as twilight deepened into night. Along the coast, the cliffs drew a jagged silhouette, and lights from the high-up mansions shimmered dimly through the dark like a dusky string of pearls. Farther out on the jutting bluff, the beam from the tower of Ocean Watch cast its glow across the sea. It didn't move, but it seemed to, following the *Alma* like a vigilant, amber eye. When Harley and Liam sailed at night, they never failed to mention the human quality of that light. Harley thought it had something to do with what had been seen inside that room. Tonight, its gaze unnerved him. Maybe because Pugs had mentioned Teddy Flynn. Maybe because he was falling in love and he felt the eye was watching, beaming its warning from the shore.

∽

The wheels of the car, which Red Legs had let Harley use, crunched on sand and pebbles as they passed through the tall, stone portals that marked the entrance to Ocean Watch. The meadow was dark, and the house itself seemed deep in sleep.

Cassandra unhooked her seatbelt, and slid into Harley's arms. Gently, he flipped the headlights off. He lowered his face, pressing his mouth against her hair.

"Tonight was beautiful," she said. She nuzzled deeper, as if burrowing in for a place to sleep. "I wish it didn't have to end."

"Yeah, me, too." Harley kissed the side of her face.

In a second-floor window, a light snapped on. It made no sound, yet Harley felt its solid click like a tiny fracture in the glass.

Cassandra slithered from his arms. "Don't get out. I'll be all right."

"Just a few more seconds—"

"I have to go."

"I guess I ought to wish you luck. For Thursday, I mean—"

"Don't say 'good luck'. Say '*merde*' instead. That's French for—"

"I know what it means," said Harley. It was just about *all* the French he knew. He wanted to kiss her, but she was gone—had slipped away with that snap of light.

Harley watched as she headed quickly toward the house through the patch of lamplight on the drive. At the doorway, she turned and waved to him, and then she disappeared. Harley backed out. For some strange reason, he didn't turn the headlights on. He stopped again near the tall, stone posts. In the second-story window, the light flicked off and darkness filled the empty space. It happened so fast that Harley wasn't certain if he'd actually seen the silhouette, or if it was a memory, an image fixed inside his eye, of a tall and slender woman with a fall of long, black hair.

Chapter 9

After work on Monday, Harley headed into town. It was nearly six o'clock but the day had been warm, and the heat hung on in the windless air. He ambled slowly up the street past the jumbled storefronts and the wood-framed houses in between. Nothing in town had changed for years, except for the renovation at the Smits's Plumbing & Hardware Store. From blocks away, Harley could see the bright façade, a jutting eyesore of poured concrete.

A few doors up, Wally Callister exited the grocery store. "Remind your dad," he hollered out, "that Saturday is poker night."

Harley shouted a "yeah, okay," and then said hello to Mrs. Bundt, who was sitting outside the laundromat. A few years back her husband, Westy, had had a stroke and couldn't go out with his lobster pots. Now, Mrs. Bundt worked part-time at Speedy Kleen, folding people's clothes. Harley walked on, peering into windows, remembering the good old days. He and his friends stealing gum and candy bars. Buying icy drinks with their last few dimes, then heading to their pirates' lair, where everything was cool and damp, dark and green with the smell of sea. He was thinking of this, of that cave along the ocean, when up ahead Mairin came out of the Smits's store.

He knew her at once by her blue-black hair. Walking along beside her was a mini version of herself. This was Tierney, the youngest of the bunch of them—at least for the moment anyway. Both were laden with shopping bags, so many bags Harley didn't understand how they were holding onto them. Elbows, wrists, and shoulders—a body had only two of each. Mairin was hunched, walking at a turtle's pace, while Tierney moved lightly, a little ahead. The street sloped up with the rise of the hill; it wasn't an easy walk in heat. Harley sped up to catch them. As he passed the Smits's store, he peered inside. Smits was leaning against the wall, talking on the telephone. A wave of anger, much too hot for a day like this, rose up from Harley's stomach and fired in his brain. Why in hell wasn't Smits helping Mairin with those bags?

"Mairin! Tierney!" he called from behind as he approached. Tierney turned first, and her face lit up. A witchy, little fairy's face framed with those knotty curls.

"Harley, hi! Mairin, look! Look who's here!" Mairin stopped. She couldn't seem to turn her head without turning her whole, slumped body. Harley stepped out in front of her so she wouldn't have to try. Her face was pale and beaded with sweat, her skin a queasy shade of green.

He reached for her arm and yanked two bags right out of her hand. He went to grab a couple more, but Mairin pulled away from him.

"What are you doing? I'm all right." She tried to strike a sturdy pose, but wobbled a little on her feet.

"If you're all right," said Harley, "why do you look like you're going to faint?"

"She just threw up," said Tierney, swinging her bunch of bags. Mairin flashed around at her but didn't have the strength to snap.

"I mean it," said Harley. "Give me those bags. I'll walk you home."

"I don't *want* you to walk me. Go away." Mairin stepped back, and Harley noticed her sack-like dress. He'd never seen her in this dress, but he guessed it was new and probably cool for weather like this. And girls who were pregnant didn't wear tiny, cut-off shorts. On her feet, were a pair of sneakers. One of her ankles looked much too big.

"If you don't let me help you, I'm going for Smits." Harley glanced back toward the door of the store. What he wanted to do was storm inside and deck the guy.

"Oh, thunderation!" Mairin said. That was one of her mother's words, and Harley chafed at the weird, archaic sound of it. Angry, he grabbed a few more bags. He turned around to Tierney, intending to take another from her, but she'd stuck the bag on top of her head.

"I'm an African," she told him, walking in a stately way.

Mairin spat out, "You look like the Cat in the Hat to me!"

"No, I don't! I'm from Eeth-ee-o-pia."

"And I'm from Gehenna," Mairin said. Gehenna was Hell, Harley had learned in a class this year. An accursed valley under the earth southward of old Jerusalem.

Bewildered, Harley looked at both of them. "What the heck is wrong with Smits? Why couldn't he give you a hand with this?"

"He's working, that's why," snapped Mairin. "He can't just walk right out of the store." *Why not?* thought Harley. Plenty of stores had back-in-five-minutes signs on the door. And Mairin was pregnant. She'd just thrown up. The hatred he had for Smits right now was like nothing he'd ever felt before. Mairin was so much better than Smits—smarter, nicer, funnier—and it pissed him off beyond all words that he'd treat her like something less.

"Plus, the food's for my mother," Mairin said.

"Does your mother know how much was on that grocery list?" Mairin's stupid mother could send him off on a whole new rant.

"She's sick," said Mairin, wiping sweat from her pale, green face.

"And what are you?" pressed Harley.

"I'm pregnant. Not sick. There's a difference, you know."

"But she's getting married," Tierney chirped. "And I'm going to be the flower girl." Harley himself was starting to feel a little green. Hearing Mairin say it out loud—the two blunt words: *I'm pregnant*—made something inside him deconstruct. He'd known she was. He'd seen the thickness under her shirt. But not until now, not until she'd said it, had he truly realized what it meant. After that, he couldn't speak.

They turned off the street onto the road where the two girls lived. He wanted to tell Tierney what a beautiful flower girl she'd be. He knew she would—wild-eyed and excited with a wreath of roses in her hair, which her mother for once would comb and fix—but he still couldn't seem to find his voice.

They carried the bags to the front of the house. Harley noticed that Mairin's drunken father had never bothered to fix the door. He remembered kissing Mairin there, flakes of paint coming off in her hair as he pressed her against the wood. Why was he thinking of that right now? Of all the things that could never come back.

"Just leave the bags," she told him.

Harley nodded. Dredged up the single word "okay." It was better this way. He didn't want to go inside. It was always dark. And her mother would be sitting there, fingers knitting rosary beads, a game show blaring on TV. He carefully put down the bags, leaning them against the house.

"Thanks," said Mairin, her voice so soft Harley barely heard it above the hum of insects whining in the unkempt grass.

"Bye-bye, Harley," Tierney said. He suddenly had to turn away. It was crazy, really crazy. He was going to cry if he opened his mouth. It was Tierney's face. Her luminous, enchanted eyes, and the dense confusion of her hair. She looked more like Mairin than Mairin did. Harley's heart did not know what to do with that.

❦

He took a long time walking back to town. He needed to compose himself so Becky wouldn't ask him stuff. She was really good at reading his eyes. But even if Harley wanted to talk, he couldn't have explained to her the mess of feelings in his head. Better just to walk it off. Take the long way through the streets and think about other, different things.

Not that that was easy, ambling through this neighborhood, where memory clung to just about every tree and hedge, each broken fence and weedy yard that had once been their wild terrain. They'd been the best of friends, Mairin and he, since he was seven and she was six.

When he finally got back to the luncheonette, Becky was standing at the door, the CLOSED sign posted behind the glass.

"Is Mairin all right?" she asked him. "I was going out to help her when you came running up the street."

"Fucking Smits." Harley had to clear his throat. "He was right there in the hardware store talking on the phone."

"I figured as much. Come on in. I'll make you a bad-ass ice cream float."

Harley settled onto a stool as Becky scooted back behind the counter. The luncheonette closed at four o'clock, but Mr. O'Neill, who loved her like a daughter, let her bring friends in the afternoons.

"I just can't believe," said Becky, "how Smits can be so mean to her."

"And why she lets him," Harley said. That's what really pissed him off. This was the part he couldn't accept. "It's like she's doing penance. Like she feels some need to punish herself."

Becky paused, the ice cream scooper held mid-air. "It's not your fault, I hope you know. You waited for her an entire year. Most guys would never wait that long. Especially guys in college with millions of girls all over the place."

"It's true. I waited. I really did."

"I understand. You had to move on." Becky was quiet for a while as she worked at making the ice cream floats. She came around the counter then and sat at Harley's side. "It's just that I always pictured you two. Harley and Mairin, like names in a heart. Forever and ever, you know what I mean?"

"Maybe," said Harley, "there's no such thing as names in a heart. That's what my dad keeps telling me. Forever and ever does not exist."

"Your dad's an old creep!" cried Becky. "What about me and Billy? Don't you think we have a chance?"

"Sorry. You're right. You and Pugs are perfect." Harley smiled. "When I look at you together, I see rainbows and hearts and all these x's in the sky."

"Damn right," said Becky, grinning back. "And by the way, I really think Cassandra's great. And please don't say, 'I told you so.'"

"All right, I won't. But you know I did." Cassandra's face, upturned, sweet, came into his mind. He held it there, like a physical thing, blocking the pictures underneath.

"It's funny with people," Becky mused. "You look at their lives and think they're so perfect compared to yours. And then you find out that they have problems like everyone else. Like Cassandra with that horrid guy."

Harley nodded but didn't speak. He took a taste of whipped cream from the top of the giant float.

"Who'd ever think," Becky went on, "that a girl like that, a girl as beautiful as her, could get messed up about some boy? You'd expect it to be the opposite. That he'd be the one with the broken heart."

"You'd think," said Harley slowly. He kept his eyes on the mound of cream, on the small, bright cherry on the top. If he was very careful, Becky was going to fill him in on a bunch of stuff he wanted to know. "But bad things happen to everyone."

"*Bad*? What that bastard did was horrible. And then to tell her on Christmas Eve. With the snow and the church . . . It was just so cruel."

Harley nodded, as if he knew.

"I told her," said Becky "how lucky she is to be with you."

"Thanks for the plug. Sounds like you two really talked."

"Yeah, we did. Plus, she called last night. We were on the phone for at least an hour."

"You and Cassandra?"

"Yeah. Surprise. She says it's nice to have a friend. When all that horrid stuff went on, she had no one to really talk to. Maybe that's why it messed her up so much." Becky toyed with the tip of her straw. "I mean, I love Pugwash—Billy—but if he decided to call it quits, I wouldn't get deranged like that. I certainly wouldn't try to—" Suddenly she stopped herself. She stared straight into Harley's eyes. "Oh my God. You don't know any of this stuff. She never told you about this guy."

"That's not true! She told me a lot. Just not the details—the Christmas part."

"If you don't know the details, Harley, you really don't know anything. And you should have told me, you little rat."

"Just tell me what happened, will you? It's important that I know this stuff, if only for Cassandra's sake."

"Oh, shut up, Harley. You're full of shit."

"All right, I am, but I have to know. What the hell did he do to her?"

Across the room, there were three short raps on the glass of the door. Pugs's grinning face appeared, striped by the slats of the half-closed blinds.

"Guys can be such bastards," Becky said in a tone of disgust. "And there's never any consequence. I wish there was a hell for them where they'd feel what their girlfriends have to feel." Harley made no comment. He knew what hell she was talking about, and all its occupants weren't girls.

"Come on," he said as Becky wriggled from the stool. "You've got to tell me what you know."

"I've already told you far too much. You'll have to get the rest from her." Becky turned and wove her way through the maze of tables that crowded the floor. At the door she paused, fingers resting on the lock. "I'm not like Cassandra, that's for sure. If Billy ever did something like that, I'd do harm to *him*—not to myself."

Chapter 10

"I washed the Jeep," said Liam, sliding down the cabin stairs. "Inside and out. The upholstery, too." Harley looked up from the laptop screen.

"I was actually planning to get to that."

"When?"

"Whenever. One of these days."

Liam grinned. "Know where you are taking her?"

"I was looking around on the Internet. There's a restaurant called Lulu's. And another one called Green Banks Grill."

"I'd take her to the Harbor House. It's right on the water. Tables outside. I'd make a reservation now." Harley stared at Liam. There wasn't a thing to read on his face. But Liam had been inscrutable ever since his Boston trip. And he'd stayed a couple of extra days. Were things heating up with Vanessa, never mind Liam's claim that he liked his solitary life?

Liam pulled out a couple of beers as Harley called the restaurant. The woman who answered spoke in a cultivated voice. In the background, he heard soft music and the hum of a quiet dinner crowd. What time would he like? the woman asked, and Harley had to calculate. He'd fetch Cassandra at five o'clock. An hour's drive. Maybe a walk along the beach. Green Banks had an awesome beach. Seven o'clock, he finally replied. The woman checked. She had only one table, for eight fifteen. Harley took it gratefully.

Hanging up, he popped his beer. "Guess I'm not used to doing this yet."

"You'll get the hang of it," Liam said. He sank to the bunk in front of Harley's laptop, peering at the screen. "Well, what do you know? You're not as clueless as you look." He leaned in close and read out loud: "'*Giselle,* Act One. Synopsis.' You're actually studying for your date."

"Yeah, ha ha," said Harley, tipping the screen away from him. "I just thought I ought to look it up so I'm not a total idiot. That's the ballet they're putting on at the show they do in Sandy Bluff."

"I've seen *Giselle*. It's creepy as hell." Liam leaned back and sipped his beer. "Giselle's this innocent peasant girl. She falls in love with a stranger who wanders into town. She thinks he's a peon just like her, but he's actually a count, disguised."

"Yeah, that's Albrecht," Harley said, glancing at the screen. "But there's also this real-life peasant who's always wanted to marry her."

"I forget his name."

"Hilarion."

"Hilarious?"

"No, that's you."

"I have my moments," Liam said. "Anyway, as I recall, Hilarious reveals the count for who he is and Giselle gets all upset."

"She's more than upset," said Harley. "She loses her mind and then she dies."

"I wonder if that can happen. I mean medically," said Liam. "Can you really die from a jolt like that?"

"Broken heart," said Harley. "I hear it happens all the time."

"Yeah, I know. But it's not that quick. It takes long years. And, in the process, you start to rot."

"Really? That explains a lot." Harley meant this as a joke, but when he actually gave it thought, it seemed more sad than laughable.

Liam chuckled all the same. "Giselle," he went on, "is one of those *very-very* girls. Very happy or very sad. Nothing's ever in between. 'Bipolar,' they call it nowadays."

"She's just emotional," Harley said. "That doesn't mean she's mentally ill."

"She's also a dancer," Liam said. "She has the artist's temperament. And dancers, more than others, tend to be on the crazy side. Take it from one who knows."

"With you," said Harley, smirking, "the women are always the crazy ones. *You're* intact. Completely sane."

"So are the guys in the ballet. They may be cheats and liars, but they know what they're doing. They plan and think. It's the girls who are totally out of their minds. And it's not just Giselle. When she dies and goes to the land of the shades, she meets a bunch of *Wilis* who are just as crazy and weird as her. Pretty soon, she's one of them."

"*Wilis?*"

"Yeah. I guess you didn't read that far." Liam paused for a slug of beer. "The *Wilis* are all these beautiful ghosts who've died from a broken heart. They have this queen, I forget her name—"

"Myrtha?" asked Harley, skimming the cast.

"Myrtha, yeah. I knew her well." Liam plunked down his bottle of beer. "I'm not kidding. I really did." He got up from the bunk to fetch the scotch and his favorite glass. "On moonlit nights, Myrtha leads the *Wilis* into the forest to hunt for men. They're dressed like brides and look so sweet and innocent, but woe to any guy they find. Myrtha gives the order and they round him up and make him dance until his heart gives out. It's all about revenge, you see. Alive, the *Wilis* were jilted by men. And now it's happened to Giselle." Liam took a sip of scotch. "I remember that crazy guy I saw. Jumping up and down, doing weird little twiddles with his feet. Anyone would die from that."

"'Twiddles,' I guess, is a ballet term. I didn't know you were such an effing expert, Dad."

"When you see the guy do it, you'll know what I mean." Liam looked at Harley. "I just realized what a rube you are. Nineteen years old and you've never been to a ballet. That's pretty pathetic, actually."

"I didn't grow up in a cultured home."

Liam laughed. "You didn't even grow up in a home." He glanced around at the dimly lit boat, where the last of the twilight shadows pooled on the cluttered bunks.

Harley scanned the end of the synopsis. "So the *Wilis* kill Hilarious first. Then the count comes wandering into the woods to leave some flowers on the grave of Giselle. Queen Myrtha gives her orders, and now they go for him."

"That Myrtha's a bitch," said Liam. "Bitter, you know. The way women can get when they wake up old and realize that they're all alone."

"Shut up, Dad. Plus she's not alone. She's got dozens of *Wilis* all around."

"But don't you get it? They're all dead."

"But listen to this. *'Giselle resolves to protect Albrecht from the dreadful fate met by Hilarion. All through the night, she dances with him, guarding him from the* Wilis, *who lose their power at the light of dawn.'* Sounds to me like the count survives."

"But Giselle's still dead."

"It doesn't matter. Their love goes on. *'Giselle's ethereal shadow fades in the rays of the rising sun, but her love will live forever in Albrecht's memory, transcending the power of death.'"*

Liam eased up and looked straight into Harley's eyes. "Do you believe in any of that?"

"Any of what?"

"That stuff about love going on and on. After death and into all eternity."

"Why the hell are you asking me that?"

"I'm asking because I'm wondering." Liam paused for a sip of scotch. "Didn't you think, ever since you were twelve years old, that you and Mairin would be in love till the end of time?"

Harley sank back against the wall, where the bulkhead shadows hid his face.

"I guess I did. But I guess I was wrong."

"I thought it, too," said Liam. "When I saw you two together, even when you were little kids, I really believed in that crazy, never-ending love. You were soulmates, I thought, like Giselle and her count. Chosen by the fates."

"Well, whatever you thought, it's over now. She doesn't want to look at me."

"Why?"

"Why *what*?"

"Why doesn't she want to look at you? Is it maybe because she loves you still?"

"Shit, Dad. Really. What's the point of talking like this? She's fucking *pregnant* by somebody else. She's going to marry the stupid jerk."

"That doesn't mean she can't still be in love with you. And it doesn't mean you can't be—"

"I'm *not* in love with her anymore!" Harley pushed forward out of the dark. "I met someone else and I'm happy with her. I thought you might be happy, too."

"Hey, didn't I wash the Jeep for you? Didn't I give you the name of a goddamn restaurant so you wouldn't show up in Green Banks with no place to take your nice, new girl?"

"Yeah, okay. And I told you thanks. So let's just leave it at that, all right?"

"What did you say her name was? Oh yeah, Cassandra. I like that name."

"Good. I'm glad. It would really suck if you hated her name."

Liam smiled in a way that Harley couldn't stand. That wise, omniscient half-a-smile that said he could see through Harley's bones.

Liam got up and pulled out his phone. "Let's order some clams from Wally's place."

∽

Harley lay in his narrow bunk. The night had been weird. Beer and clams and Liam in a chatty mood. Later on, when his father dozed off, he'd gone back to his computer and read some more about *Giselle*. He'd watched some YouTube videos, too. The ballet was strange and beautiful. He'd never seen anything like it—rows and rows of beautiful ghosts moving in perfect unison on the eerie moonscape of the stage. It could almost put you into a trance. Yet Liam was right: The story could really creep you out.

There was something about the *Wilis* that made your skin feel prickly. It was their silence, Harley thought. How they came out of nowhere all at once, like flashes of light between the trees. How their feet made no sound on the forest floor, and the swish of their dresses was like a breath. Or maybe it was their beauty itself, so delicate and ethereal you didn't know how to process it. Like the way he'd felt the day he met Cassandra and she'd seemed to him like some hybrid being, not a totally human girl. Then, there were the numbers. One *wili* alone you might not fear, but the *Wilis* roamed in a swirling pack, making dizzying patterns and winding loops. When they finally closed in like an intricate net, you realized the frenzied chaos was really order in disguise. They were beautiful white zombies, one body, one mind, one single hunger in their souls.

Lying in the darkness he struggled to imagine Cassandra as a *wili*. He could see her in the costume, the white tulle dress and the airy veil, but he couldn't imagine her playing such an evil role. He was thinking of this when her name lit up on his cell phone screen.

"Harley," she said, her voice like a breath. "I hope I didn't wake you up."

"You didn't, no. I was lying here thinking about *Giselle*."

"*Giselle?*"

"That's right. I looked it up online tonight."

"Are you serious, Harley? That's just so sweet. I'm going to do the same for you. I'm going to learn about boats and things. Tide and wind and the names of fish."

Harley smiled. "Is that what you think I care about?"

"I don't know. You tell me. I want to know all there is to know."

"What I care about now is how your audition went today."

"Really well. I had to call and tell you."

Harley eased upward in the bunk. "You'll make a beautiful Giselle."

"Don't be silly! I'll never get picked to dance the lead. There are so many wonderful dancers here. And they're more experienced than me. Blanca, Christina—all of them. Even little Pia dances like a dream."

"But if the audition went so well—"

"It's something else. Something that happened afterward. I was walking from the studio when Madame Ravenska called me aside. She's that famous dancer I told you about who's staging the ballet for us. You won't believe what she said to me."

Harley waited for her to go on.

"She said that I was . . . *beautiful.*" Cassandra's voice was quiet and shy. "She said I'd *bloomed* in the last three weeks—"

"I could have told you—"

"Told me what?"

"Told you that you're beautiful."

"Oh, Harley. God. Now, I'm really going to cry."

"So, when you're Giselle—which I bet you are—who will your Count Albrecht be? Who should I be jealous of?"

"I *won't* be Giselle!"

"Just say you are."

"You shouldn't be jealous of anyone. But as for Count Albrecht, I don't know. We thought it would be Julian. He's the best of the boys, and he looks the part. But his ankle's messed up, so he's out of the mix."

"His ankle?"

"Yeah. It happened that day. Remember the storm?"

"I thought you told me he was fine."

"He was," she said. "It was just a sprain, but now it's worse."

"Cassandra, that's really terrible."

"Yes, it is, but it's all his fault. Everyone knows about treating a sprain. He just refused to give it rest."

"How long will it take for him to heal?"

"It all depends. Two to six weeks is what they say."

"Six weeks? For real? Summer will be over then."

"I know. It's sad. I feel bad for him."

"Yeah, me too," said Harley. He really and truly did.

"Anyway," Cassandra said, "we'll know who's who by Saturday. Whatever happens, whatever part I get to dance, I'm just so happy. It's hard to explain. It's been so long since I felt like this."

"I'm happy, too," he whispered.

"Can't wait to see you Saturday night."

"Yeah, same here. Thanks for calling. You sleep tight."

Harley clicked off. He was suddenly wide awake again. Stretching toward the port-side bunk, he reached for his laptop and flicked it on. He pulled up the YouTube video, the last one he'd watched. He wasn't sure why he did this, but he felt compelled to look again. His gaze homed in on the dancer playing Albrecht, and something shifted in his brain. Instead of the dark-haired dancer, he envisioned the sleek, blond Julian. Julian surrounded. Encircled by the swirling girls. Tortured and twirled and forced to leap as the beautiful, icy queen looked on. Something shivered up his neck. Harley did not like Julian. But it didn't seem right—or normal—that his injured ankle hadn't healed.

Chapter 11

"Guess what," said Liam. "You're not the only one with a date." It was Saturday morning, and Harley had just made coffee. Liam was wearing his "Paris jeans" and had shaved his usually scruffy jaw. A faint aroma of Eau Sauvage lingered in his wake.

"A breakfast date?" asked Harley. "Where? Who with? You're freaking me out."

"Pour me some coffee," Liam said. And when Harley had passed a mug to him: "Mrs. Pell over at the Palmer Club."

"I know you like older women, Dad, but—"

"It's a job, my boy. A good one. Restoring the library at the house, including a big, old mantelpiece. Dates from the eighteen hundreds. Lots of flourishes. Art Nouveau."

"Wow," said Harley. "That's really cool. When did all of this transpire?"

"It's been in the works, going back and forth. Didn't want to mention it until I was really sure."

"Well, congratulations," Harley said. "It's been a while since you've had a job you care about."

"I need the Jeep, but I'll have it back in plenty of time." Liam sipped some coffee and then reached for his portfolio, a worn-out Gucci folder filled with photos of his work. Ninety-year-old Mrs. Pell was sure to like this better than trying to look at things online. Harley imagined her diamond-weighted fingers turning the pages one by one to gaze at the gloomy altars and dark Venetian saints.

"Hey, Dad," he called as Liam swung up the cabin steps, "can I dress like that, the way you're dressed, when I go to the Harbor House tonight? I mean, jeans are okay at a place like that?"

"Yeah, they're fine. As long as they're not full of holes. And bring a blazer just in case they've gotten weird. Shove a tie in the pocket, too."

"A tie. Oh, shit."

"You never know. And check your shirts. If they're wrinkled as hell, which I'll bet they are, bring one up to Annie Bundt." Liam tossed some money onto the counter next to the steps. "She'll be glad to iron it for you."

◦◦◦

A half hour later, Harley was heading up the hill with his balled-up, wrinkled shirt. Before he left, he'd checked to see that his blazer was pressed. It lived inside a garment bag, and he never wore it, so it was fine. At the Speedy Kleen, Mrs. Bundt was folding towels.

"Hi there, Harley. That all you got for me this week?" She squinted her eyes and swept back a strand of long, white hair.

Harley pulled out the crumpled shirt. "Just wondered if you could iron this."

"Going somewhere fancy, eh?" Steam hissed out as she dragged the iron back and forth.

"Just into Green Banks," Harley replied.

"Bet you anything it's a girl."

Harley's eyes wandered out the window toward Nellie's Luncheonette. Becky would be working now. It was crazy busy on Saturday with the people from the fancy boats hiking up for the kind of breakfast they'd never cook. The towels Mrs. Bundt was folding also came from one of those boats. Harley knew by the *Sea Dream* embroidered into the plush.

"I remember the days," Mrs. Bundt went on, "when it was you and Mairin. Never thought she'd end up the way she is." Harley started to fold a towel, but Mrs. Bundt barked at him to put it down. "Hands off, skipper! I've got my technique." She picked up where she'd broken off.

"Well, at least she's getting married now. Two weeks, I heard. Up by old St. Brendan's Church. Father Neale wasn't all too pleased; that's the reason it took so long. I guess they had to talk things through." Harley made no comment, staring at the thin, blue stripes as she pulled the iron over his shirt. It seemed like forever until she was done. But at last he was heading out the door, the shirt on a metal hanger draped in a plastic bag. She'd refused to take any money, so he left ten bucks on the ironing board, where she'd see it when he was gone.

As he started down the street again, Becky called out from the luncheonette. Harley went over to say "hello."

"Hey," she said. "Just wanted to tell you, have fun tonight."

"How did you hear?" asked Harley. This town knew things you sometimes didn't know yourself.

"From Cassandra."

"Really?"

"Yeah. She called. So you're going to the Harbor House?"

"You think it's okay? My dad's idea."

"It's more than okay. It's perfect." She stared at his shirt through the plastic bag. "Is that what you're planning to wear tonight?"

"Yeah. What's wrong?"

"Who said anything was wrong?" She lowered her voice and made her eyes mysterious. "I know what Cassandra's wearing, too. She sent me pictures on her phone. She's going to look beautiful." Becky slipped back inside the door.

"Wait," said Harley, "There's something I need to ask you." The metal hanger dug into his hand. "Is it true what I heard? Mairin and Smits, two weeks from now?"

Becky nodded. "Yeah, it's true. I can't believe they're actually doing it in the church." She squinted at Harley and forced a smile. "Don't think about it anymore. Just focus on Cassandra and what a great time you're going to have. Anyway, I've got to go." She blew him a kiss and disappeared into the fray of the luncheonette.

Back on the boat, Harley hung up the ironed shirt. He pulled out the jeans he was going to wear and took the blazer from its bag. He tried to recall when the hell he'd worn it last. It might have been with Mairin when her uncle died and he went to the wake. Mairin was in a pale-gray dress. Small, white stitches along the neck, *but you can't start thinking of Mairin's neck.*

Harley climbed off the boat again. Leaving the docks, he crossed the street. The air in the chocolate shop was cool, tinged with a scent that was heavy and sweet. In the long, glass cases, the candies looked like precious gems, each on its own gold doily or nestled in a fluted cup.

"If you have any questions?" the woman behind the counter said. She was wearing a brown-striped apron that matched the awning over the shop. A spidery net engulfed her hair. *What's in the middles?* That was Harley's question as his gaze swept over the vast assortment on the shelves. He was just about to give up when he caught a glimpse of the chocolate swans. They swam in a line at the counter's end, black and brown and creamy white. What could be more perfect? Ballerinas were crazy for swans. Harley asked for one of each, and the saleswoman carefully packed them up in a fancy box with a bright pink bow. Clasping his tiny shopping bag, he hurried to the boat to change.

Liam had already come and gone. His portfolio lay on the starboard bunk, and the half-filled mug was sitting on the table. He'd left a note and the keys to the Jeep. There was also some money lying there.

Have a great night. Take the dough. It's the Christmas gift
you never got.

L

Harley picked up the five crisp bills. Typical low-key Liam. It was true about the Christmas gift. From an early age, Harley had known there wasn't any Santa Claus. Gifts arrived when Liam was in a giving mood. Harley sat down and took out the box of chocolate swans. It would fit in his blazer pocket, the inner one against his chest. He'd wait until after dinner and then pull it out like some big surprise. He smiled when he thought of that. Of how Cassandra would react, all teary and touched the way she got. He wondered how she'd wear her hair. He loved when it was in a braid, thick as a rope, with a few loose strands around her face.

He was thinking of this, and of what to write on the card that came with the box of swans, when suddenly his cell phone rang.

"Harley?"

"Cassandra."

"You'll never guess what!" Her breath ran out as she said the "what."

"What?"

"I'm Giselle!"

"You're—" It took a second to register. "Oh my God, you got the *lead*?"

"Yes!" Cassandra uttered, and again she seemed to lose her voice.

"That's totally fantastic. I mean, really, Cassandra. Yay! Hooray! Tonight we can really celebrate!"

The pause that followed was long and still, and as it played out, Harley felt its hollow ring.

"The thing of it is," Casssandra said, her voice just over a whisper now, "I can't come out to dinner tonight. I'm so sorry, Harley. I really am. But we're having a special meeting, some of the girls in the cast—and me."

"Can't you tell them you have plans?" Harley's stomach had dropped to his feet.

"Oh Harley, I would! At any other time but this. But I can't say no to the party tonight. Madame *Ravenska* invited me."

"I thought you said a meeting. If it's just a party—"

"It's a *meeting-party,*" Cassandra said. "Madame calls them her *soirées.* It's a combination sort of thing. She holds them in her private rooms, and only certain girls are asked."

"Cassandra, come on. She'll invite you again."

"No, she won't. You can't say no. Plus, I feel I owe her in a way."

"Owe her for what?"

"She was the one who gave me the part."

"What do you mean? I thought you auditioned like everyone else."

"I did," said Cassandra softly. "And all the teachers had a vote. But, in the end, the only vote that matters is hers. She told me after class today."

"Told you what?"

"She told me she's had her eye on me. That she'd picked me out the very first day she saw me. She said that I was *her* Giselle."

Harley felt his mouth go slack. He didn't have the words arranged—didn't completely know what they were—but in his gut he felt a cool unsettling, a shiver like a wisp of dread.

"I'm so sorry!" Cassandra said again. "And I hate myself for doing this. But Madame Ravenska, oh my God! You have no idea how famous she is. She's the queen of ballerinas, and just the thought that she's singled me out—oh, Harley, try and understand. I promise I'll make it up to you." She stopped for a breath. "We'll do something really special soon. If you want to, I mean. If you don't completely hate me now."

"I don't hate you," Harley managed to stammer out. But he did feel something akin to hate for the Russian witch who had ruined his night. Part of him wanted to burst Cassandra's bubble and tell her the truth about what her idol was really like. How crazy she was. How years ago she'd taken a pair of scissors and—but he knew it would be pointless. She was smitten with the woman. She wouldn't believe a word of it. And who the hell would blame her? Even he had trouble imagining his father winning the heart of the world-class ballerina, the Russian beauty, the queen of them all.

Cassandra's voice was quiet now. "Maybe tomorrow we could meet."

"Maybe, yeah." He drew a breath. "Have a fabulous time at your *soirée*." He said the last sarcastically, but Cassandra didn't seem to hear.

"Thank you, Harley. You're the best."

Harley flopped lengthwise on the bunk. The *Alma* stirred in the shifting tide, and the plastic bag with the ironed shirt swayed gently back and forth. Next to it, the blazer hung, buttons winking in the sun. He got up again and yanked the shirt and jacket down, hurling them through the forward door. He headed for the icebox and started with a Heineken.

Chapter 12

Theodosia Ravenska
A Life of Triumph and Tragedy

Harley slumped over the glowing screen. He'd made the switch from beer to scotch, and anything in italics blurred. She was born in Moscow. Orphaned at six. Raised by a ballerina aunt. Admitted at nine to the Bolshoi Ballet Academy. Onstage debut at the age of twelve.

Harley took a long, slow sip.

When she's twenty-five, Ravenska defects to England—"an offstage drama that stuns the world." She is wined and dined by royalty. Courted by distinguished men. Demands of career, however, make romance impossible. A Chilean ambassador "seems to make inroads into her heart," but he *disappears* during Pinochet's regime. Three years later, she moves to the United States.

Harley bit into a chocolate swan, lopping off its head.

The "still young" Ravenska throws herself into dance again. Declares that she is now a nun, devoted only to her art. These are her most productive years and she "catapults" to worldwide fame.

Harley tried to picture that, the elegant ballerina flung in the air by a great machine.

When Ravenska reaches forty, love comes into her life once more. He is younger by at least ten years, "a jet-setting heir to a South-American cargo line." Two weeks before the wedding, he is killed in a skiing accident.

Harley dipped the second swan into the glass of scotch. Poor Ravenska. She sounded a bit like Liam. Unlucky in love, though only one of Liam's had died. At least the camera loved her. It lingered on her milky skin, her dove-like hands, and her thick, black hair. She was gorgeous in every photograph. Posing in front of the Taj Mahal. On the deck of a ship. In a green gazebo who knows where. There were pictures of her dancing, too, with explanations underneath. Letters swam in Harley's eyes. White Odette, Black Odile.

His vision cleared abruptly as he neared the bottom of the screen. The photograph showed two long, white lines of dancers in a blue-lit forest under the moon. In the center, a figure seemed to float. She was dressed in incandescent white, and on her head was a glittering crown.

"*Though a prima ballerina, Ravenska seemed born for one superb supporting role: that of the cold Queen Myrtha in the deeply romantic ballet* Giselle. *Hers was a deadly* wili *queen—ruthless, cruel, her sorrowing beauty hard as ice.*"

⤬⤬⤬

Harley stared at the solitary figure poised between the two white rows. He realized that he knew her. That he recognized that silhouette, the swan-like neck and the perfect oval of her head. He could see it in his memory like the afterimage of a flash. But he hadn't seen it on a stage. He'd seen it in a window frame, black against the amber light, shadows in the hidden eyes that were riveted on him.

⤬⤬⤬

Harley couldn't fathom how he'd ever gotten to Becky's house. When she opened the door, he didn't remember why he'd come, only that he felt hollowed out and didn't want to be alone.

"Harley, God! What's going on?" Her face looked soft, framed in the cloud of strawberry hair. She was wearing a light pink sweatshirt; that, too, seemed plush and cozy like a pillow on a nice, warm bed. "What on earth are you doing here? Aren't you supposed to—" Her voice broke off as she looked more closely at Harley's face. "You're totally drunk. What happened tonight?"

"I don't know. Can I come in?" Harley stepped forward toward the door, but Becky blocked his way.

"I really don't think it's a good idea."

"Come on, Becky. Let me in."

"What's going on?" called a voice from inside. Mairin appeared in the splotch of light just over Becky's shoulder. She took a look at Harley, and gently pushed Becky out of the way. "Let him in. Before he falls down."

Then Harley was in the living room, sitting on Becky's old, blue couch with Mairin gazing down at him.

"I didn't know you'd be here, Mair. I'm sorry for busting in on things."

"What things?"

"Whatever. I didn't know you'd be hanging out."

Mairin emitted a shallow laugh. "We weren't hanging out," she said. "I mean, not in a social kind of way. I came here to get away from Smits." She was wearing the baggy dress again, the one she'd had on the other day with the tiny flower print. One of the shoulders had slipped away, revealing her narrow collarbone and the strap of a pale-blue bra.

"Why do you need to get away?"

Becky stepped forward into the light, taking Mairin's arm. "You don't have to tell him any of this."

"What does it matter?" Mairin said. "It's not like Harley doesn't know."

"Did Smits do anything to you?" Harley asked, more lucid by the second now.

"Anything like what?"

"Like he didn't . . . touch you, did he? Because if he did—"

"Oh, shut up, Harley," Becky said. "You're stupid and drunk, all ready to go and pick a fight."

"He's just being courtly," Mairin said. "But no, he didn't touch me. He doesn't *touch* me anymore." She narrowed her slender, cattish eyes, and something in Harley's stomach swirled. Mairin blurred as he rose from the couch. Details lingered in his eye—the crooked neckline of the dress, blue bra strap, and her bone exposed—as he rushed to the bathroom down the hall.

When he got back to the living room, Becky had made coffee. The two girls sat on the lumpy couch. Mairin poured Harley's cup for him. She loaded it with sugar the way she knew he liked it, clinking the spoon as she always did.

"So you got stood up," she said to him, passing the coffee into his hand.

"It's not like that," said Harley; it sounded pitiful put that way.

"What is it, then?" asked Becky. "How could she just call things off?"

"She couldn't help it. Something important came up at the school."

"A ballerina," Mairin said in a strange, faint voice. She seemed to be talking to herself. "I guess I can see that happening. I didn't expect it, I have to admit. I thought it would be some Colby girl. I mean, all those months, didn't you meet *anyone*?"

Harley looked into her pale-green eyes, but he couldn't anchor himself inside. If he could, if Mairin would let him past the wall, his gaze would tell her everything. She'd remember what he'd promised and she'd know why there'd never been a girl. But he couldn't get through the surface now. He wondered if eyes could form a seal, like skin growing over an open wound.

"I still don't get it," Becky said, breaking the silence in the air. "What could be so important that Cassandra would bail out on you? You had reservations! You ironed your shirt!"

"She got the lead in the ballet."

"Yeah. That's great. I still don't see—"

"It's that woman!" Harley blurted out. "That woman who teaches up at the school."

"What woman?"

"You know. Ravenska. The one she always talks about. That woman's got some hold on her."

Becky laughed, but not in any cheerful way. "That's really pathetic, Jamison. So now it's not Cassandra's fault that she totally stood you up?"

"She was under pressure. She had no choice. When Ravenska calls, you can't say no."

"Who *is* this person?" Mairin asked with interest. She had curled herself up at the end of the couch. "And why can't people say no to her?"

"She's this really famous dancer. Anyway, she used to be. By the way, she's the one Liam got involved with back when we were little kids."

"This woman is *her?*" yelped Mairin.

Harley nodded. "One and the same."

"You knew and you didn't tell me this?" Becky demanded, incredulous. "Oh my God. Does Cassandra know?"

"She'd never believe it," Harley said. "She worships the ground she walks on."

"Tell me about her," Mairin said.

"First of all, she's crazy. At Ocean Watch, she lives in the freaking chapel and tells the girls they should be like nuns. I'm pretty sure she hates all men. She has this group of minions who do whatever she tells them to—"

"You're making that up," said Becky. "You don't know that she hates all men."

"She says that men devour your soul! Cassandra told us that night on the boat." Harley rushed on, "Up at the school, she has these little parties. She calls them *soirées*, and everyone wants to go to them. But she only invites a 'chosen' few."

Mairin spoke softly into the dark. "What sort of things does she tell her minion girls to do?"

"She tells them to break their dates with boys," Becky dubbed sarcastically.

"No, really," said Mairin. "I want to know." Her finger twirled a strand of curls.

Harley's head felt heavy. His coffee looked like a blot of mud.

"I think she told them to hurt this guy. Or to scare him, at least. But it all went wrong and now he can't be the count." Becky and Mairin stared at him. "The day of the storm when I brought Cassandra back to the school, we rescued him from the cellar. A bunch of girls had locked him in. But Julian has asthma, and he lost his inhaler and dropped his phone. He might have died if Cassandra and I hadn't come along."

"You're shit-faced, Harley," Becky said.

"But I wasn't drunk that afternoon. The guy was freaked. He said the girls attacked him. And now Cassandra is one of them! Ravenska chose her. She told her as much. That's why she picked her for the lead." Harley paused for a breath of air. "Cassandra's *Giselle!* Do you get it now?"

Becky and Mairin sat mute as rocks.

"The ballet explains the way they work. If a guy does anything bad to a girl, the *Wilis* attack him in the woods. They're dressed like brides, but they're really basically killer ghosts. They surround the guy and catch him. Then they make him dance till his heart gives out."

"That's it, Harley," Becky snapped. "You need to go home and get some sleep."

"Listen to me! I'm serious. There's this bitter queen named Myrtha, and she's in charge of all the ghosts. She gives the sign—like she throws some petals into the air—and the *Wilis* do whatever she wants." Harley could hear his own strained voice. He sounded crazy even to himself, but couldn't seem to stop.

"Don't you see? Ravenska *is* Queen Myrtha! She has this power over those girls." Harley looked up, and his eyes locked into Mairin's. He couldn't tell what she actually thought. The thinking was still going on.

"Why?" she asked, when a moment had passed. "I mean, why would this woman tell the girls to hurt that boy? What did he do that was so bad?"

"He went after one of the younger ones. She's twelve years old, and Julian is seventeen. The others were protecting her. They were trying to get even, just like the *Wilis* in *Giselle*."

"I wonder if they'd help me out," Mairin said with a bitter smile.

Becky stepped in before Harley could react to that. "I thought I liked Cassandra. But maybe all those people are right. The ones who say, like Billy, that there's something weird about those girls." She gestured toward the coffee, and Harley took another sip. His stomach roiled, and he rushed down the hall to puke again.

When he came back, he decided to leave.

"Are you sure you're all right?" asked Becky. "I could try to get Billy to walk you home."

"Yeah, that'd be fun," said Harley. "Anyway, thanks. The coffee was great."

"I could tell you liked it," Becky quipped.

He was stumbling down the front porch steps when Mairin poked out from a slit in the door. "Forget her, Harley. That girl's a dope." She paused for a beat. "I know you're drunk, but you aren't crazy, Captain Blood. I believe that stuff you said inside. Be careful. I mean it. Go straight to the boat."

Chapter 13

All Sunday long, Harley checked his cell phone, expecting Cassandra to send a text. Another sweet apology. Or a beautiful description of how she was going to "make it up." But evening came and he hadn't heard a word from her.

"Dancers aren't like regular girls," Liam tried to explain to him. Like the way he'd explained the facts of life when Harley was eight years old. "The dancing always comes first for them. They'd miss their own damn wedding if the lead girl tripped and they got to fill in. Take it from me. I know this stuff." He looked up from the sketch he was working on, an elaborate frond of flowers and fruit. "You take things much too personal. It's one of your most charming flaws."

∽

On Monday, Harley had to put up with Pugs. Becky, of course, had told him what had happened, and the told-you-so's ran on and on. On Wednesday, when Cassandra still had not called, Harley stopped defending her. The excuses he'd given Pugwash began to sound stupid, even to him. At the end of the week, he sent a one-line text:

Pls just tell me you're all right.

His anger by then had faded and was turning into missing her.

He kept playing back scenes inside his head. The night on the boat when he held her at the steering wheel and the lights of the land went drifting by. The day he'd rescued her in the storm. How tiny she'd looked in his big, blue sweats. The first stunned sight of her combed-out hair. In all his thoughts, she was light and frail, and his muscles ached with memory.

Friday was hot, and Harley and Pugs trawled for hours in the banks of eel grass along the shore. The shade of the stalks didn't reach the boat, but the green reflections made them imagine coolness and remember how it felt. They were sweaty and tired and reeking of fish as they motored back to port. But it had been a productive day. The buckets were full of killies, and Pugs had caught a bluefish, trolling from the stern. Back on shore they stowed the catch. Pugs reminded Harley that the gang was having pizza and watching baseball at Red Legs's that night.

"I'll be there," Harley promised as they parted ways at the end of the dock. Shortcutting through the yacht club grounds, he suddenly stopped cold. Where the lawn cut off at the water's edge, Julian sat in the yellow sun, dangling his legs. Looking more closely, Harley saw that one of his feet was cuffed in a therapeutic boot. He would have kept on going, but Julian had spotted him.

"Harley," he called, waving his hand. Harley was stunned that he knew his name.

Reluctantly, he crossed the lawn. "Stay where you are. No need to get up."

Julian stopped struggling and sank back down to his seat on the wall. He was dressed in white. Immaculate. Like someone's baby boy. Harley felt even more filthy and rank.

"I was hoping I'd see you," Julian said.

Harley didn't respond to that.

"Want to sit down?"

"I'm okay."

"Just for a minute. Please." Julian looked at Harley, a sheepish expression on his face. "I wanted to thank you for that day. That day of the storm, I—"

"It's no big deal," said Harley.

"It is a big deal. You saved my life."

"I wouldn't say that."

"Ten seconds more, I would have passed out."

"It was kind of a happy accident."

"No," said Julian, shaking his head. "There are no accidents up there. By the way, have you seen my foot?" He stretched his leg, displaying the boot. "Peroneal tendon. Just hope I don't need surgery."

"I'm really sorry," Harley said. "But you—"

"I wish you'd sit."

"I'm not sure you'd like that. I kind of stink."

"Fishing?"

"Yeah."

"I don't care."

Harley eased down, placing himself on the upwind side.

"Is that what you do?" asked Julian.

"It's a summer gig," said Harley. He shifted another inch away from Julian's drastic cleanliness, shirt and jeans crisp as a brand new handkerchief.

"I'd starve to death if I had to catch a fish to live," Julian said with a slender smile. "Pretty pathetic, don't you think?"

"I'd starve to death if I had to do a dance to live."

"I can't do anything but dance. It's really all I've ever done. It's all I want to do in life. And now, I've got this ankle mess."

"I'm sure if you rest, you'll be just fine."

"Yeah, let's hope. Anyway, I'm going home. Back to New York. Getting the hell away from here. If I were you, I'd do the same."

"I happen to live here," Harley said.

"Oh yeah, that's right. You live on a boat. Well, in that case, I'd just sail away. Head out to sea and never come back."

"Actually, I like it here."

"I did, too," said Julian. "I've come every summer since I was nine. I liked everything about the place. The water, the boats, the houses where I got to stay. I even liked the whole idea of the feud between the town and school. I liked being one of the 'evil ones.'" He gazed across the harbor. Everything was calm and bright, the sailboats bobbing gently on the ripples of the waves. "I used to think that all of you were crazy. The 'townsfolk' we used to call you. Sometimes 'the inbred.' Take your pick."

Harley shrugged. He knew all that. "We had names for you as well."

"Yeah, I bet," said Julian. "The thing of it is, I don't think you're crazy anymore."

"And why is that?"

"It's because of this," said Julian, lifting his booted foot again. "I've come to believe the town was right about that guy. The one that went out the window. I don't believe he fell or jumped. I think he was pushed by a pack of girls."

"Wow," said Harley, staring at him. "I know you're upset about your foot, but I think there's a major difference between the prank that was played on you and what happened to Teddy Flynn. That, by the way, was the name of the guy."

"You still don't get it. I could've died."

Harley knew that this was true. He remembered Julian that day, covered in mud and gasping for air. "So what's your theory? The girls who pushed Teddy five years ago also locked you up that day?"

Julian squinted into the sun. "We're not the only ones, you know. A few years back there was this dancer at the school. He was older than me, but we were friends. Really good looking, a movie star. He had a fling with a girl who came from Michigan. Summer ended, they kissed goodbye, and all of us went home. That winter he had an accident back in Boston, where he lived. Was drunk at a party, people say, and got too near the fireplace. He was horribly burned. His face destroyed. They'd never put him on a stage."

"That's really awful," Harley said. He paused for a spell, not wanting to let the image in. "But what's it got to do with—"

"That party was full of dancers, and eighty percent of them were girls. Some had been to Ocean Watch, and were friends with the one from Michigan. Turns out the guy had a serious Boston girlfriend, too; he'd been cheating on the both of them."

"And what?" said Harley, incredulous. "The girls who'd been at Ocean Watch shoved him into the fireplace?"

"I wasn't there, so I couldn't say. And I didn't know that Teddy guy, but I'd bet you anything I own he was having a thing with one of the girls. Something must have happened, or maybe he wanted to break it off." Julian paused and stared at him. "Don't you get it, Harley—why I'm telling you this stuff?"

Harley didn't answer. A breezy chill was cooling the sweat along his arms.

"I know you like Cassandra. She's a really nice girl, but they've got her now, and you need to watch out."

"Watch out for what?" said Harley, a tingle spreading up his neck.

"She's part of Ravenska's little cult."

"Her *cult*?"

"That's right. From what I hear, it started a bunch of years ago when Ravenska first came to Ocean Watch. It's hard to believe, but people say she was jilted by some local guy. After that, there was kind of an unwritten rule."

Harley swallowed audibly. "Hard to believe," he echoed, glancing away from Julian.

"It's been passed along from year to year. The sacred vow, whatever, to right the wrongs that are done by guys. Right now, there's a certain group of girls, the current keepers of the flame."

"I don't get it," Harley said. "If you really believe a thing like this, why would you keep coming back? It sounds pretty hazardous to your health."

"I thought it was over," Julian said. "Nothing had happened—not at the school—since that guy went out the window. But now with Ravenska here again . . . It's starting all over, don't you see?"

"And you think Cassandra's part of it?"

"She was at the 'party' the other night, and as you probably know by now, was picked to dance Giselle."

"She auditioned," said Harley weakly. He could smell himself, the reek of fish wafting from his moistened skin.

"She's a pretty good dancer," Julian said. "But Christina and Blanca are better than her, and everybody knows it's true. Ravenska gave the role to her as a way to mark her as her own."

"But why Cassandra? Why would Ravenska pick her out?"

"How the hell would I know? I only know that you better be good if you don't want to end up dead or maimed."

Harley drew his gaze away. Off to the right on the yacht club porch, some people were having cocktails in the glow of the late-day sun. He couldn't hear their voices, but he knew they were talking of normal things—weekend plans and weather—and it made him feel displaced and strange.

"I don't know if it was Ravenska who told them to track me down that day, or if it was their own idea." Julian shook his golden head, a weighty curl falling over his brow. "I only know this: I should have been Count Albrecht. I shouldn't be on my way back home, possibly facing surgery."

"Cassandra would never take part in something like that," Harley said with certainty. "You just have to look at her to know."

Julian uttered a bitter laugh. "Don't be stupid, Harley. That's how they get away with it. They look so sweet and delicate. Moonbeams. Moths. Mere wisps of air. But let me tell you, they're strong as hell. And they work together, like a pack."

"If all this crazy shit is true, Cassandra doesn't understand. She doesn't know what's going on."

"It doesn't matter. They'll rope her in."

"I won't let it happen," Harley said.

"It's already happening. It's too late."

"I don't believe that, Julian."

"Yeah, all right. But if you stay together, you better be really nice to her. Don't lie or cheat or even look at another girl. They know who you are. They're watching you."

"Let them watch. I'd never do anything bad to her." Harley paused. The truth, which he didn't mention to Julian, was that he'd probably never see her again. It was almost a week since she'd stood him up, and he hadn't heard a word from her.

From the pocket of his pressed, white jeans Julian pulled a small, white card. "Here's the number of my cell. My e-mail's printed under that. Give me your contact info, too. I'd like to keep in touch with you." He glanced around. "I think my taxi's finally here."

"Where's your stuff?"

Julian pointed across the lawn to a jumbled pile of bags. "The people I live with brought it down. I didn't want to wait up there. Something could happen, you never know." Harley helped him onto his feet.

Red Legs appeared at the yacht club gate. "What's up?" he asked suspiciously, surprised to see Harley with his fare. He tossed the luggage into the trunk. "You coming to watch the game tonight?"

Harley told him that he was, and Red Legs slid into the driver's seat.

Julian slipped into the back, dragging the clumsy boot. "So long, Harley. And thanks again." He extended a hand, which Harley shook.

"Yeah. Good luck. I hope that ankle heals up fast."

"It better," answered Julian. "If it doesn't, I have no life."

Chapter 14

The text came in on Saturday.

I'm alright we have to talk.

Harley's stomach took a dive. He knew what that meant, and it wasn't really a big surprise. All the same, the message hit him with a jolt. He must have been clinging to a thread of hope.

Glad you're ok. No need to talk.

He typed in the heroic words and sent them with a click. Then, taking his mug of coffee, he retreated to his private space. Liam would know if he looked at his face, and Harley didn't want to chat. Liam was pretty cheery these days. Artistic work always had that effect on him. He was drawing right now, his fine-lined sketches covering the table, the entire cabin strewn with books.

Harley sank down on his narrow bunk. The whole thing with Cassandra had lasted only about two weeks. Talk about brief and fleeting. Butterflies lived longer than that. *You're better off,* Julian would have told him. Hell, everyone would say the same. Even Becky, who'd thought Cassandra might be her friend, wondered what was going on. She'd called her twice but hadn't heard from her all week. Yet Harley didn't feel better off. When he thought about her smiling face, her weightless presence in his arms, the pain he felt was physical, a whining tug just under his heart. The ending was all so unexplained. The last time he'd said goodnight to her, she hadn't seemed like someone who planned to break things off. She was soft and sweet; she'd nestled her face against his chest as if she'd wanted to climb inside. So what the hell had happened? He suddenly wished he hadn't sent that text. Maybe there *was* a need to talk.

From beyond the door he heard the boom of his father's voice.

"Who goes there?" Liam called theatrically, quoting (he'd say) from *Hamlet.*

Harley wearily shut his eyes as Liam's steps sounded on the cabin floor. Probably Wally Callister come to grab a beer. He was glad he'd make his quick retreat.

A few seconds later, knuckles rapped against his door.

"Hey," called Liam. "You've got a guest."

"Tell him I'm out," Harley replied.

"It's not a him. And she knows you're here."

Harley sprang up and opened the door to Liam's smirk. "She's gorgeous, man. I can see why you're such a frigging mess."

"Where is she?" Harley whispered.

"She's on the dock. I tried to get her to come aboard."

"I look like hell," said Harley, running a hand through his stubby hair.

"You look the way you always look."

"Thanks, Dad, really. That helps a lot."

"Just get up there before she leaves." Liam motioned with his head and then moved from Harley's path.

Cassandra stood on the sun-washed dock. The sheen of her hair, the creamy yellow of her dress, and the gauze of a shawl looped around her shoulders, everything hot with midday light, blurred in a dazzle in front of his eyes. Harley could only see half her face. The rest was obscured by a huge bouquet. He stood transfixed as if by some apparition his brain could not absorb.

"Hi," she said. "These are for you."

Even that did not compute, although he guessed she meant the flowers. But why on earth would she bring him flowers?

"Can I come on the boat?" she asked him. She tipped the bouquet, so he saw her face. Sky-blue eyes and rosy lips. Star-white rope of silky hair.

"Yeah, of course." Harley shivered from his daze. He stepped from the cockpit and onto the deck. He could see up her dress to her smooth, lean thighs, everything tinted yellow like the inside of a buttercup.

Light as fluff, she landed on the *Alma*'s deck. She thrust the flowers into his hands. "I felt like I had to bring you these."

Shit, thought Harley mutely, what a way to say goodbye.

"Welcome aboard!" Liam called from the cabin door. He'd switched from his thunderous *Hamlet* voice to the one he used with women; Harley knew its milky tones.

"That's my dad," he murmured, guiding Cassandra along the deck and into the cockpit's cushioned space. "Dad, Cassandra. Cassandra, Dad."

"Call me Liam. Please sit down. I'd invite you into the cabin, but I've got it all a mess right now." He glanced at Harley, smirking. "You look like Miss America."

Harley shifted the huge bouquet. He'd never been given flowers before, and he didn't know what to do with them. He looked at Cassandra. "You didn't have to bring me these."

"I didn't know what else to do. Words can't say how sorry I am."

"It's all right."

"It isn't all right. You planned our date so perfectly, and I feel so bad for ruining the night. I hate myself, but I couldn't say no."

"He understands," said Liam as he shot a grin at Harley and slid back down the stairs.

Harley stood there, staring over the pungent blooms. Cassandra's eyes were soft and damp, and he started to feel confused. She didn't seem on the verge of breaking it off with him.

"What did you want to talk about?"

"*That*," she answered. "How awful I was and how sorry I am."

"That's all?"

"That's all. What did you think?"

"I don't know," said Harley, flinching from her gaze. A surge of relief that almost made him dizzy was pumping through his chest. "I'm sorry, too," he told her, not really even meaning it. "I was acting like an idiot. Sometimes stuff just happens. Important stuff and you have no choice."

"It would have been bad if I didn't go. Everyone was there that night, and I was the special guest." She smiled at the memory. "No one was jealous I'd gotten the role. Back in New York, they'd all be scratching out my eyes." In a softer voice, she added, "Still, I know, it was mean to you."

Liam showed his face again, a blot in the cabin door. To Cassandra, he said, "Tell me, do you like little, heart-shaped cakes?" She answered with a giggly laugh. "I'm serious. Do you like those teeny sandwiches with the crusts cut off and an olive on top?"

"Dad—"

"She does! She likes that stuff!" Briefly, Liam disappeared. When he came back, he handed Harley the keys to the Jeep, along with a plastic card. "We now belong to the Palmer Club. Take her for tea. She'll love the place."

"You serious?"

"Yeah. Give me those flowers. We've got a bucket somewhere here. I'll pass your blazer up to you."

⁂

They were halfway out to Palmer's Point. Harley had finally absorbed the fact that Cassandra wasn't dumping him. One of these days, he was going to have to tell her never to say *We have to talk*. But that could wait for another time. Right now the world was perfect. She was sitting as close as the seatbelts allowed, her fingers resting on his leg, her head against his shoulder, a light but burning weight. Sometimes he'd reach and take her hand, its smallness restoring his sense of strength and the power he liked to think he had. He wanted to ask her a million things—questions about

Ravenska and what her party was really like, and if she knew that Julian had gone back home. But he held this, too, for another time. It was just so good to be with her, to have her sitting next to him in her yellow dress in the splash of sun, after thinking it was over and he'd never have the chance again. So he left it at that. At the holding of hands and the gentle talk that didn't tell him anything except that she was there.

They were driving along the sandy stretch, which wound its way toward Horsehoe Bay, where the Palmer House and the summer hotels nestled high above the shore.

Suddenly Cassandra said, "Let's not go to that place for tea."

Harley's foot eased down on the brake. He drew to a stop and pulled the Jeep to the side of the road. Her face had a way of startling him, and today its beauty took his breath. He didn't know why, but her eyes looked bluer than ever before, her mouth more pink, more petal-soft.

"Take me somewhere else," she said. "Somewhere I would never go unless I was with you."

⚬☙⚬

Harley turned the Jeep around and they circled back toward town again. They reached the road that wound up to Ocean Watch. Halfway up, he slowed the car. He pulled to a stop in a patch of scruff and stunted pines.

"We're going in *there*?" Cassandra stared at the small, gnarled trees.

Harley didn't answer. He climbed from the Jeep and came around to open her door. He had a flash of serious doubt as she stepped from the car in her spotless dress and airy shawl. But peering down at her smiling face, he knew she wanted to go with him. He could feel the pulse in her clasping hand as he pulled her across the sandy road and through the field of the Black estate. She gasped when they reached the edge of the bluff.

It was not as high as the dizzying perch of Ocean Watch, but the view was still dramatic, a sweep of ocean, a stretch of sky. The difference here was the shape of the land. It wasn't sheer but sloping, and a kind of natural stairway descended to the shore. Still not speaking, Harley drew her forward and down the craggy path.

She had no trouble scaling the rocks, and they quickly reached the ledge below. Its width was maybe fifty feet, and along its rim, the ocean crashed.

"I love it here!" Cassandra cried. Her cheeks were pink and wet with spray. She stopped to pull her sandals off and reached for Harley's hand again. She was light, so light, so sure and graceful on her feet, it was nothing at all to bring her along. Even when the rocks grew sparse, she flitted easily over the gaps above the dark green swirls.

"There it is!" called Harley as he spotted the landmark up ahead. They'd reached a section of the coast where the cliff receded inward and the shore stretched out in front of it. Huge, black boulders jutted from the sheer stone wall. They looked like a jumbled pile of rocks that an angry ocean had flung to shore.

Harley slowed down as they approached. Cassandra's face was radiant, her mouth half open, and her eyes blue o's. He leaned to kiss her shining cheek, inhaling the taste of salt. Then, clasping her hand, he drew her through the high, black door, back through the years, back into his childhood, into the cool, damp dark of the pirates' den.

Cassandra froze as she stepped inside. Harley, too, had to take a breath. The cavernous space was awesome. He felt the same strange mystery he'd felt when he first saw this place, a nine-year-old boy who'd thought he'd fallen through a hole to the center of the earth. His eyes roamed over the rugged walls, multicolored with moss and salt, and along the pitch-black niches, up to the roof and the jagged chinks filtering shafts of light.

"It's beautiful!" Cassandra cried. Her voice was small in the vaulted space. "How did you ever find this place?"

Harley's voice was just as faint. "I found it with my friends one day. We claimed it as our pirates' lair. There's our symbol on the wall." The skull was pretty badly drawn, but it somehow looked good on the craggy rocks. "We practically lived here, my friends and me."

"You came here when you were little kids? All by yourselves? How wonderful!"

"Nowadays, they'd probably call it child neglect. But we were happy, the guys and me. Especially in the summertime."

"I can't imagine a life like that. I would have loved to come here, too!"

"Sorry," said Harley. "No girls were allowed in the pirates' den." As he said the words, he knew they really weren't true. Mairin had followed them here one day. Although they posted warnings, she came whenever she wanted to and took the name Queen Anne's Revenge.

Cassandra ambled around the space, running her hands on the bumpy walls. "What did you used to do in here?"

"Pirate stuff," said Harley. "We cursed. Took oaths. Cooked hot dogs. And sometimes we counted our booty up."

"Your booty?"

"Yeah." He glanced back over at the skull. It was probably still hidden there in the murky niche just underneath. He couldn't imagine that Red Legs or Pugs would have taken it out. He moved to the spot, and reached inside the cool, black hole. There it was, small but solid in his hands.

Cassandra drew close as he pulled it out. It was shaped just like a captain's chest but about the size of a box for tools. Black-green mildew scarred the wood, and the hinges were thick with rust.

"What *is* it, Harley?"

"I'll show you. Look." He set the chest on a flat-topped rock, working the stubborn latch. Then, lifting the lid, he revealed the cache of precious jewels. Memory came flooding back. Those blood-red plastic rubies had been swiped from Pugs's sister, June. Red Legs had stolen that giant diamond ladybug when his grandmother came for a weekend stay. Harley himself had pilfered the pearls from the ninety-nine cents store in town.

He turned to Cassandra. "Come here. Sit down."

First he slipped off her gauzy shawl. It slid down her arms and pooled on the rock. He untangled the strand of mildewed pearls. Draped them carefully over her head, lifting the heavy braid. Next he put the rubies on, gleaming beads that dribbled down her small, high breasts. He layered the gold on top of that, the long, fake chains and shiny ropes. On her fingers he slipped the gone-green rings, and around her wrists the bangles that clinked with silver coins. Into her braid he pinned the diamond ladybug.

"I'm the queen of the pirates," Cassandra announced as he took a step back to gaze at her. Harley didn't argue. The bright junk jewelry looked real on her. The silver shimmered; the rubies blazed in the shaft of slanting light.

"Step forward, pirate," she ordered next. "What's your name?"

"I'm Captain Blood."

"Very well, Blood. I now command you to kiss your queen."

The pirate complied. Leaning over her small, bright form, he tipped her head and kissed her mouth. She jangled as he eased her down, her back against the rock. He kissed her again until his lips felt bruised. Then, he traced his mouth along her neck, nudging the pearls on her shadowed throat. He could feel her pulse against his lips. He followed the strand of rubies, allowed his mouth to linger for a heartbeat as a moan escaped from the narrow seams of her yellow dress. He kissed her hair, biting the braid between his teeth. When he eased her up to sit again, she looked like someone wakened from a long and languid dream.

For a moment, neither of them spoke. Cassandra's fingers twirled around the scarlet beads, an interplay of red and white. Then she said, "It was sort of like this the other night."

Harley looked up and into her face.

"At Theo's party on Saturday night, she let us put her jewelry on. She has three huge cases filled with things and we got to try whatever we liked. Necklaces, brooches, bracelets, rings. You should have seen the bunch of us."

Something inside Harley—a pulse, a flutter, a racing joy—skidded to a stop.

"Theo?" he echoed, drawing away. The word left a taste at the back of his mouth.

Cassandra giggled. "She said that we could call her that. But only at her parties and never when we're in class." She gathered the shawl from around her hips. "And she gave me this. Isn't it too beautiful?" Harley stared at the length of cloth, which she drew across her shoulders now. "It's very old. She used to wear it when she was young." Her eyes roamed through the cave again. "Her room is a little like this place. Mysterious and beautiful with thousands of candles everywhere. It still feels like a chapel. And yet it's not like a chapel at all."

Harley reached for the chain of plastic rubies and eased them from her neck. He was careful not to touch the shawl. It suddenly looked like spider web cloying to her skin. "What else did you do at Theo's place?"

"Mostly we talked. It was really nice."

"Talked about what?"

"About lots of stuff. She told us stories bout her life. The roles she danced and all the places she's traveled to. She has hundreds of pictures around the room. She's been everywhere in the world."

Harley removed the string of pearls. "And you don't get bored listening to all that stuff?"

"Bored? God no! Plus, it's not just Theo. *We* talk, too. She loves to hear about our lives. And we eat the most amazing food. We had prawns and figs and the smallest eggs I've ever seen, served on these tiny spoons. Maybe I shouldn't tell you this, but she also let us drink some wine."

Harley didn't care about that. Or what kind of crazy food they ate. He treaded lightly as if on glass. "So what did you tell her about your life?"

Cassandra was quiet for a while as he slipped the bangles from her wrist. "You're wondering if I mentioned you. And the answer is yes. I told them all about you. How sweet you are. How you saved me in the storm that day. How you live on that boat and know how to sail. And I told them that I stood you up to go to her *soirée*."

Harley's finger snagged on a clasp, and a bracelet clattered to the ground. His hands were damp as he picked it up.

"Theo felt bad," Cassandra went on. "And she wants to make it up to you. She gave me a gift—for the both of us."

"I don't want anything from her," Harley said, a touch of sharpness in his voice. "Listen, Cassandra. There's something I have to tell you. Something that you need to know. Madame Ravenska is not the person you think she is—"

"Oh, Harley, please. Don't stay mad. It's an absolutely special gift. I was going to tell you later on, but I guess I might as well show you now."

"Really, Cassandra—"

"Just wait till you see what it is, all right?" She reached for her purse, which lay on the rock beside the chest. She drew out a slender envelope and slid two tickets from under the flap. "Do you know what these are?" she whispered. And before he could answer or make a guess: "They're ballet tickets—to see *Giselle*. Theo bought them for herself, but she wanted us to have them. It's the Boston Ballet. Next Saturday night. Please tell me that you'll come with me."

Harley was at a total loss. His mind had spun at the thought of *Theo* giving them some sort of gift. He couldn't imagine what it might be, but he knew he didn't want it. He didn't want anything from her. But this, two tickets to the ballet, was an absolute surprise. It meant they would be together, Cassandra and he, away from the school. In *Boston*. Ravenska was sending them on a date, which Harley had thought she was trying to thwart.

"Please!" Cassandra begged again. "It's important for me to see the ballet since I'm going to be Giselle myself. And I want for you to see it, too!" There was one last piece of jewelry Harley hadn't yet removed. Lifting Cassandra's long, pale braid, he flicked the latch on the giant diamond ladybug. She grabbed his hand and held it, her eyes reaching deep inside his own. "Please say yes," she whispered, each word drawn out like the notes of a song.

"Yes, of course. I'll come with you to see *Giselle.* Tell Madame Ravenska thanks from me."

Cassandra squealed with pleasure and threw herself against him, wrapping him in her arms.

"Harley," she murmured against his chest, "what did you do on Saturday night?"

"What?"

"When I broke our date. I can't stop wondering what you did."

"I got shit-faced drunk."

"All by yourself?"

He nodded.

"That's just so sad. I could almost cry," She let out a sigh, sinking deeper into him.

Harley leaned down and kissed her hair.

"I love you," she whispered into his throat.

And Harley answered, "I love you too."

He stowed the chest in its hiding place. As he slid the box deep into the niche, he glimpsed the pile of whitish stones clumped against the wall. In the dark of the hole, he couldn't see the spots of blood. But he knew they were there, and it bothered him still that Pugs had ever gathered those stones. Someday, he thought, he'd take them out and throw them in the ocean to the deep, cool grave where they belonged.

Chapter 15

It was Liam's idea that they spend the night in Boston. Vanessa, he said, would be more than glad to put them up. Her place was big with bedrooms to spare. They could spend the night on Saturday, and on Sunday they could walk around and see the city's sights. Harley was unsure at first.

"I don't know," he mumbled. "I think I'd feel weird at Vanessa's place." He'd met her twice. One of those faded beauties Liam was always drawn to. Tall. Long hair. Decidedly unmaternal. She stood at open windows to smoke her hand-rolled cigarettes.

"You'll hardly see her. I promise you." Liam was already on the phone.

Harley knew why his father was pushing the Boston plan. The other night at Red Legs's he'd heard the whispering of the girls under the roar of the Red Sox game. He'd found it funny, that secrecy. Did they really think he didn't know about the wedding on Saturday? Liam had reached Vanessa. His back was turned, but Harley could hear his quiet voice, setting his proposal out. He was probably right; the Boston trip was a good idea. The wedding would happen anyway, but at least he wouldn't hear the bells ringing from St. Brendan's Church. When he got back, Mairin would be Mrs. Smits and the whole thing would be signed and sealed.

❧

It was almost too easy how things worked out. Vanessa was "jazzed" to have them stay. Could hardly wait to see Harley again. Cassandra was thrilled and screamed ecstatically into the phone when Harley presented the plan to her. She called her mother to get permission to spend the night. Liam, too, later talked to Mrs. Birch, affecting his best real-father voice, not failing to hint at the millions of rooms in Vanessa's place.

The Jeep was washed for the second time in as many weeks. On Saturday at two o'clock, Harley pulled up at Ocean Watch. Cassandra flew out, looking totally hot in skinny, white pants and T-shirt, carrying a garment bag and a tiny suitcase the color of sand. Harley jumped out to take her stuff and plant a kiss on her upturned face.

Cassandra was smiling and out of breath. "I can't believe we're doing this! This summer's like a perfect dream!" She turned to the house and waved at a window to someone there. "Pia's jealous," she explained. "Did you know she has a crush on you?"

"Really?" said Harley, smiling. He stuck her things in the back of the Jeep. "She's already forgotten Julian?"

"Julian's gone."

"Yeah, I know." Harley opened the door for her and Cassandra slid into the passenger seat. He eased himself in on the other side.

"So now it's you," Cassandra teased. "Pia has eyes only for you. What's he like?, she asks me. Which boat does he live on? What's its name?"

"I feel bad for Julian," Harley said.

Cassandra laughed. "Don't worry. I'm sure that he'll get over her."

"I don't mean that. I'm talking about what happened. I saw him in town the other day, waiting for his taxi cab. He was pretty upset about his foot."

"I told you, Harley, it's just a sprain." She clicked her seatbelt into place. "If he lets it rest, he'll be just fine."

Harley backed out of the pebbled drive. The day was warm, but a breeze blew through the windows, carrying the smell of sea. "He told me he might need surgery."

"Don't believe that, Harley. They never operate on sprains. He was trying to get your sympathy."

"I do feel sympathetic. He really wanted that Albrecht role."

Cassandra didn't answer. She was gazing out the window, watching the scenery along the road. "Hey, look!" She pointed. "That's where we parked when we went to the cave. They've mowed the meadow, haven't they?" Harley turned. He hadn't noticed it driving up. The stretch of field on the Black estate had been flattened to a sprawling lawn, smooth enough for a game of golf.

"Cassandra?"

"What?"

"What if he does? What if he does need surgery? What if he can't dance again?"

Cassandra's eyes flickered from the window. "Why are you so concerned with this? And why do you believe him? Julian's always telling lies."

"I don't think that he was lying. He was really scared the other day." Harley paused. "He could hardly wait to get away."

"That's crazy, Harley. He's paranoid." She placed her hand on Harley's thigh, sending squiggly shivers down his leg. "We all feel bad about Julian. But his injury was minor. He's the one who made it worse. We can't be blamed for that."

"Don't say 'we,'" said Harley.

"What?"

"Don't say 'we.' You weren't there that afternoon, and you'd never have taken part in that."

"It's true, I wouldn't," Cassandra said. "But you have to know, they only meant to scare him away."

Looks like they did, Harley almost said aloud. But her fingers were making pictures, wavy patterns along his leg, and he told himself to let it rest. What the hell, they were getting away from that crazy school. And that crazy town, where a strange, sad thing that should not be allowed to happen was taking place the following day. There'd be plenty of other times to talk. Now was not the moment. They were making their break. Escaping. It was time to leave the crap behind.

At the base of the hill, Harley turned on to the two-lane road that headed out of Ocean Watch. For a long, blue stretch, beach grass wavered on either side and sand kicked up beneath the wheels. By the time they reached the highway, the lingering thoughts had flown away. As he hit the gas, he started feeling really good.

It was not unlike those moments on the *Alma* when the sails first winged and caught the wind and suddenly you were off. He hadn't left town since he'd been back, he realized as they sped along. It was easy for that to happen. To hit that place and just stay put. But now that he was on the road, flying north with a beautiful girl beside him, he remembered again how much he loved to get away and how sitting in that little town could strangle you to death.

Cassandra seemed to feel it, too. Harley could hear the bright excitement in her voice as she chattered and laughed and pointed out sights along the road. She read from the guidebook she'd brought with her and talked about things in Boston she wanted them to see. She flicked on music and sang along. Then, she turned it off and they drove in silence for a while. Now and then, he'd drop his hold on the steering wheel and reach to take her hand. Or she'd rest her hand at the back of his neck, leaving a sweet, dark burn.

"Hey," she said after one of their lengthy, quiet spells. "Let's play a game. The letter B."

Harley smiled. "What does that mean?"

"You look for things that start with B. Like there's one! *Bend*—the bend in the road."

"That's not a bend. It's hardly a curve."

"Okay. Bird. And don't try to tell me that's not a bird."

"I have one," said Harley. He turned his face to look at her. "Beautiful. That starts with B."

⸎

Vanessa opened the shiny door of her high-rise apartment on Boylston Street. "Harley. Wow. You've really shot up." She'd seen him last year at Christmastime. He hadn't grown an inch since then, or even in the last three years.

"Hi, Vanessa." He kissed her cheek. "This is my friend, Cassandra."

"Thanks for letting us stay with you," Cassandra said in her sweetest voice.

"Wow, you're pretty," Vanessa replied. "She's really pretty, Harley. Wow." Vanessa used to be pretty, too. Not that she wasn't attractive now, tall and thin with long, black hair that was clearly dyed. She looked like a rock star's girlfriend, the kind who dresses forever young, and who still wears her thick mascara and wobbly high heels. "Come on in. I'll show you the place."

Vanessa's apartment, unlike her, was modern and sleekly elegant. The furniture was low and white, and her big, steel sculptures loomed in the corners of the rooms. "So how's your crazy dad?" she asked as she led them through the loft-like space and down a white-walled hall.

"Good," said Harley. "He got a commission to restore some big, old library."

"Cool," said Vanessa, and Harley wondered if he should have let Liam tell her the news. "The guy's a freaking genius. He ought to work more. He ought to do his own damn stuff. Like me, you know. I'm busy these days. Lots of cool shit." She opened a door to more white space. "Here's bedroom one. Across the way is bedroom two. I'm upstairs, so do what you want. Bathroom's down there. Kitchen, oh yeah, it's back where we entered. There's not much food, but whatever's there, you're free to eat."

"Your apartment's great," Cassandra said, stepping inside the stark, white room. "It could be in one of those magazines."

"Thanks," said Vanessa, handing Harley a set of keys. "I'll be going out tonight myself. Not with a guy, you can tell your dad."

"He'll be glad to know that."

"Yeah. I bet." Vanessa offered a crooked smile. Her teeth were kind of crooked, too. "So you're going to the Opera House? You can walk from here. There are nice cafés along the way. I have no idea when I'll be home."

Harley said thanks, and Vanessa walked down the gleaming hall and through a door that led to stairs.

"She's really nice," Cassandra said. She put down her purse and draped her garment bag over the bed. Then she moved to the window to peer outside. Harley stepped in uncertainly, carrying their bags.

"Come look!" she called. "It's fabulous!"

The city sprawled beneath them: the tops of buildings, the blot-like trees, and off to the north, the big, green splash where the Commons and Public Gardens cut the blocks of gray.

Cassandra giggled. "I feel so old. Nice old, I mean. Like people on a honeymoon."

Harley smiled. He wrapped an arm around her, and pulling her close, kissed the top of her tilting head. He knew what she meant. It was just the two of them alone, far away from everyone and all the things that tugged at her. He began to wonder if he could change the way of things. If he could saturate her heart, so *he'd* be the one she'd tell her stories to at night. So *he'd* be the small, dark chapel, and the one she was devoted to. He was going to try, he told himself, as they turned from the high, bright window and back into each other's eyes.

Chapter 16

Harley could see heads turning as they climbed the marble stairs. Cassandra's dress was shimmery white. It showed off her smooth, bare shoulders and the beautiful bones at the base of her throat. Her hair was coiled in a seashell twist, a fat, white pearl pinned into the cleft. Looped low around her elbows was Ravenska's gauzy shawl. People were looking at Harley, too. He could feel their eyes drifting from Cassandra to see who he was, the lucky guy.

Their seats were in the balcony and Harley liked the high-up view. He could see the whole theatre from this perch—the walls with their ornate carvings and the scalloped pattern the arches made along the rising tiers. He could see the orchestra in the pit, black and white specks beneath the curtain, huge and red. As the lights went down, Cassandra reached out to take his hand. He leaned and kissed her on the cheek. The music began and played for a while in darkness. Then Cassandra's fingers fluttered, and the curtain drew up on a scene of a sunny village, a rustic house to either side.

Harley wanted to love ballet. But he found it kind of silly—that phony set and all the nonstop pantomime. The girls were cute, that he'd admit, in their ruffled dresses and petticoats. But the guys in those tights, oh, cripes, every inch of them defined, front and back and all around. He kept thinking of Pugs and Red Legs and what they'd have to say about this. Plus, the peasants seemed like fools to him, dancing around, all chummy, slapping each other on the back for no real reason he could see. *Townsfolk,* Julian had said. The word came sailing into his head as he watched them leap and kick their legs.

Then, a hunting horn sounded from off to the left. The peasants got all excited. But Albrecht, disguised as a peasant to woo Giselle, quickly ran to hide. A few seconds later, some servants with a wolfhound led "the Aristocrats" onto the stage. The Aristocrats were fully dressed. The men's long jackets covered their butts. The beautiful daughter of the prince wore a trailing ermine cape. Right away, the townsfolk prepared a table and chairs, and crazy Giselle began to dance. The peasants were always dancing, it seemed, while the royals sat there calmly, sipping from big brass cups.

Once the Aristocrats were gone, Hilarion found Albrecht's sword and hunting horn, which revealed who he really was. To prove his point he blew the horn, which summoned back the Aristocrats. Cassandra leaned forward slightly when they got to the part where the truth comes out: Albrecht is a nobleman betrothed to the princess in the cape.

"Watch," she whispered. "Giselle is going to lose her mind."

As Harley gazed at the scene below, he found himself thinking about the guy, the one who'd broken Cassandra's heart. Suddenly, he could picture Cassandra as Giselle, stumbling madly across the stage, spinning Albrecht's sword. It took the dancer a while to die, but when at last she collapsed in a heap, Cassandra let out a sigh. Her hand went limp in Harley's, and she softly fell back against the seat. Down on the stage, the Aristocrats seemed vaguely sorry about Giselle. But in the end, they just furled their robes and headed back from whence they'd come. Hilarion was left distraught.

❧

At intermission, Harley and Cassandra walked out onto the mezzanine among the buzzing crowd.

"Want something to drink?" he asked her as he noticed the bars along the wall. Cassandra seemed distracted.

"Not now," she said. "I have to write a few things down." She pulled a notebook from her purse and quickly began to scrawl. "Giselle is sweet and trusting. She's loved by her friends and sheltered by her mother.

She's never been deceived before. Ravenska says I have to understand her if I want to really dance her well."

Harley nodded. "That makes sense." He'd hoped the "R" word wouldn't come up too much tonight.

"I used to think Giselle was just so stupid. I mean, why would someone lose her mind all because of some horrid guy?" She stuck the notebook back in her purse. "But now I know it's possible. You can really go crazy. You can *die*."

Harley wanted to take her hand. He wanted to pull her close to him, so she'd think about now and not about then. But she was busy adjusting her shawl, pulling it around herself as if it could actually keep her warm. From down the curving corridors, a melodic bell began to chime, signaling intermission's end. She drew a short ecstatic breath.

"Oh, Harley, just wait until you see Act Two."

∽⟡∽

The audience applauded when Queen Myrtha emerged from the painted woods. Cassandra clapped, too, her hand slipping out of Harley's clasp. Queen Myrtha was all in white and was wearing a crown that reminded him of icy twigs. She flitted around the stage a while, surveying her terrain. Then, she tossed two stems of flowers into the wings on either side. Something swished. A breath-like sound. Harley felt a crawling chill as an army of ghosts pushed from the black beyond the edge. Misty veils covered their downcast faces, and they moved in a strange, bent posture, as if there was something wrong with their legs. Harley shivered in the dark. The chill seemed to rise from the soles of his feet straight into his scalp. There were so many brides, long lines of them, slow and sad, so he knew they were dead, like Mairin, whom he hadn't thought of all day long.

For the rest of the act, Harley watched as if alone. The music, haunting and repetitive, was marked by the drum of the *Wilis's* feet as they wove their patterns across the stage, synchronized and strange. Then came the sudden flurry as Hilarion wandered into the woods. Queen Myrtha gave her order, and the *Wilis* circled in a hoard, roping him into their pale corral, where they danced him to his death. Harley felt exhausted by the time Count Albrecht's life was spared and Giselle, like a fading candle, melted in the dawn.

The applause went on for a very long time. There were half a dozen curtain calls, and the ballerina who'd played Giselle was showered with bouquets. Harley's legs were sleepy and stiff, and the chill still lingered on his skin. Cassandra's hand had never come back. When at last the lights went up, she was in a world all by herself, rooted to her chair. People around them were streaming out, pushing past her knees. Harley waited, giving her time, but before too long the balcony was empty and the ushers were urging them to leave.

"Come on," he coaxed. "We have to go." He touched her arm and she rose from the seat like a ghost herself. He led her through the vacant aisles, down the stairs, and through the ornate doors.

"Oh, Harley," she breathed, as they stepped out into the tepid night. "How will I ever dance like that?"

"Cassandra, hey. You'll be a beautiful Giselle." He looked into her glassy eyes. There was nothing to see beyond the daze. "I think you ought to have something to eat."

On the way to the theatre, they'd stopped for a snack at a little café, but Cassandra had hardly touched a thing.

"I couldn't eat," she told him now. "I'm too . . . I don't know. Too *bodiless*."

Harley could not have said the same. His stomach was suddenly begging for food, tweaked to life by the scent of bread wafting from a restaurant. But it would have seemed rude to break into Cassandra's mood; she was still caught up in the moonlit realm of the ballet.

She suddenly pulled out her phone.

"Who are you calling?" Harley asked.

"I need to talk to Theo."

"Now?"

"I just want to thank her, Harley. And tell her how beautiful it was."

Harley opened his mouth to speak, but Cassandra had already hit speed dial. Traffic was thick along the street, and he looked out into the sea of lights. A taxi cab drew up to the curb, and a group of people crammed inside, their laughter trailing after them. Cassandra was hunched, the cell phone pressed against her cheek. She was mostly giving answers to whatever Ravenska was asking her.

Suddenly she turned to him. "I told her that you said thank you. And how beautiful you thought it was." Harley thought she was off the phone, but she bent again to listen, a hand against her open ear. "She wants to know if you understand what it's about."

The question startled Harley. He wanted Ravenska to go away. But Cassandra was waiting breathlessly, so he nodded; yes, he understood. Cassandra exhaled and reported back. A few seconds later, she slid the cell phone into her purse. "Theo's a little worried. I won't have a lot of extra time with all the rehearsals coming up. She hopes that you can understand."

"I understand that. And I understand the story, too." Harley stopped, trying to center in her eyes. He could not dispel the feeling that Ravenska's question was a threat. "Here's what I think the story's about: A guy's in love with a girl who comes from a different world. He has to learn the dances if he wants to fit in and win her heart. What do I not understand?"

Cassandra reached out and took his hand. "Do you understand this? That the girl's in love even more than the guy. That she loves him so much she'd die for him."

Harley took a long, slow breath. "And defy her queen to save his life?"

❧

The apartment was dark and silent. It almost seemed like another stage, pale-blue light glinting on the sculptures, illuminating the vast, bare floor. If Vanessa was home, she had gone upstairs.

"I think I'll take a shower," Cassandra said as they headed toward the bedroom. "I suddenly feel so tired and drained."

Harley went to the kitchen. Vanessa had said there wasn't much food, but whatever was there they were free to eat. There were three brown eggs. A bottle of vodka. A bowl of grapes. Harley pulled out the bowl and devoured half the fruit. He would have eaten all of it, but then Vanessa might starve to death and Liam would have no girlfriend. He looked inside the cabinets. Foraged and found some crackers. Paper-thin and just as dry. Back to the fridge for a swig of the icy Belvedere. He flicked off the light and turned to leave the kitchen.

Cassandra was standing across the floor at the entrance to the hall. She was dressed in a long, white nightgown, the light in back showing her body underneath in curving silhouette. Her hair was loose, a moon-bright stream coursing down one side of her. Harley froze. He tasted the vodka in his throat.

"Harley," she said. "I don't feel bodiless anymore."

❧

It all had the quality of a dream. The strange, blue light. The slowness. The sense that they were floating somewhere high above the world. Cassandra's body was stretchy and ethereal, and even his own rough substance—muscle, hair, bones that seemed enormous measured against her fragile frame—had a lightness and a glow. Harley looked beautiful to himself. Open palms against the bed. Wrists and thigh and a light-struck foot. It was beautiful, too, when they wound themselves together, her willow-supple arms and legs curling in complicated shapes. Knots and twists. The arch of her steely, pliant spine.

When he woke later on, he felt confused. He turned to his side, realizing slowly where he was, yet still not sure what had really happened and what had been a dream. Cassandra was not in the bed with him.

Harley got up. He drew on his jeans and slipped from the room. Silence hung in the loft-like space beyond the hall. The night had grown darker with the hours but was still a ghostly shade of blue. In the liquidy air, the thin, veiled figure dancing along the windows was luminous and white. Harley stopped at the edge of the space. He said her name. *Cassandra.* It whispered out across the floor. He said it again, but her figure continued dancing, floating, ungrounded, back and forth along the length of the room. Harley treaded slowly. He didn't want to startle her. As he drew in close, she spun around as if she'd heard his soundless steps. But her eyes were blind under the long, white bridal veil that had formerly been her shawl. Harley drew back. He saw Vanessa standing in the doorway where he had stood a moment before.

"What the fuck!" She exhaled the sentence into the dark. "Should anybody wake her up?"

"I don't think so. I'll keep watch."

"I'm going to have bad dreams," she said, moving backward down the hall.

Harley stood in the dim, blue glow. He hardly breathed as he watched Cassandra dance, alone, across the starless panes of sky, where he did not exist.

Chapter 17

The *Alma* cut through the cold, black waves. This nighttime sail was just what Harley needed, and he dropped back his head and let the wind rush over his face. He'd felt funny all week since coming back from Boston, oddly heavy and ill at ease as if something were hanging over him.

"Gives you perspective, doesn't it?" Liam said from his post at the wheel. "Wind and water. The great-big sky." He was doing his mind-reading act again.

Harley nodded. "Yeah, I guess."

"Did you ever think how easily we could sail away? I mean, right off the radar. Disappear."

"I think about it all the time."

"You're full of shit. You'd never leave your crazy girl."

"Is that what Vanessa called her?"

"Yeah. But who the hell is she to talk?" Liam coaxed the steering wheel. "She also said she likes her. 'Fucking angelic' were her words."

"All she said to me was 'fuck.'"

"I told her I thought it all made sense. The girl's obsessed with learning her role and you'd just come back from the damn ballet. What else is she going to dream about? Unless it was you in a pair of tights."

Harley didn't bother to laugh. "She didn't remember anything. When I told her in the morning, she said *I* must have had a dream. We went out for breakfast and it was nice. It was her idea to buy Vanessa flowers and stuff."

"That was good. I'm glad you did." Liam paused. "So what's the problem, son of mine? Who cares if she dances in her sleep? Have you been in touch with her this week?"

They had definitely been in touch. It was Friday now, and they'd been in contact every day. In between classes she texted him. Every night they talked on the phone. *She* talked, that is, and Harley listened tirelessly as she told him about rehearsals: every tiny detail, corrections Madame Ravenska had made, comments, suggestions, technical points he didn't begin to understand. It wasn't that this bothered him. He loved that she told him everything; he could listen to her voice all night. The problem was that talking was all they got to do.

"She has no time," he said aloud to Liam now. "All day long she dances. And now they're rehearsing every night. When she's not doing that, she's at Madame Ravenska's weird '*soirées.*'"

"Does she know about us, the madame and me?"

"No," said Harley bluntly. "I can't seem to find the moment. She loves that woman. I don't think she'd believe the truth."

Liam shrugged. "So what goes on at these *soirées*?"

"Apparently they talk a lot. And Ravenska tells them about her life. She feeds them figs and sparrow eggs. They all drink wine and probably say too much."

Liam laughed. "I can see it now. Candlelight and sherry. The glow of the stained-glass windows. And a coven of whispering, half-buzzed girls. Sounds like a dangerous mix to me."

"And Cassandra's all wrapped up in it. Something's different about her now. I can't explain it, but it's there."

"I'm not surprised. Ocean Watch has always been a spooky place. There's something odd and female there. Hostile to the likes of us."

"Us?"

"Yeah, us. Those of the male variety." Liam eased off the wind a notch. "You know what I think? I think you need a little space. Cassandra, I know, is a beautiful girl, but she's under a lot of pressure now. You could use a breather, too."

Harley stood up and worked the jib as Liam prepared to come about. The *Alma* turned, and the tall sails puffed with wind again. "You were with her last weekend," Liam said. "Give it a break. Spend some time with your townie pals."

∽

It was something they'd done each summer since Harley was thirteen. Full moon in July, they had a bonfire on Horseshoe Beach. It had started out with just their class in high school, but before too long, everyone was joining in. Along the shore, the fires could be seen from miles around. Harley's group was super-organized by now. Coolers and hibachis. Blankets, chairs, and music. A prime location on the sand. Harley arrived at eight o'clock. The sun was starting to go down.

"Harley's here!" called Lacy to the guys around the fire pit. They all looked up and welcomed him.

"We need you, pyromaniac!" Fitz yelled out with a sweaty grin, referring to a fire Harley had stoked one Full Moon Night with some highly explosive boatyard junk.

"What you need is kindling," Harley replied. "Weren't you a Boy Scout, man?"

"So get us some!" yelled Tommy Roy.

"How's it going, Roy Boy?" Harley went over to say hello. He hadn't seen Roy since he'd been back, and they pummeled each other's arms.

"Looking good," Roy told him. "How's college, man? Are they making you smart?"

"Smarter than you guys," Harley said. "You can't even build a fire."

"Get the fucking kindling, man," Johnny called from across the pit. Harley grinned and dropped the stuff he'd brought with him. Three six-packs of beer and a canvas bag with a sweatshirt and towel. He turned and headed up the beach to the line of scruffy shrubs. Along the way, he bumped into Pugs and Becky, who were hauling a giant cooler filled with food and drinks.

"Harley, hi. So glad you made it!" Becky called.

"You really think I'd miss Full Moon?"

"You never know these days," said Pugs.

"Oh, shut up, Billy," Becky said. She pushed back a flop of straggling curls. "I was actually hoping Cassandra would come. She'd love it, and she needs a break."

"When did you talk?"

"The other day. We were actually planning to take a drive out to the mall in Sandy Bluff. She canceled, of course. As usual."

Pugs broke in. "If it's all right with the two of you, can you save the chit-chat for later on?" He was holding one end of the cooler, the two back wheels sinking into the sand.

Becky rolled her eyes at him. "Talk to you later, Harley. Come on, grouchy, haul away."

From where he stood at top of the beach, Harley looked down at the shimmering bay. The surface was golden close to the shore, but beyond the horseshoe of the land, an orange blaze spanned the whole horizon, almost painful to his eyes. He had the strange sensation that he and everyone on the beach were being tinted by the light, and that when it got dark their incandescent skin would glow. Walking back down with the branches and twigs, he thought about Cassandra. Wished she was here to share the light and awe with him.

At least there were Becky and Pugs to watch. They'd parked the cooler and had wandered down to the water's edge. They were holding hands and their shoulders touched, dark silhouettes against the gold. Something in Harley's body ached, a physical longing centered underneath his ribs that thrummed like a deep, low chord. He walked to the pit, dropping the kindling onto the logs. He watched as Johnny struck a new flame. The sky was brighter than the fire.

By the time the edge of the sun dropped down, they were all in their places around the pit, beers in hand or clasping cups of cheap, pink wine. Harley sat on a big, red blanket Becky had brought, with Pugs and her and Roy Boy's dog, who had joined the group. Red Legs and Johnny looked like kings in a couple of legless beach chairs, and Lacy and Sue were perched on rubber tubes. Next to them sat Jim and Walt and some other guys who used to be on the football team. The cheerleaders huddled next to them as if time had stopped one golden, autumn day last year. Harley liked the changeless scene. In the mood he was in, it soothed him. It was nice to know there were things that he could count on. Steady things like girl-pink wine and people in their slotted places.

Harley relaxed as the moon floated up in the purple sky. He'd built a backrest out of sand and had fortified it with his bag. He was barefoot and cool, the bonfire's heat drifting west and out to the bay. Breathing deeply through his mouth, he could taste the salty water, the seaweed tang, and hot dogs charring on the grill. The summery scent of Becky's OFF! drifted like an undertone. *Sand fleas*, she'd said, passing the plastic bottle as if she were the mom.

The conversation drifted. Bluefish were running. Johnny's dad had spotted two sharks. Lobsters were big, and jellyfish had stayed away. Wally's seawall was caving in, and Mairin had made a pretty bride. Harley flinched as he caught the words.

"That was her grandmother's dress, I heard," said Jane O'Neill from across the way. "With that empire waist Mairin didn't show at all."

"Real Irish lace," said Lizabeth.

"I loved the veil. That crown of flowers. She looked like a saint."

"Some saint," said Jane and the others laughed.

"I'm surprised her mother went for it," Lizabeth said in serious voice. "With the party afterward and all."

"Yeah, me, too. Talk about a hatchet face."

"Her mother thinks she hit it big just because Smits's father has an in-ground pool behind the house."

"Shit. Three o'clock!" snapped Sue Malone, tilting her head as if knocking water out of an ear. Everyone spun around to look. Harley turned too, as Smits and Mairin, loaded with bags, approached the group.

"*Be nice!*" rasped Becky under her breath.

Everyone pasted a smile on.

"Look who's here! The newlyweds!" That was Lacy, obeying orders way too hard.

"Hey there, Mairin!"

"What's happening, Smits?"

"Congratulations," said Johnny and Roy.

"Yeah," said an echo from off to the left. Smits went around for handshakes as if he were mayor of the beach.

Harley got up, not for him. "Mairin, hi. Sit here with Becks."

She met his eye. And the look in hers said everything. *Thank you. Hello. I need this seat. I hate my life, and what have I done? Has there ever been such a big, white moon?*

Harley sank down in the still-warm sand a little ways off. He'd left his canvas bag behind, and he liked the idea that it served as Mairin's pillow. He wanted to give her something, some tiny comfort, whatever he could. She looked tired and pale, slight in the baggy, cotton dress. His mind roamed off against his will, and he pictured her in a wedding gown. Irish lace, the girls had said. A wreath of flowers. A long, white veil. He snapped off the image in his head and looked at Red Legs across the way. He was sitting with Jane and the two of them were laughing. A cheerleader. Wow. Could it really be true? Red Legs had always wanted one.

Harley got up for another beer, and when he came back, Smits had weasled onto Becky's blanket. He was sitting next to Mairin, possibly leaning on Harley's bag. His arm was around her shoulder in a tight, possessive-looking clutch. As Harley sat down, he shot him a gloating smile. Harley didn't smile back. The others on the blanket were asking about their "honeymoon"—two short days in a tourist town an hour away—and Smits described the beach hotel as if it were the Ritz. The girls told Mairin how much they'd liked the wedding and how great she'd looked in the antique dress. They asked about her new apartment over the shop. How was she going to decorate? Was she fixing up the baby's room?

"If only you knew what it actually was," Jane remarked through a sip of wine. "I mean, boy or girl. Pink or blue."

"You can always do yellow," someone said. "My cousin Eileen did yellow and it really looked adorable."

Smits got up. "I'm out of here." Like the subject of domestic life had nothing to do with him. He joined the guys at the barbecue, who were slugging shots from a bottle of bourbon Fitz had brought.

"You should eat a burger," Becky said to Mairin. "You don't even have to eat the bun."

"I'll throw it up," she answered. "Eating anything makes me sick."

"Aren't you feeling better yet?"

Then Lacy murmured something, and the other girls leaned inward, forming a protective ring. Harley caught the whispered "blood," and knew he should follow in Smits's tracks. He climbed to his feet, but didn't join the other guys. They were already getting dumb and loud. He ambled down to the water's edge, where the moonlit waves came lapping in. The entire bay was bathed in light. It was silvery and luminous, tinted at the dampened rim with streaks of mirrored fire. Harley waded slowly in, to the edge of his cut-off jeans. The water was cold like its silvery hue. The voices of partiers on the shore bounced from its chilly surface, so the silence it held seemed deep and vast.

Tonight it felt like Harley's realm. He loved his friends, but something was missing back on the beach. Something that used to be there. Or was he the thing that had gone away? He took another forward step and plunged into the bay. He started to swim, stroking hard, away from the shore and into the night.

❦

When Harley got back, winded and cold, the girls were wearing sweatshirts and had drawn the blankets close to the fire. Red Legs was cozied up with Jane, but most of the guys were playing some rule-less, improvised game involving driftwood and two dead crabs. Smits was clearly drunk. Harley looked for Mairin. She wasn't in the group of girls. Just as he realized she was gone, Becky suddenly reappeared.

"I tried," she said to all of them and no one. She looked exhausted, her curls awry. "At least I got her up to town. She said she wanted to be alone."

"He's such an asshole," Lacy said, glancing vaguely across the sand. "Someone ought to bring *him* home."

"Or not," said Becky grimly. "She'd rather he just passed out down here."

"Did she actually say that?" Lizabeth squeaked. Harley didn't listen for an answer. Grabbing his bag, he turned and started up the beach.

"Harley, no!" gasped Becky. "If Smits sees—" But Harley didn't give a damn. Plus, Smits was so drunk he could lay him flat if it came to that.

Chapter 18

Her small, dark form moved slowly up the dimly lit slope. Now and then she stopped in place, bending slightly forward as if she might be sick. There was nobody else on the silent street, and Harley's footsteps echoed as he broke into a jog. Mairin turned when he was several yards away. She was holding her stomach in both her hands.

"Mairin, hey, are you all right?" He knew how stupid the question was. "You look like you're in pain."

She stared at him, her green eyes glazed. "I thought you were going to swim away. Just swim and swim to Portugal."

"Mairin—"

"I saw you go in and I wished that I could follow you." She shook her head, black rings falling over her cheek. "Remember we used to do that, swim out to Parrot Island? And sometimes I'd even beat you there."

"*Sometimes?* Always," Harley said.

"But now I can't do anything."

"Yes, you can."

"No, I can't." She drew a breath. "I thought you had a girlfriend. Why didn't she come to the party tonight?"

"She's busy at the ballet school." Harley paused. "They have to rehearse and stuff like that."

"I'm curious to meet her. I try to imagine what kind of girl would win your heart." She clutched her stomach, emitting a groan. Then, glancing back up Harley: "I'm not in pain. I just feel nauseous all the time. In the morning. At night. In the afternoon."

"Is that normal?" he asked.

"How would I know?" Her pale lips stopped at the edge of a smile. Then, something flickered across her eyes and she asked him in a nervous voice, "Did Denny see you coming here?"

159

"I don't know, and I don't care."

"*I* care, Harley. That wouldn't be good."

"I'm not afraid of Denny Smits."

"Good for you," she answered and started to turn away from him.

"What the hell does that mean?" Harley reached out and grabbed her hand. "Are *you* afraid of Denny Smits? Does that asshole ever—"

"No," said Mairin. "At least, not yet."

Harley's heart was doing a war dance in his chest. He had to struggle to slow his breath. "Don't go home," he suddenly said. "Come back with me and stay on the boat."

"What? You're crazy."

"No, I'm not. My dad wouldn't mind. He'd want you to."

"Denny is my husband now."

"I don't care. He's shit-faced drunk and stupid, and I think that you're afraid of him."

"I'll be all right. I'll lock the door."

"Are you kidding me, Mairin? You'll *lock* the *door*? What's this guy been doing to you?" Harley was really on the edge. He was starting to hyperventilate.

"He hasn't done anything," Mairin said. "He's just loud and awful when he's drunk."

"And just how often is he drunk?"

"I don't know. After the wedding, he drank a lot. And one of the nights when we were away."

"You were only away two freaking days!"

"I think he's feeling a little bit stressed."

"Screw it, Mairin. You're coming with me."

"No, I'm not." She took a step back beyond his reach. "I have to make this marriage work."

"You don't have to do that!" Harley practically spat at her. "Not if he's a goddamn drunk! Not if you're afraid of him."

"You don't understand," said Mairin. "Something happened recently."

Harley waited, trying to catch one good, long breath. "What?" he finally snapped at her.

"It moved. He moved. My baby *moved.*" Mairin's pallid face transformed. The tension melted from her jaw, and a gleaming tenderness filled her eyes. Harley suddenly found himself staring at someone he didn't know.

"I already love him," Mairin said. "I don't care about his father. Who he is or what he's like." She threaded her long, thin fingers over the insubstantial mound. "I've never loved anyone as much."

Harley found that he couldn't talk. Whatever he'd thought about their separation—how *he'd* been the one who'd gone away—reconfigured on the spot. His move from town, the distance of miles from here to Maine—none of this meant anything measured against her distance, the faraway place where she had gone.

Harley leaned forward and kissed her cheek. "Okay, Mairin. I'll leave you be."

She smiled faintly. "Thanks for coming after me."

"Take care of yourself," he murmured. Then, turning, he started down the hill, the lights of the moonlit harbor fuzzing in his eyes.

Cold as he was, Harley could not go back to the boat. He pulled off his shirt, which, like his jeans, was plastered icily to his skin. He wrapped himself in the long, wide towel, and walked in a plodding rhythm past the darkened storefronts, empty porches, and narrow houses along the way. When he reached the street that ran along the harbor, he dragged past the row of silent shops, looking in the windows at the faint reflection of himself, a strange, dazed figure in a cape. He trudged to the very edge of town. Then, passing the chocolate shop, he turned. He found himself walking up the hill on the lightless road to Ocean Watch.

As he hiked along, he started feeling better. The exertion helped and the air was slightly warmer here. In one of the mansions, a party was still going on. He could hear the drunken chatter, the ringing laughter, the clink of glass. They were probably out on a seaside terrace under the moon. The sounds grew faint as he climbed the slope. Now and then, something stirred in the undergrowth, small, nocturnal animals, whatever they were, who lived in the sea pea and stunted brush. Harley didn't have a plan. All he knew was that something had changed, and he needed to be near someone who still loved him. Someone from *now*, this moment, and not some dream from the finished past. Suddenly his footsteps froze.

Through the trees ahead, he thought he glimpsed a flash of light. Or maybe not light, just whiteness—a glimmer of something bright and pale, flickering through the ragged limbs. He stood in place, not breathing. And then he saw the flash again. He heard a *whoosh*, a whisper like curtains in the wind, and all at once there were many bright flashes among the trees. The flashes began to take on shape, transforming into figures. They were slender and white, their faces shrouded in mist-like veils. Barely seeming to touch the ground, they wove their haywire patterns through the branches of the pines. He knew what he was looking at, but he couldn't say it to himself. He couldn't name the horror. He had no word for how it felt to be in danger as strange as this.

But the *Wilis* didn't see him. Blind, entranced, they swarmed from the woods, a legion fanning across the moonlit field of the Black estate. Harley exhaled. And then he saw the boy. He was tall and thin and seemed to be lost. Who the hell *was* he? And what on earth was he doing up here? Harley knew they'd spotted him. Already the *Wilis* were circling in, surrounding him in their wide, white ring. They swirled and spun, pushing him back when he tried to break loose from the tightening chain.

Harley felt a scream rise up. It was all so unreal, yet he knew that it was happening. Those girls were real. That boy was a breathing human being. Like Teddy Flynn. Like Julian. Like the one whose beautiful face was burned.

He couldn't let it happen again. He leapt from the cover of the trees.

He heard the music as he did. Faint and blurred, it drifted softly across the field as if carried on the moon's white light. He halted in place. Derailed. Confused. Then, he saw the people. A clump of them, there on the side of the road. Some were taking pictures. Others were aiming hand-held phones at the eerie scene playing out on the field. As Harley stood there paralyzed, one ghostly girl danced in from the edge. He drew a breath that stuck in his throat. Like a sequence in a slowed-down film, the pieces began to fall in place. The girl was Giselle—*Cassandra*—and this was a rehearsal out in the air under the full, white moon. Harley stared as she glided across the silver grass. She did not look like a human being. She looked like a glowing specter risen from the grave. In all his life, he had never seen anything like this. He felt caught in a place, a strange and shady vestibule, between reality and dream. Transfixed, he watched as Giselle protected the weary prince, alternately dancing and imploring the bitter queen. Long minutes passed until at last the *Wilis* disappeared into the reaches of the field.

When the ghostly performance came to an end, the audience on the roadside cheered. The dancers formed a long, white line and curtseyed in swishing unison. The girl who'd played Queen Myrtha—it looked to Harley like Princess Ice—stepped out to take an extra bow. Then came two boys. Hilarion and Albrecht. Harley stared at the slender count. He was tall and dark with a regal face and shimmering, jet-black hair. A bookend to golden Julian. The line of *Wilis* parted and now Cassandra tiptoed through. There was more applause and some shouted "brava!" from the crowd. Cassandra curtseyed several times, and the whole ensemble bowed again. On impulse, Harley gathered a wild bouquet of sea pea and pine. He edged in closer to the crowd in the shadow of the trees.

"What on earth are you doing here?" The growl of a voice took him aback. Harley turned, meeting Hannah's stormy face. She looked him over from head to toe. "You must have lost your blooming mind."

Harley knew he was a sight. Soaking wet and shirtless. Wearing the towel like a Roman cape and clutching his bouquet.

"I just want to see her . . . to give her this." Hannah scowled at the clump of foliage in his hand. "Put on your shirt. You look like a fool." She grabbed the branches out of his hand so he could pull his T-shirt on. It was wet and cold, horrible against his skin. The unpleasant sensation coincided with more applause, and as Harley looked up, a tall, thin woman emerged from behind the line of girls. In the midst of all that whiteness, she moved like a shadow, black as black. Sleek, black dress and raven hair. Everything dark and elegant, the only spot of brightness the icy diamonds around her neck. She blew black kisses into the air. With a gentle push of a long, sleek arm, she urged Cassandra forward again as if to tell the audience to cheer for her student, and not for her.

Cassandra was dressed like the other girls in an ankle-length skirt of swishy tulle. But draped across her shoulders was the gauzy, cloying shawl. It seemed to wrap her in a mist that Harley wished he could blow away. He took a step forward onto the road so Cassandra would have to see him there. He caught her eye. Surprise and pleasure lit her face. She seemed about to come to him. Then, a sinewy arm slipped around her shoulder and drew her back into the soft, black folds. Harley met Ravenska's eye—or the place where he knew that her eye must be, in the angled shadows of her bones—and felt the cooling of his blood. Cassandra glanced back as her body was slowly turned away. In only seconds she was lost, another white bride in a flock of identical-looking brides who floated slowly up the hill behind the tall, black queen.

"Do you want me to bring her the bouquet?" Hannah appeared at Harley's side.

"It's all right," he murmured. "It was probably stupid, anyway." He turned and started down the slope, and Hannah let him go. After several seconds, he threw the bouquet to the side of the road. He was shaking all over from damp and cold.

Chapter 19

From where he stood in the white foyer of the Breeze Hotel, Harley could see Cassandra and her mother crossing the reception room through the shafts of late-day sun. Mrs. Birch was also blonde. Not cornsilk like her daughter, but a golden type with short, swept curls that twinkled in the light. They were both in pale-blue dresses as if they'd made a formal plan, and Harley felt a little awed by the picture-perfect look of them. He took a glance down at his khaki pants and the polished deck shoes at the hems. Liam had found that funny, trying to gussy up those shoes, and had called him Blazer Boy again. But what the hell. What was he supposed to do when the mother of the girl he loved was taking them to dinner at the fanciest hotel around? He cleared his throat, getting ready to talk.

"You must be Harley!" cried Mrs. Birch as he stepped from the foyer. She reached for his hands and smiled warmly into his face. Her eyes were blue, brighter than Cassandra's, and her skin was tanned with a spray of freckles around her nose. She exuded cheerful energy though her voice was soft and whispery, almost like a child's.

"My mom," said Cassandra glumly. She looked airy and pale next to her vibrant mother, and Harley thought she'd lost some weight, if such a thing were possible. Looped around her shoulders was the ever-present shawl.

"Call me Sandy," said Mrs. Birch.

"It's great to meet you," Harley replied. He knew he'd never call her that. He'd never call her anything. He turned to Cassandra and mumbled, "Hi." Almost kissed her, but lost his nerve. Mrs. Birch attached herself lightly to his arm.

"It's so lovely here. I've asked for a table out on the veranda." She reached to take Cassandra's hand and they walked in a threesome across the room toward the double doors that led outside. Harley felt self-conscious as people turned to look at them. Yet he had to feel grateful to Mrs. Birch. If not for her sudden visit, Cassandra right now would be in New York with Madame Ravenska and some of the girls. They were going to see the Bolshoi Ballet Company and spend the night at Ravenska's grand apartment overlooking Central Park. Cassandra had planned to be part of that. It was practically all she could talk about. Then, her mother called to say that she'd be passing through on her way to Boston College for a reunion of her sorority. Cassandra had practically had a fit. She could see her mother any time—she'd be going home in a matter of weeks—but when would she get the chance again to be a guest in Ravenska's home? *Never*, she'd whimpered into the phone when Harley spoke to her last night. She was still a little sulky now. Harley had heard it in her voice. That bored "my mom" she'd managed to drawl.

Out on the veranda, the glassed-in candles were not yet lit, and the white-clothed tables bathed in the glow of the setting sun. A host in a short, white jacket tinted with the same rare light escorted them to a table at the edge of the rambling porch. Harley sat where Mrs. Birch suggested, next to Cassandra, across from her. Mrs. Birch ordered a daiquiri at once and asked if Harley wanted a drink ("I know you college boys all do"). Harley declined, though he actually could have used a beer. Cassandra requested a Perrier, and he said he'd just have one of them.

Mrs. Birch unfolded the napkin on her plate. "So I hear you go to Colby. I have a friend, well, someone I play tennis with, whose daughter goes there, too. Mariah Clark; you should look her up."

"No, he shouldn't," Cassandra snapped.

"Just to say hello is all."

"'Hello,'" Cassandra mimicked. "'Do you happen to be Mariah Clark?' What's the point of that?"

Harley had the feeling it was going to be a lengthy night. He turned from the table and looked at the vista beyond the porch. The Breeze Hotel perched on a hill over Horseshoe Bay. From where they sat, he could see the beach where he and his friends had had their party the other night. A man-made ledge of piled rocks walled it off from the fine-combed beach of the hotel. But the sky, he noted, looked the same on either side, and the same bright bay gathered the light of the same red sun.

The drinks had arrived, and Cassandra's mother drew a sip. "My daughter tells me you live on a boat. All year round in this climate up here? You and your father must be very hardy souls." Harley explained that the *Alma* had heat and a small, wood-burning fireplace, but Mrs. Birch remained impressed. "I also heard that the boat is filled with your father's work. I read all about him. He's very well known."

"You *Googled* Harley's father?" Cassandra slammed down her water glass.

"Well, yes. I did. What's wrong with that?"

"It's like spying on people! It's just not done."

"I don't understand. I see you doing it all the time."

"No, you don't," Cassandra snapped.

"Yes, I do. You're on those Facebooks every day."

"It's not the same. I don't Google people to check them out like the CIA."

"Oh, don't be so dramatic. Nobody's like the CIA." Mrs. Birch signaled for a waiter. To Harley, she said, "I really wasn't spying. I just wanted to see your father's work. The way Cassandra described it, well, it made me very curious."

"It's okay," said Harley. "I'm sure my dad would be glad you did." The waiter arrived with the menus then, which saved him from meeting

Cassandra's glare. They ordered dinner. Caesar salads, then lobster tails. Cassandra said she only wanted salad, but her mother insisted on ordering the entrée, too. She also requested another drink.

"So, Harley," she said when the waiter had gone, "Cassandra told me how you met. How you came to her rescue in the storm. That's very romantic, I happen to think. Like a knight in—"

From inside Cassandra's white straw purse, her cell phone suddenly started to ring. She grabbed for the bag and pulled it out.

"Who is *that*?" groaned Mrs. Birch. "Don't they know it's dinner time?"

Cassandra glanced down. "It's them," she said.

"Them?"

"The girls. Christina."

"Well, shut them off, for goodness' sake."

"I just want to say a quick hello."

"Then take it somewhere, would you please? People are having cocktails here."

"Be back in a second," Cassandra said to Harley. She slipped from her chair, and before he had time to answer was gliding between the tables, heading back toward the double doors.

Mrs. Birch watched until she had disappeared. She picked up her glass and took a sip, then said to Harley confidingly, "You probably think I'm horrible. For not letting her go to New York with the group."

"I don't think that," said Harley. It was weird to be alone with her.

"Her father and I don't want her back in the city just yet. I mean, that was the whole idea of this." She gestured vaguely with her hand. "To get away and forget it all."

Harley nodded but didn't speak.

Mrs. Birch leaned forward, both hands on the tablecloth. "So, tell me, Harley. How does she seem?"

The question disconcerted him. Big and vague and not what he thought she was going to ask. He glanced at Cassandra's empty chair. "Right now she doesn't seem too good."

Mrs. Birch drew back with a fluttery laugh. "I don't mean *now*. I know she's furious with me. I mean how does she seem when you're together and I'm not here?"

"To tell you the truth, I don't get to see her all that much. She's really busy at the school."

"Yes, I know. But the two of you went to Boston. How was she then? Did you have a good time?" Mrs. Birch was staring intently at Harley's face. Something ticked at the edge of her eye.

"It was nice," he said, attempting a smile. "And I finally saw my first ballet." He was not about to tell her about Cassandra's dreaming dance.

Mrs. Birch let out a breath. "I can't *begin* to tell you how glad I am that the two of you met."

"Yeah, me, too."

"I probably shouldn't mention this. But back in New York, there was this *boy*. Things ended really badly, and Cassandra took it very hard. She's always been so sensitive." She paused for a second and glanced behind him at the doors. "That boy lives in our neighborhood. I see him walking around the place like no one knows what a horror he is. My husband and I just don't think she's ready for that—to meet him suddenly on the street."

She was hungry for information, Harley saw as he looked at her. Though the same, he knew, could be said about him. Drawing a breath, he ventured, "What did he do that was so bad?"

"Cassandra didn't tell you?"

"No. Just that it really messed her up."

"Anderson truly broke her heart. That's his name. Anderson Pitch. Are you sure you wouldn't like a drink? I mean, something more than that seltzer and lime? No one will care. I'll order it."

"Thanks. I'm fine."

"It's a rather ugly story, and I can't go into detail now. I just want you to know that we usually let her do what she wants. And I know how much Ravenska's invitation meant. We just feel she needs a bit more time. When we brought her here to Ocean Watch, she'd just gotten back up to ninety pounds and had finally stopped walking in her sleep." Her eyes flashed back to the doors again. "Maybe I shouldn't be telling you this, but my daughter is very fragile. After the Anderson incident, she actually tried to—"

Harley waited. She didn't go on.

She reached in her purse and pulled out a pad. "Will you do me a favor, Harley?" She scribbled at a frenzied pace and tore out the page to give to him. "Call me, please. If something seems *off*, just let me know."

He felt his mouth jerk into a smile as Cassandra breezed back, swinging her purse. He climbed to his feet, which Liam had told him would score ten points, shoving the folded paper in the pocket of his jeans.

Cassandra's dress made a swishing sound as she settled in her chair. "I hope you behaved," she said to her mother, smiling. She seemed much cheerier than she'd been.

"You'll never know if I did or not," Mrs. Birch responded. "So what was so important that it couldn't wait 'til a civilized hour?"

"It was intermission. When else could they call?" She stopped to drink some water, and then went on in a rapturous voice, "Christina said Ravenska's place is beautiful. It's huge and old, filled with art and statues. There's a marble foyer and a grand piano that Arthur Rubinstein used to play. The room that Christina and Blanca are sharing opens to a courtyard. There's a fountain in the middle with actual trees and these little, red birds that fly around. Christina said that the—"

"Little, red birds," mused Mrs. Birch. "And they aren't in a cage?"

"She doesn't believe in keeping birds in cages." Cassandra stopped to drink again. "They're going backstage after the performance. Then they're having midnight supper at a Russian restaurant downtown. It's strange," she said as the waiter arrived and set their salads in front of them, "I suddenly feel hungry. I suddenly have an appetite."

Harley didn't get it. He thought the phone call would get her depressed and angrier still at Mrs. Birch. He was glad it had done the opposite. But it was disconcerting that simply talking to those girls had totally changed her mood.

Darkness fell, and candles flickered along the porch. Beyond the bay over the slender spit of land, the lights from the harbor twinkled, and over it all hung the gibbous moon. Conversation was easier now with Cassandra taking part in it. They covered a range of subjects from rehearsals to Cassandra's friends. Mrs. Birch chatted about her tennis game and the beastly weather in New York.

She reached to take a piece of bread. "By the way, I saw Julian last week, limping along in a big, black boot. I can't help feeling bad for him."

"We all feel bad," Cassandra said. "While the girls are in the city, they're going to try and visit him."

Harley glanced up. "Does Julian know about this plan?"

"It's a surprise."

"Cassandra—"

"I think that's sweet!" Mrs. Birch enjoined. "It might surprise you, Harley, but the world of ballet is tiny. Everyone knows everyone. It's probably not so different from living in this little town."

Harley wondered if that was true. He'd started to think the ballet world was smaller, and measured against its tininess, Ocean Watch was huge. The girls would know where Julian lived. If they wanted to pay a "visit," they would simply show up and knock at his door.

Mrs. Birch went chattering on. The town was so quaint and charming, she gushed. Maybe next year if Cassandra came back, she'd rent a house for a couple of weeks.

Cassandra laughed when she said that her husband might come along. "If you can get Daddy to take a break . . ."

"Leonard's a workaholic," Mrs. Birch explained to Harley. He was a sports physician who ran a center in New York. Famous athletes were on his list of patients, and his greatest joy was getting to hang around with them. Harley said he'd take them sailing if they came. Mrs. Birch said the offer might just lure her husband up. The conversation turned to Harley's father then. It was terribly sad, said Mrs. Birch, he'd lost his wife at such a young age. And left with a child to raise alone! Liam must be a wonderful man. Harley knew she wouldn't find him wonderful. They weren't similar types at all. She'd find his father juvenile. Delinquent, in fact, a teenage boy. Cassandra giggled. She knew it, too.

They ordered dessert and Mrs. Birch had a *crème de menthe*. The conversation wandered. Maine. *Giselle*. The reunion tomorrow of Mrs. Birch's sorority. The "sisters" were still the best of friends even after twenty years. That's how it is with girls, she said. Under the table, Cassandra's tiny fingers rippled over Harley's leg.

After dinner, they ambled inside from the glowing porch. In the spacious, lamp-lit sitting room, guests relaxed in armchairs, reading books and talking with friends. They paused near the reception desk.

"I'm going upstairs," said Mrs. Birch. "It was lovely to meet you, Harley. In the fall, you should visit us in New York." She kissed his cheek and he thanked her for the dinner. To Cassandra, she said, "Don't stay long. I'll be waiting for you. I took the suite so we could spend a little time."

Alone at last, Harley grabbed Cassandra's hand. He drew her through the lobby and down the wide front steps. A path led into the breezy dark around the side of the old hotel. In a grove of shrubs and wild grass, he pulled her close and kissed her. She melted away inside his arms.

"The other night," she murmured, "after rehearsal out in the field, I wanted to come and talk to you. How did you know that we'd be there?"

"I didn't know," said Harley. "I just wandered up. I'm not sure why." He smoothed his mouth along her cheek.

"So how did I do? Was I an acceptable Giselle?"

"You were beautiful, Cassandra. Watching you dance, I could hardly breathe." For a second, he paused. "The strange thing is, I thought it was real. At first, I mean, when I saw those girls, the *Wilis*, and that guy out in the field alone. It felt like a scary dream."

"Poor Harley," she said with a little laugh.

"Who was the guy? Who finally got the Albrecht role?"

"His name's Joaquin. He's not so bad."

"I thought he was great," said Harley. "But I couldn't help thinking of Julian." He drew a breath. "Listen, Cassandra, your friends in New York shouldn't visit Julian. He doesn't want to see them. They're the whole reason he went home."

Cassandra pulled slightly back from him. "You don't get it, Harley. Julian left when he realized he couldn't be the star. He has an ego as big as France. Despite that fact, the girls want to go and cheer him up. I think it's really nice of them."

"It *isn't* nice. It's threatening."

"What?"

"I'm sorry, Cassandra, but it's the truth. He doesn't want to see those girls, and you have to tell them to stay away."

Cassandra moved from the ring of his arms. "It makes me feel really horrible when you talk about my friends like that."

Harley knew that the ice was getting thinner, and he had to be careful where he stepped. He looked at her face and the cloud of hurt that had shadowed her eyes. He wanted to shout *They aren't your friends!* But feeling her sudden distance, knowing she didn't understand and that truth at this moment would ruin the night, he settled with a limp request: "Just tell them to call him before they go."

"That would ruin the whole—"

"Please. Just tell them. Do it for me."

Her face seemed to soften along the edge. She sidled back into Harley's arms. "Okay. For you. I think I'd do anything for you." Harley drew her close again. She *had* lost weight, he could feel it now as his arms engulfed her tiny form and she pressed against his chest.

"Tomorrow," she whispered, "come up to the school. There's something I want to show you."

"I'm not sure that's a good idea."

"You don't have to worry. No one's there. All my friends are in New York, and Hannah spends half the day at church."

"When?"

"I'll call you when my mother leaves."

"What is it you want to show me?"

"You'll see tomorrow when you come." Her hand reached up behind his head, and she pulled him down to kiss her. The shawl slipped off her shoulders, and he kissed her neck and the pulse of her throat. Again and again, he kissed her, drowning in the taste of her, which was cool and sweet with a tinge of salt.

⸙

Harley's eyes snapped open. His heart was pounding in his chest. He could still hear the swish, the wind-like *whoosh* of the long white skirts. He could smell the heavy dampness that cloyed to the veils as they circled in. Not daring to breathe, he lay there, paralyzed, in the bunk. Moving would bring them back again. Out of the walls or wherever they'd gone with their weepy eyes. Two pale stars shimmered in the porthole, and he stared at the points of brightness until his breath slowed down and the smell of the grave went drifting through the open hatch. He eased up slowly and reached for his phone. He flicked on the light above his bunk and scanned for Julian's number. The coldness of the nightmare clung as his shaking fingers typed the words.

Thought u should know Ravenska's girls are in NY.
Might be coming to visit u.

Chapter 20

Harley slipped past the pillars and onto the grounds of Ocean Watch. He glanced toward Hannah's garden. If she were there, she'd notice anything that moved. But Cassandra was right; she'd be off at church. And all her friends were in New York. So he didn't know why he lowered his head as he hurried down the graveled drive and clung like a thief to the side of the house. Habit, maybe. Or just the funny feeling that if he looked up, there'd be someone in a window or the shadow of someone slipping away. He came to the slanting cellar door and thought again of Julian. When he first woke up that morning, he wasn't sure if he'd actually sent that e-mail in the middle of the night. In the light of day, it all seemed really crazy to get so rattled by a dream. Yet checking his phone and rereading the two-line message, he was glad he'd sent the quick heads-up. Averting his eyes, he hurried past the cellar door. He'd told Cassandra he'd wait behind the wall of rocks at the bottom of the house.

The day was bright and breezy, a sudden break in the August heat. The ocean was flecked with whitecaps, friendly ones that skirted the tops of the sun-struck waves. Squinting his eyes, he could see the sails of some far-off boats, skimming along the sky. Minutes ticked as Harley waited at his post. He hadn't wanted to come here today, except to pick Cassandra up and take her somewhere else. Liam had said he could use the Jeep. They could have taken a nice long drive. They could have gone to Green Banks for that dinner date they'd never had. But Cassandra was excited to show him whatever her secret was, and Harley couldn't say no to that. Time dragged on, and he found a stone to sit on from which he could see the door of the house. She was at rehearsal, Harley knew, but she'd told him she'd be done by three. One of the teachers who coached the boys had wanted to work with her and Joaquin on their Act Two *pas de deux*. That meant "dance for two," he'd learned, and it made him jealous to think of it. He'd seen the ballet, and he knew how romantic the whole thing was. Plus, he'd seen Joaquin in the meadow that night. Tall and dark, the classic Latin heartthrob type. When he let himself look at his watch again, it was almost four o'clock.

He pushed from his seat on the lumpy stone and took a last glance at the ocean view. The breeze had settled down a bit, and the whitecaps were thin and scallop-shaped, like a series of fading smiles. As he wriggled through the fence-like rocks, he saw her coming from the house.

She'd just slipped out of the door on the side and was rushing toward the shore. She was dressed in her clothes for practice. Black leotard, those pale-pink tights. Over that, a pair of low-slung, cut-off shorts. There were sweater-like things around her legs that jumbled at the ankles as she sprinted through the grass.

Harley stepped out and waved to her, and in an instant she was there.

"I'm so sorry!" she cried. "I couldn't leave. Stupid Joaquin kept screwing up, and Boris kept saying, 'One more time!' I thought I was going to *explode*!"

"It's all right. It's not your fault." Harley swept her into his arms and eased her back behind the rocks. Cupping her face, he kissed her cheeks. More slowly then, he found her mouth. There were things in the world worth waiting for.

Cassandra drew back and looked at him, a sleepy smile on her face. He watched her eyes as they drifted past his shoulder, and then suddenly blinked and widened as they reached the jagged precipice, and she realized where they were.

"Harley. God. Is that really the *edge*?"

"Don't worry," he said. "You won't blow off."

"It's so scary," she said. "But beautiful."

Like you, thought Harley, kissing her lips. His fingers encircled her fragile neck, touching the tight, low bun. He wanted to undo it, shaking it loose in his open hands.

"Look," she said. She took a small step backward and dug in the pocket of her shorts. Then, smiling through her narrowed eyes, she opened her rosy palm.

"Come on. Let's go. Christina let me borrow it."

Harley stared at the object nestled in her hand. For one long second it didn't compute. It looked like a key, an old, archaic sort of key, long and thin with the shape of an ax. His heart began to hammer. Did this mean what he thought it meant?

"Don't you want to?" she asked with a smile.

Of course I want to, a chorus screamed in Harley's brain. *Why would she even ask?* Yet his voice came out all wavy. "Now?"

"We may never have another chance." She was doing something with the key, digging it into Harley's hand as if nudging a secret keyhole in the center of his palm. "It's the perfect time. They're all away."

"There are other people in the house."

"But they won't see us. We won't get caught. The stairway's close; it's right inside." She was slipping slowly out of his arms, holding the key like shiny bait. Harley followed her through the rocks, across the grass, and straight through the heavy door.

It was silent and cool in the dim foyer. The floor and the walls were made of stone; the large and chilly vestibule had probably served in bygone times as an entrance for the servants. An archway ahead led into a hall, which threaded, guessed Harley, into the house. To the right was a hefty, wooden door. It creaked as Cassandra opened it, emitting a moldy breath. She motioned for him to follow her.

Once, when he was little, Hannah had taken him up these stairs. But that was in the wintertime when the school was closed and no one was there, and the tragedy hadn't happened yet. Harley must have been very young because way back then the stairwell felt large and drafty. Hannah had had a lantern, a great big thing that lit the walls in front of them. The passage felt oppressive now as they circled up in the glow of their phones, the space contracting with every turn, like the tapering of a screw. The higher they climbed, the stronger Harley could hear the sea murmuring through the walls. The sound of it made him want to stop. But then he'd glance up and see Cassandra's long, lean legs dipping into shadow where they met the tiny shorts. And the sea's faint message died away.

One last turn and Cassandra finally halted. She wasn't the least bit out of breath from the long and twisty climb. Harley came up behind her, holding his cell phone next to hers as she worked the key in the rusted slot.

The door gave way, and they tumbled into light-filled space. Harley stopped to take a breath. He felt as if they were in the spire of a church. The room was shaped like a hexagon, all six tall windows filled with sky. The ceiling rose up maybe twenty feet, and dangling from the center hung a huge ship's lantern on a chain. It was weighty and still, like a silent bell.

"Isn't it too beautiful?" Cassandra asked in a whispery voice.

Harley didn't speak at once. Beautiful, yeah, but something was wrong. He looked around the sun-washed space and realized what it was. All the windows had been glassed in. The rumor he'd heard in town was true. When he'd come here with Hannah those years ago, the wintry wind had swirled through one portal and out the next with a high-sung howl that to Harley's young ears had sounded like a crying girl. The stillness seemed strange, unnatural, and he didn't like the feel of it. Slowly, he moved across the room. He stopped at the central window, the one in the middle that faced the sea.

Cassandra came up behind him. Her arm slid warmly around his back, and she nestled close as he gazed outside. To the south there were several islands, small, green shapes with ferries scurrying back and forth, but off to the north and eastward there was only ocean and cloud-flecked sky. Harley inched closer to the glass. Forehead pressed, he could see straight down. The drop to the rocks was dizzying. The drop beyond that was a blue abyss.

"Are you glad you came up?" Cassandra asked. Her voice was soft and kittenish, and it pulled him back inside the room. He turned and looked at her smiling face. Sometimes she seemed so simple. Last night, for instance. Her childish behavior with Mrs. Birch. Or the way she'd thought that flowers could fix his mangled heart. But sometimes, like now, when he looked inside her sky-blue eyes, there were hazy mysteries he couldn't see his way around. Why, he wondered, did she want to do it in this room?

He touched her face, tracing a finger down her cheek. She closed her eyes, and he watched for a moment the flutter of the tinted lids, the skin so pale and tender, it almost ached to look at it. He kissed her brow, that eggshell bone, the plush of her cheek, the delicate jaw. His fingers did what they'd wanted to do since she first came slipping into his arms, and hairpins clattered to the floor.

Hundreds, thousands, it seemed to him, like a silvery summer rain. Her hair fell loose and tumbled, and Harley gathered it in his hands, lifting it toward his face. That was when he saw the nails.

She must have felt him stiffen. "Harley, what's wrong?"

His hands went limp, and the heavy hair cascaded free. He stared at the window. "It's nailed," he said. "Someone nailed the window shut."

Cassandra turned around to look. "I didn't notice that," she said. "Whoever it was didn't do a very neat job."

Harley inched away from her. He circled slowly around the room. "It's all of them," he mumbled as if speaking to himself. "Someone nailed all the windows shut." The thing of it was, they weren't ordinary nails. They were six-inch spikes, their heads bashed down and twisted, folded backward on themselves. There were ten, at least, along each side of the window frame. A shudder rippled Harley's spine.

"I don't think we ought to be up here."

Absurdly, Cassandra's phone began to ring. She blinked at the screen and flicked her eyes to look at him. "That was Christina. They just got home."

"They're here in the house?"

She nodded.

"Do they know where you are?"

"How would they?"

Harley reached out and grabbed her hand. He pulled her to the stairwell and started to lead her down. It should have been easier going in this direction, but instead it felt more dizzying. Harley clawed along the walls, and the spiral never seemed to end. The air was claustrophobic, humid and thick with the smell of mold. His thoughts wheeled round in circles, too. Why the hell was he afraid? Why was he running away like this? He hadn't committed any crime. They hadn't even *done* it, and she was the one who'd asked for that. Yet he couldn't slow down. He needed to get out of there. He thought about how he'd make his break as the stairs began to widen out and they neared the drafty vestibule. Cassandra would have to hurry inside. Divert the girls with questions. Keep them from noticing anything strange. Harley circled back again: *Why was he afraid of them?*

One last bend, and he landed at the wooden door. Cassandra pressed behind him, panting softly against his neck. "When am I going to see you again?"

"I'll call you," said Harley through his breath.

From the stair behind him she kissed his ear. "I'll go inside and find them. Wait two minutes and then take off."

She pushed around him through the door and hurried through the vestibule. Her footsteps echoed down a hall. He listened briefly for other sounds. Two minutes, she'd said, but he didn't wait.

Back outside, he skulked in the shade along the house just as he had done before. From one of the rooms, he heard some notes of music and the slam of a distant door. He glanced toward Hannah's kitchen as he passed the formal entranceway and bee-lined for the gate. By the time he reached the two stone posts, he was almost at a run. It wasn't the fear of being watched. Or even of being caught. It was something much worse than any of that. Something he'd never thought about and could only allow inside his mind now that he was out of there: what it must have been like for Teddy Flynn. The tall and gaping window. An instant at the very edge. Seconds of breathless freefall. Nothing but air and the whoosh of wind. The rocks floating up like scattered clouds.

Then, like a scene from some grade-B horror movie, he pictured Teddy's father, that raw-boned hulk with the ruddy face, who used to hang around the docks. He imagined Flynn, a madman at the window—who else on earth would have a need to do this?—pounding, slamming, twisting back the iron bolts so that no one's son could ever fly away again.

Chapter 21

"This place is a mess," said Harley. "What the hell should I do with this crap?"

"Don't touch my papers," Liam barked. He leaned in from the cockpit, a big, dead flounder in his hand. "Just clean up all the other stuff. I'll put the drawings away myself."

"We should call that Tidy Cabin girl," Harley said as he scooped up a pile of rumpled towels.

"You call, you pay," snapped Liam. "When you're off at school, this place looks great. Immaculate."

"Yeah, right," said Harley under his breath. He picked up Liam's sweatshirt, a pair of old socks, and a couple of newspapers from last week. In the cleared-off spot on the cushioned berth, another piece of clothing lay. It was something he knew and recognized, but for several dragging seconds he couldn't remember why. Then he touched it and right away knew. It was washed-out blue. A sweater. Thin as a bedsheet worn for years with frail, chipped buttons shaped like hearts. On the neckline was a label. *Fairy Island,* it used to say, but now it was too pale to read.

"Dad," said Harley, moving to the cabin door. "Why is Mairin's sweater here?"

Up in the cockpit Liam froze. His eyes slid down to Harley's hand, then up again and into his face. "She comes to visit me sometimes."

"Mairin's been coming to the boat?"

Liam slid through the cabin door with a bucket holding three large fish. "Got to get these on ice," he said. "Have you heard from the gang? Are they coming tonight?"

Harley ignored the questions. "How many times has she been here?"

"I really haven't kept a log." Liam shut the icebox lid and turned around to face him straight. "Maybe three or four times. We went out for a sail the night you were with Cassandra's mom. Mairin hadn't sailed in months. You should've seen her at the wheel. She actually looked like herself again."

Harley was at a loss for words. He was not even sure what he thought or felt. Finally, he asked in a gruff-sounding voice, "When were you going to tell me this?"

"Never," answered Liam.

"Never?"

"Yeah. She asked me not to tell you. She doesn't want you all jammed up."

"What the hell does that mean?"

"You know what it means. Don't play dumb. If Smits ever thought she was visiting you—"

"Now," said Harley, "who's playing dumb? What do you *think* he'd figure if he knew she was coming to this boat?"

"Frankly, I don't give a damn. But if he found out, I'd tell him the truth. That Mairin comes to visit me. He knows you work with Pugs all day."

Seconds passed. "I don't get it," Harley said. "Why would she come to visit you?"

"I know it strains credulity, but Mairin likes to talk to me. There's no one else who gets who she is."

"So you're the—" Harley broke off before he said something hurtful. It was hard to picture Liam as surrogate father of the year.

"Don't be jealous," Liam said.

"I'm not jealous."

"Really? Then why are you grinding that sweater up?"

Harley felt his cheeks grow hot. "I just didn't know she was coming here."

"Yeah, okay. So the secret's out. How about we let her do what she needs to do? If she wants to visit some dumb, old coot, let her visit the dumb, old coot. I love that girl. I always will. I've loved her since she was two years old."

Harley flinched from his father's gaze. Sometimes he hated the dumb, old coot.

⸞⸟

The night was cool and starry, but the cockpit was warm with the lingering heat of Liam's old hibachi, still simmering on the stern.

"The fish was great," said Pugwash, swabbing his plate with a piece of bread. "Tomorrow, Harley, you and me should take some poles when we go out."

"Yeah," said Harley. "We've got the bait."

"Question is, do you have the touch?" That was Liam, gloating over his glass of scotch.

"Where'd you catch these anyway?" Red Legs asked from his cushioned camp near the cabin door. As Liam launched into his fishy tale, Harley's cell phone started to buzz.

"Wonder who?" said Becky, who was sitting at his side.

Harley glanced down. "It's just a text."

"Yeah, I know. That's all I ever get these days. She never calls me anymore."

"She's really busy."

"Yeah, I heard."

Harley scanned the message.

Rehearsal bad. Theo doesn't like Joaquin. during adagio called him oaf. almost dropped me en penche Miss u lov u C

"Anything new?" asked Becky. Harley let her see the screen.

"What does that mean? Translation, please." Becky glanced back and read again. "And who are Theo and Joaquin?"

"Joaquin's her partner in *Giselle*. Theo is Ravenska. As you can see, they've gotten close."

"Is that what you call it?" Becky said. "Cassandra's, like, obsessed with her."

"I better text back. Should I tell her 'hi'?"

"Tell her hi to Theo, too."

Harley typed in his clumsy style.

Sorry. Sounds bad. Hope that u can wrok it out. Beky says hi. We're having diner on the boat. love u H

He stowed his phone and peered straight into Becky's eyes. "What do you know about Teddy Flynn?"

"*Teddy Flynn?*" Becky's whisper was like a shout, and the whole group turned to look at her.

"What's going on with you two?" Pugwash wanted to know at once.

"Sorry," said Becky under her breath.

From across the darkened cockpit, Lacy said in a quiet voice, "I saw his mother the other day. She's crazier than ever. Had a baby carriage filled with junk. Bicycle tires and winter coats with a Barbie doll sitting on the top."

"It'll be five years in a couple of weeks," Red Legs said through a sip of beer. "Time goes fast. We were just fourteen."

"I'll never forget that night," said Sue. "My dad and his were really close."

"What was he like?" asked Harley. "Teddy, I mean. You must have known him pretty well."

"He was older, of course. Kind of a nerd ball, but he was nice. He had a lot of comic books. When we went to their house, I'd sit and read those things for hours. He liked all those stupid heroes. Captain Marvel. Spider-Man. He had this antique Airboy lamp that he wouldn't let me touch."

"And he played in the band," said Lacy. "Something goofy, like xylophone."

"Yeah." Sue smiled. "I forgot about that."

Pugwash turned to Liam, who sat on a cushion out on the stern. "What do you think? Did you ever believe Teddy fell out that window?"

"Or jumped?" said Red Legs with a sneer.

Liam took a sip of scotch. The last of the dying charcoals tinted his face with an orange glow; to Harley, he looked sinister. "I never believed he fell," he said. "But I couldn't say if he jumped or not. Everyone's a mystery. Most of the time you have no idea what's going on in someone's head."

"And he was pretty weird," said Lacy. "I don't think he ever had a girl."

"Yeah," said Sue. "I always had to wonder why he was in that tower. Maybe he thought he really could fly, like one of those guys in his comic books."

"Or maybe," said Pugwash, "he *did* have a girl. One of those girls from Ocean Watch."

"Oh, right," said Lacy. "A dweeb like him."

"That drives me crazy!" exploded Pugs, slamming down his beer.

"Take it easy," Becky coaxed. She reached for his arm, but he brushed her off.

"But that's what everybody thinks. Like a regular guy, a guy from town, could never get a girl from *there*. Like they're so special, and we're so lame."

"What the hell are you talking about?" Red Legs said with a dopey grin. "Harley's got one, doesn't he?"

"Harley's different," Pugwash growled. He turned to Harley. "I'm sorry, man. But it's the truth. You don't really live here anymore. You're here for the summer, yeah, that's great. But, face it, man. In a couple of weeks, you'll be off at school. And in the end, you know you aren't coming back."

"For God's sake, Billy!" Becky breathed.

"I'm just being honest," Pugwash said. "Harley isn't Teddy. He's a college man and not some townie misfit, so Harley can be with one of those girls. That's all I'm saying. That's all I mean." A weighty silence filled the air. Harley reached for his bottle of beer. He could feel the beam of Liam's eye, watching from his distant post.

"You're an idiot, Billy," Becky said. She placed her hand on Harley's leg. "People can go to college. People can go away from here. It doesn't mean that somewhere deep inside of them they aren't one of us anymore."

"Becky's in college," Sue put in. "Is she some kind of *reject* now?"

"Yeah," said Lacy in distress. "Let's shut up and have a beer." A general murmur filled the air, and Red Legs popped the cooler, passing bottles all around.

The night itself was soft and calm, the moonless sky speckled with a zillion stars. Harley had always wondered, even as a little kid, where he fit in with all of it. The town, the world, the universe. He wondered vaguely if Pugs was right, that somehow he did not belong. But he didn't believe this really, not when the night was full of stars that faded into galaxies, and not when he was sailing and the ocean and sky merged into one and he knew, like faith, that he was a part of it. His cell phone started to buzz again, but he left it in his pocket, shivering on his thigh.

When everyone was leaving, Pugs came over and gave him some version of a hug.

"I'm sorry if that came out wrong," he said up close to Harley's ear.

"Forget it," said Harley. "It's okay." He thought it was. He hoped it was.

Yet he had to wonder as Pugs took off, trailing behind the group of friends, how it would be tomorrow out on the boat with their nets and poles, and for all the rest of the summer days now that he knew what Pugwash really thought of him.

∞

"You know what I think?" said Liam. He was lying flat out on the starboard bunk in the threadbare sweats he wore to sleep. He took a sip from the dregs of scotch. "Becky was right and Pugs was wrong. You're still who you are. You haven't changed. I mean, not in the fundamental ways. I wouldn't like you if you had. And I like you. I do. That's how I know."

"That's some brilliant litmus test."

"But Pugs *was* right about one thing." Liam set down the empty glass on the ledge along the bunk. "Poor nerd ball Teddy *did* have a girl. A dancer up at Ocean Watch."

Harley stopped mid-motion, his fingers stuck on the forward door. "How come you never told me that?"

"I promised Hannah I'd keep it mum."

"Hannah?"

"Yeah. Hannah knows everything up there. Like she knows you were there last Sunday."

"Shit. You really could've told me that."

"What's to tell? You know you were there."

"Jesus, Dad." Harley's fingers played along the rim of wood. "So what did Hannah tell you? About Teddy, I mean, not me."

"Just that he was seeing this girl. She was beautiful, said Hannah, and quite a catch for a guy like him. They both seemed really happy. Then something apparently went wrong."

"Something like what?"

"Hannah figures that maybe she broke it off with him and Teddy got depressed and jumped. That's all she'll say. She doesn't like the subject much."

"Pugwash swears that he was pushed."

"Which, of course, is also possible. He got me thinking tonight, that Pugs. Maybe Teddy *did* break it off with the girl. Some chicks can't handle a thing like that."

Harley gazed through the cabin over the bunk where Liam sprawled. He caught the allusion, plain and clear. "Maybe," said Liam, "the girl was too much work for him. Too much drama and up and down. Maybe she had no time for him."

Harley caught this allusion, too.

"Okay, Dad. Let's say it's true." Harley leaned against the wall. He pedaled the conversation back. "Teddy broke up with the beautiful girl. Marvel Comics Teddy. Teddy who played the xylophone. He tells her it's all over. Wouldn't *she* be the one to jump, not him?"

"Listen to Pugs. Maybe there was no jumping, man."

Harley uttered a mocking laugh. "I'm guessing Teddy was not too big, but there's no way in hell some little ballerina could lift him up and throw him out a window. You're crazy if you think she could."

"Unless," said Liam softly, "she had some help from a few of her friends."

The violet sky in Harley's frame of vision froze. For a second it looked like a wall of glass. Then the center cracked and it all collapsed inside his head. His eyes shot down to Liam, but all he could see was a thatch of hair, a blotch on a pillow in the dark.

"You're crazy," he muttered. "You're out of your mind."

"Hope I am." Liam didn't turn around.

Harley lurched forward, shutting the door. Inside his quarters, he flicked on the light. Its glow was dim, and his shadow was long; it stretched right up and out the hatch into the starry night. He yanked off his jeans and dove into the narrow bunk. A scrap of nightmare was coming back; he could feel it there like something glimpsed at the edge of his eye. He warded it off. Refused to see its blueness or hear the wind-like swish. He had to be drunk, he told himself. And Liam, of course, was very drunk, or he'd never have said that crazy thing. That cold-making thing; that could *not* be true. Yet hadn't Julian said the same that day in town when he left for home? And hadn't Harley thought it himself? Why else had he almost panicked when, up in the glassed-in tower, he learned that those girls were in the house? Freeing one arm, he reached to the bolster along the bunk, pulling something from under it. He pressed the fabric to his face. The old, familiar feel of it. It smelled like Mairin, whatever that smell was, and it made him feel safe to hold it, that frail, worn sweater, broken buttons shaped like hearts.

Chapter 22

Harley and Pugs were busy all day on the fishing boat, and neither mentioned the comments of the night before. There'd been only a minute of awkwardness. Harley had bought Pugs coffee, and their eyes had locked as Pugs said "Thanks" and took the bag. They were quiet as they motored out, but they were always quiet then, watching the sun float up from the sea. It was pearly and bright, and it made their petty crap seem small. By the end of the day, they were back in synch, lugging the catch of killies up to the bait and tackle shop. All the same, Harley didn't check his phone until he and Pugwash had said goodbye. He was halfway across the yacht club grounds when he finally paused and pulled it out. Cassandra's message seemed to scream.

OMG!!!! NY last wknd ACCIDENT!!! I relly need to see u C

Harley stared at the pulsing words. How could she send a message like that? How could she mention ACCIDENT and then not tell him what it was, or at least who was involved in it? He started to text a message back. All at once, his fingers froze. He lifted his eyes and looked across the gleaming lawn. Julian was sitting there. Or at least an image of him was there, all in white, immaculate, his booted leg hanging over the edge. Something in Harley's stomach lurched. He shut his eyes so tight it hurt. When he looked again at the space of wall that edged the lawn, there was only air, summery and golden on a scrim of dancing waves. Beyond all that was the placid harbor, the smooth, blue sky. What he was thinking could not be real. It could not occur in a world of summer afternoons where grass was green and sunlight winked on the rippling waves. *Pretty girls on weekend trips did not cause terrible "accidents."*

And yet. They'd said they were going to visit him. Harley should have called him instead of just sending the e-mail that night. He lowered his eyes to the phone again. He didn't reply to Cassandra's text. Instead, he clicked his contact list. With a lump in his throat and a feeling of dread like a rising tide, he typed the message and clicked on SEND.

Julian. Hi. U doin OK?

Stowing his phone, he continued his trek across the lawn. He hurried along the quiet docks, sprinted down the ramp and climbed aboard the boat. Down in the cabin, Liam and Mairin were sitting at the table, Liam's sketches scattered about. Harley uttered an audible gasp.

"I didn't know—" His voice trailed off.

"Someone chasing you?" Liam asked.

Harley didn't answer. He could hear the thumping of his heart.

"Hi," said Mairin.

"Hi."

"I hear you've discovered our affair. It's all my fault; I was indiscreet." She paused and smiled. "Do you happen to know where my sweater is?"

In Harley's brain, the gears were crunching out of control. Full stop. Full speed. Everything gone off the track. He took a short and stabbing breath. She was wearing another baggy dress, but this one was sort of lavender. Her hair was loose, a squiggle of purple ribbon holding it back from her face. "I think it's up forward. I'll go see."

Up in his quarters, Harley sat down on the edge of the bunk. The shock of finding Mairin there—and thinking she looked beautiful—was more than he could handle now. He groped behind the bolster and numbly drew the sweater out. He folded it the best he could, but it wouldn't stay fixed in any shape.

Back in the cabin, Mairin was getting ready to go. She was standing near the doorway, a crocheted satchel on her arm. "Thanks," she said as she took the sweater from Harley's hands. She held it up and laughed at what a rag it was. "It's a hundred years old and it doesn't actually keep me warm."

"But it's nice," he said. "I remember it."

"It's more like a blankie than anything else." She turned to Liam. "Thanks for the tea."

"Thanks for the company," he replied. "Come on. I'll walk you to the street."

He offered his hand to help her up the cabin steps, and she took it as if she needed it. Which Harley knew she didn't and wouldn't have taken from anyone else.

"See you, Harley."

"Yeah. Goodbye." He started to say something more—*Come when you want, it's okay with me*—but she already came when she wanted to, and it didn't matter if it was okay with Harley or not; her visits had nothing to do with him.

Alone in the cabin, Harley checked his phone again for any word from Julian. No e-mail. No text. No nothing. Sick at heart, he punched Cassandra's number in. From where he stood, he could still see Mairin walking along with Liam on the upper dock that led to the street. Suddenly, from out of nowhere, Cassandra appeared at the end of the wharf, heading in the opposite direction.

She was walking quickly, her long hair loose, rushing, Harley knew, for the boat. She seemed to acknowledge Liam, saying something as she passed, and then broke into a wobbly run. Harley threw the cell phone down and hurried up to meet her as she clattered down the ramp. Shaky and pale, she practically threw herself into his arms. She was dressed in her clothes from dance class, a skirt pulled over the camisole leotard and tights. The shawl she always wore these days was tied in knot around her waist.

"Come on," he murmured. "Come to the boat."

It was warm in the cabin, drowsy-warm, but her body trembled under his touch.

"Calm down," he coaxed against her hair. "Just try to relax and take a breath."

"I can't!" she cried. "Everything's so awful, and I feel like it's all my fault."

"What's your fault?" Harley gripped her shoulders, drawing her back to find her face. "You said there was an accident. Tell me what happened. Who got hurt?"

"I wished it," she said in a wisp of a voice. "I told my friends I wished he'd die. I wished he'd have an accident. That something awful would happen to him." She shook her head, her hair falling forward around her face. "Maybe I didn't kill him, but I wished he was dead and now he is!"

"Julian's *dead*?" Harley's heart stopped like a clock. He had to sit down or his knees would buckle under him. Cassandra stared as he sank to the bunk. Her face looked dazed. There was blurred confusion in her eyes.

"Julian?" she murmured. "Why are you saying *Julian*?"

Harley stared. He felt like his brain was inside out. "Isn't that who you mean? Isn't that who—"

"You think something happened to Julian?" Cassandra violently shook her head. "It was *Anderson,* not Julian. He was at a party. He was on a balcony and *fell*."

As Harley slowly digested her words, relief came sweeping over him, wavy as a thrill. He plunked his head against the wall. Julian. God. He was all right. Nothing had happened to Julian!

"Anderson," Cassandra repeated numbly. She eased down next to Harley, peeling sticky hair strands off her face. "I said I wished that he

was dead. But I didn't mean it. It wasn't the truth. I just wanted him to
. . . understand."

Harley didn't get it yet. But somehow the syllables struck a chord.
Anderson Something. An-der-son. He knew he'd heard the name before.
Then it came back: the Breeze Hotel. Mrs. Birch telling secrets in the
dark.

"Your *boyfriend*, you mean?"

"The old one. Last year." Cassandra gulped. "I wanted it to happen.
I wished him that kind of awful death."

"Cassandra, hey. Everyone thinks stuff like that when someone hurts
them really bad."

"But I didn't just wish it. I said it out loud." A mammoth tear ran
down her cheek, and Harley smudged it with his thumb. "Sometimes at
Theo's we do this thing—"

"We?"

"The girls. We call it The Wrongs. We sit around and talk about stuff
that boys have done. Bad things, I mean. The sins they do." On Harley's
neck, the skin went cold. "We say what we wish would happen to them.
Sometimes it's funny and everyone laughs. But I said things that weren't
a joke. Things that could really happen, not crazy things like the other
girls said." Two more tears slid out of her eyes. "But I swear to God, I
didn't mean them, Harley. I know that now by the way I feel."

Harley wanted to comfort her. But the frost on his neck had spread
to his scalp, and he couldn't think straight enough to speak.

"Do you believe," Cassandra went on, "we can make things happen
by wishing them? Do you think that wishes have that power?"

"No," he answered, finding his voice. "It's people that make things
happen."

"So it's not my fault? I really didn't do anything wrong?"

"It's not your fault, but maybe you—" Harley groped around for words.

"Maybe I *what*?"

"Just maybe you shouldn't have told those girls. Whatever Anderson did to you—"

"He was awful, Harley! Awful! I feel like he split my life in half. I was one way before I met him, and another way when he was gone."

"I've already told you I hate this guy. I mean it, Cassandra, I really do. But falling off a balcony, that's a scary way to go."

"I know it is. But let me tell you, Harley, it was also scary for me. I mean, finding out who Anderson was. Learning about the things he'd done and just how many girls he'd hurt."

"Some guys are jerks. It's who they are."

"You make it sound so simple. Almost like it's not their fault."

"That's not what I mean—"

"What *do* you mean?" Cassandra's voice teetered at the edge of tears. "If a guy's a jerk—even if he was born a jerk—does it give him the right to lie to you? To make you trust like you've never trusted anyone, to make you love so much you feel you'd die for him—that you'd give him everything you have, even that thing you're supposed to keep until you find the perfect one?"

Harley knew what Cassandra meant. She'd told him once that Anderson had stolen from her. Something you could not replace.

"I really loved him, Harley. I'm sorry. It's true. He had smooth, black curls and beautiful eyes. It was Christmas Eve and we'd gone to church. Joy to the world and fa-la-la." There was no point in interrupting her, and Harley didn't try. She drank in a breath and swallowed. "I couldn't remember ever being happier. We were going to a party next. It was snowing outside and Central Park looked magical." Harley could almost see the scene. He could picture Cassandra's blissful face, white and rosy in the cold.

"He suddenly tells me we have to talk. Right then. Right there. On the corner of sixty-seventh street. There's a man near the light in a Russian hat. I could make a drawing of him now." Cassandra glanced around the boat. For a second, Harley wondered if she actually wanted to sketch the man. She blinked her eyes and spoke in a voice that wasn't her own. "You know I love you, Cassie. But we can't be together anymore. Isabelle is pregnant and I have to help her deal with it."

"Isabelle? Pregnant?"

"Yes. He'd been sleeping with this other girl the entire time he was with me. Do you understand now what a bastard he was?"

"That sucks, Cassandra."

"It worse than sucks. I'd never been treated like that before. Used and thrown away like that, like a piece of garbage on the street. I almost couldn't handle it."

"I know," said Harley softly. Part of him wanted to comfort her. Just wrap her tightly in his arms and tell her it would be okay. But it wasn't okay. And Harley couldn't pretend it was.

"Did your friends at school know Anderson?" he asked when several seconds had passed.

"What does it matter if they did?"

"They were in New York last weekend. Were they at the party where Anderson was?"

"*What?*" Cassandra's voice was less than a whisper, a puff of air. "Are you trying to say my friends had something to do with this?"

"I can't help thinking of Julian and what they did to him that day."

"What's with you and Julian?" Cassandra cried in an angry burst. "You're always sticking up for him, like he's the victim in all of this. Do you ever think of Pia? She's only twelve—and a very young twelve. He was using her like a toy."

"He wasn't really going to—"

"That's only because the girls wouldn't let that happen. We know him, Harley. He's just like all the rest of them."

"The rest of *who?*"

"Certain guys," Cassandra said. "The ones who think they can do whatever they want to do. Like Anderson, for instance. He sees a girl and decides he wants to have her. He may already have another girl, but that doesn't matter to guys like him. He's special, you know. He has these needs, and one girl doesn't fulfill them all."

"The guy's a shit, I'll grant you that."

"He's more than a shit. He ruined my life! It took me a year to start to feel like myself again. To feel like I even deserved to be loved. Why can't you try to understand?"

"I do understand. And I know he really messed you up. But karma comes to guys like that. The universe takes care of them."

A flicker crossed Cassandra's eyes. "I think that, too. And I think it finally happened. Karma came to Anderson, and at last he got what he deserved."

"Cassandra, God. Don't talk like that."

"Like what?" she said. The tears were back in her voice again. "The people who love me—my friends—say that."

"That Anderson deserved to *die?*"

Cassandra nodded gravely. "That's what the girls at Theo's said."

"Listen to me," said Harley. He had to work to steady his voice. "Those girls at Theo's are not your friends. I'm sorry to have to tell you this."

"They *are* my friends! They're the only real ones I've ever had!"

"No, they're not!" said Harley. "Can't you see what's going on?"

Cassandra narrowed her gleaming eyes. "Oh my God. I think I do. I think I'm starting to understand. You're jealous of the girls at school. You hate how close I am with them. How I tell them things I don't tell you. Theo, too,—you've always felt so threatened by her."

"I'm not jealous. I'm scared for you. You're so caught up in all of this that you can't even see who these people are. Ravenska's bad. She's a crazy bitch. My father knew her years ago."

"Your father? Ha!" Cassandra emitted a shot-like laugh.

"It's the truth. They had a thing. When he tried to break up with her, she slashed his neck. He still has the scar to prove it."

"I don't believe a word of that. He has her confused with someone else. Theo is an angel, and my friends at school are really sweet. You don't even realize, do you, that if not for them I'd never have even talked to you. They helped me get over Anderson. They made me see that I could move on and be happy again."

"I thought I did that," Harley said.

"You really *are* jealous, aren't you? That's what this is all about." Her fingers twisted the gauzy shawl. "I thought that you were different. I kept telling everyone you were. That you weren't like those other guys."

"What other guys? The ones your friends decided to hurt because they're the judges of right and wrong?"

"They didn't hurt anyone, Harley. And please don't bring up Julian. Nothing happened to Julian except what *he* made happen by not taking care of his injury."

"There wouldn't have *been* an injury if they hadn't locked him up that day!"

"They were only trying to warn him off."

"Were they trying to 'warn off' Anderson, too?"

"Shut up, Harley. You don't even know if my friends were at that party."

"What about that other guy at that other party years ago? The one whose face was burned in the fire?"

"How did you even hear about that?"

"Julian told me. He knew the guy."

"Oh, God. We're back to Julian." Cassandra wrung her shaky hands. "It really hurts me, Harley, how you always believe whatever he says, while you never believe me."

"That isn't true—"

"Yes, it is. You're always sticking up for the guys. No matter what awful things they do."

"I'm not sticking up for anyone."

"Yes, you are. And on top of that, you're tearing down everything I love. First, you attack my friends from school. You accuse them of doing horrible things. Then, you lie about Theo and your dad."

"Nothing I've said to you is a lie. You're just so brainwashed, you can't see."

Instead of getting angrier, Cassandra almost seemed to deflate. "It's so sad," she said, her eyes welling up. "People told me it wouldn't work. That we were too different, you and me."

"What people?" demanded Harley. "The very same girls who helped you 'get over' Anderson so that you could move on and be with me?"

"They warned me about the people in town. How narrow-minded and small they were. But I never believed the stuff they said. And when I met you, I knew they were wrong." She sniffled and drew a quivering breath. "But now I see that they were right, and it's just so sad I almost feel sick."

"I'm sad, too," said Harley. "But more than that, I'm scared for you."

Cassandra stared into Harley's face, a pear-shaped tear running down her cheek. "I'm so stupid," she said, backing toward the cabin door. "Why did I think it was ever possible for us?"

"Cassandra, please."

"I'm going now. Don't call or text. I never want to see you again." She turned and sprinted up the steps. In the doorway she paused, the tears now streaming down her face. "I almost let it happen again. I almost let you break my heart!" She spun around and in only seconds was up on the dock.

From the cabin window, Harley watched her fly away. He could see his father not far off, talking to Wally Callister. The two men turned as Cassandra rushed by, her head in her hands, her long hair streaming out in back. She looked beautiful and crazy, like someone dangerous to herself.

Chapter 23

Harley read from the laptop balanced on his knees.

Tragedy struck the ranks of the young and privileged in the pre-dawn hours of Sunday as Anderson Pitch, son of Wall Street scion Franklin Pitch, plunged to his death from a fourteenth-story terrace during a night of partying. Pitch, 19, had been a guest at the Upper East Side residence . . .

This account came from the *New York Daily News*. He'd already read the others from the *New York Post* and the *New York Times* as Liam sat and listened and the pizza cooled in its open box. The information was all the same. A late-night party. Exclusive address. The guests were friends from prep school, most of them in college now. Lots of drinking. The suggestion of drugs. Anderson was woozy. He'd gone out to the terrace to get some air. No one knew that anything had happened until the police showed up at the door.

Liam was quiet, sipping his beer. Harley had told him everything when Liam came hurrying back to the boat. Harley was still shaken, and Liam could understand. Liam knew about weepy girls. And weepy women. And the crazy things they sometimes did.

"Read that thing again," he said. He was staring at Harley across the space. "That newspaper story. Read it again."

"Why?" asked Harley.

"I don't know. Maybe I'm looking for a clue." Harley's cell phone started to buzz. It was a text from Julian.

Scared me when I heard from u. Were they really here?

Yeah. Staying at Ravenska's place.

I was out of the city.

Good 4 u.

Harley paused, and then tapped the words:

Ever hear of Anderson Pitch?
The guy who died? U know him?
C's old boyF from NY

For what felt like half a minute, there was no response from the other end. Then, came the one-word answer:

Shit

Harley stared at the small, blue screen long after Julian was gone. "Your friend okay?" asked Liam. "The *Wilis* didn't visit him?"

"Nothing happened. He's all right."

"What about this other guy, the one who went off the balcony. Do you really think they tossed him off?"

Harley continued to stare at the phone. The dark, dead screen. The oblong contour against his palm. "It's crazy, Dad. But, yeah, I do." Julian had come to the same conclusion, too.

"I don't get it," Liam said. "How did they even know the guy?"

"They knew *about* him," Harley replied. His mouth was so dry it was hard to talk. He reached for his beer and took a gulp. "They do this 'thing' up at the school when they have their little parties. Cassandra told me this afternoon. They call it The Wrongs. They talk about old boyfriends, guys who screwed around with them. They tell each other how bad it was. Then they make up stuff, like what they wish would happen to them. Cassandra felt really guilty; she'd wished that Anderson was dead."

"Funny," said Liam. "And now he is."

Harley's brain felt splintered. Part of him knew the whole thing was ridiculous. Crazy like a movie. Stuff like this didn't happen in ordinary life.

"But maybe it's too random," he said to Liam, thinking out loud. "There are millions of people in New York. How would they know where Anderson would be that night? Why would they be at a party with him?"

"I don't know," said Liam. "Facebook. Twitter. All that shit you kids are on. Plus, they're all sort of fancy, Manhattan types. Maybe their circles overlap." Harley knew that this was true. They were all from New York, those dancers. The world of ballet was small and tight, as Mrs. Birch had explained that night at dinner. Everyone knew everyone. Plus, they all seemed to live in same Upper East Side neighborhood.

"I'm worried," he said.

"You ought to be," said Liam. "I'm getting a little worried, too."

"I mean about Cassandra. She's innocent, Dad. She doesn't see what's going on. She thinks those girls are all her friends and that Madame Ravenska's some kind of saint."

"Maybe she just *looks* innocent."

"No. It's for real. She's trusting and sweet. But *fragile*, like her mother said."

"That's putting it mildly," Liam remarked. "Wally wondered what the hell you'd done to her." He fixed his gaze on Harley. "Let me tell you something else. If she told you to stay away from her, that's damn well what you ought to do. I mean it, Harley. No fooling around." He gestured at Harley's laptop. "As for the incident in New York, I'm sure the cops will figure it out. If that kid was pushed, they'll find out what happened and who was there. You don't get away with stuff like that."

⸎

As Harley walked home on Wednesday, he spotted the notices for *Giselle*.

They were posted in almost all the shops, and he drew up close to look at one. The picture showed Giselle and Albrecht doing their famous *pas de deux* in the moonlit forest in Act Two. On either side a long, white line of *Wilis* posed, their faces cold, their pale arms crossed in front of them. In the space below the darkness, Cassandra's name was written in elaborate script. Next to it: Joaquin Marrón. Harley felt his heart contract.

For the first few days, he'd been sure that she would contact him. He'd tried to call despite her orders not to, but she never answered back. He thought of phoning Mrs. Birch. She'd asked him to call if Cassandra didn't seem all right. He took her number out one day. He'd actually started to make the call but realized how crazy he would sound if he tried to explain what was going on. *Your daughter's friends killed Anderson Pitch. They tossed a boy in a fireplace and may have crippled Julian.* She'd think that he had lost his mind. So that was the end. Cassandra was gone. His only way of seeing her was to cross the street and peer at a moonlit poster in the window of a shop.

∽∞∽

It was Friday and work was finished for the week. Tired and hot, Harley slipped through the cabin door. Liam and Mairin were sitting on the facing bunks, sharing a pot of tea. Strangely enough, Harley felt glad. He liked the sight of the two of them there. It was weird but nice. His father with a teacup. Mairin relaxed, though somewhat pale, her swollen feet drawn up on the berth. They greeted Harley, and he sat down.

"Tea?" asked Mairin softly. Harley watched as she leaned to the table to pour for him. She was wearing a silver bracelet, and it made her wrist look small and fine. She dropped in sugar and swirled the spoon with the glittery racket she always made.

"So I finally got to see her," she said to Harley, passing the cup. "Your girlfriend, I mean. Last Sunday. I might have guessed she'd be as beautiful as that."

"You saw her coming," Liam said. "You should have seen her heading out."

A week ago, Harley would have shut him up. But somehow now he didn't care. It didn't matter if Mairin knew. He knew about Smits; she might as well know about his mess. And Liam seemed eager to fill her in.

"The day you saw her she'd just found out that her bad old boyfriend from New York had fallen from a balcony."

"What?"

"He was at a party and fell to his death."

"That's horrible," said Mairin. "No wonder she was so upset."

"That's only the half of it," Liam said. "Your friend over here thinks that the girls from Ocean Watch may have had something to do with it."

Mairin turned to Harley.

"It's just a theory," he demurred. "I don't have any proof."

Mairin took a sip of tea. "The night you came to Becky's you were telling us stuff about those girls and some of the things they'd done to guys. You said there was this woman—" Her eyes flashed back to Liam. "That woman you got involved with. The one who tried to cut your throat."

"Theodosia Ravenska," Liam said. "She's back again. And she's got Cassandra in her thrall. They have these little parties where they sit around and talk about boys and the wrongs they've done. Apparently, Cassandra mentioned Anderson."

"The boyfriend?"

"Yeah."

"And what did he do that was so wrong?"

"He cheated on her," said Harley.

"And the girl got pregnant," Liam filled in.

Harley might have imagined it, but he thought that Mairin slightly flushed. He glared at Liam. He hadn't had to mention that part.

"Do you actually think," she asked a moment later, "that they'd push him from a balcony?"

"I don't know," said Harley. "But Cassandra's friends happened to be in New York that night. A pretty strange coincidence."

It was warm in the cabin, but Mairin shivered visibly. "That's how Teddy died as well. Out a window in the night."

"And it's not just them," said Harley. "I told you what happened to Julian. And another guy who'd cheated was shoved into a fire."

Mairin firmly shook her head. "I'm glad that girl is out of your life. There's something wrong with all of them. They don't even look quite normal. Their necks are too long, their backs too straight. There's this little one who comes to town. She's always in the hardware store looking at the hooks and stuff."

"What?" said Harley. Something tightened in his throat.

"She's there a lot. And she always tries to talk to me She's the weirdest-looking girl on earth. If my kid came out with a face like that, I swear I'd have to send her back."

"What face?" said Harley, his voice like a breath.

Mairin drew it with her hands. "This round little *orb* like a white balloon. The skinniest, miniest toothpick neck. Hair the color of carrot juice pulled back so tight it makes her eyebrows stretch like this." Mairin depicted that as well, turning her eyes to pale-green slits. Liam laughed, but Harley felt a cold unease creeping through his chest. She was describing Pia. Little Moon was coming to town all by herself to visit Smits's store.

"What does she ask you, Mairin? What kind of things does she want to know?"

214

"Once she asked if I knew how to sail. Another time she wanted to know if I was fond of poetry. She saw that I was pregnant—most people don't even notice yet—and asked if I wanted a boy or a girl. Girls were better than boys, she said."

"Don't talk to her," snapped Harley, his voice coming out more harshly than he meant it to. "Don't say anything else to her."

Both Liam and Mairin stared at him.

"What are you thinking?" Mairin asked.

"He isn't thinking anything." Liam stood up abruptly. "I'll make another pot of tea." He reached to tousle Mairin's hair. "By the way, do you know it's a girl? You said you'd have to send *her* back if your baby came out with a funny face."

Mairin paused, eyes still pinned on Harley, and then let the conversation turn. "Bridey, my aunt, did something with a golden ring. And my other aunt said that when you're pregnant with a girl, you want to eat sweets, not salty things, and you never have cold feet. I can tell you, my feet are never cold."

Liam smiled. "When Elizabeth was pregnant, she also swore she was having a girl. The ring went swinging from side to side. She had to have chocolate every day. The pillow was even facing south." He tipped his head toward Harley. "Then, we ended up with this."

Mairin laughed. "I bet he was adorable."

"Picture-perfect," Liam said. "Nine pounds of rash and covered with lanugo fuzz."

"You never mentioned that before," Harley said with a bit of a smile. His father, in fact, seldom talked about that time. He never said *Elizabeth*.

"As for her feet," said Liam now, "those feet could not be cold enough. She used to run barefoot into the snow. We were living up on Water Street. Our yard was a field surrounded by pines."

"She sounds like I'd like her," Mairin said.

"You would have, I'm sure. You're quite alike." Harley wondered if this was true. He did not recall his mother, but the moment he met Mairin when he was just a little kid, he felt as if he knew her from some watery place he couldn't name.

"Anyway," she was saying now, "I've decided a girl would be okay. She won't be a silly, frilly girl. I'll teach her stuff, and she'll be like me."

"Your kid will be great whatever it is," Liam assured her with a grin.

Mairin eased up. "No more tea. I've got to get home."

Liam kissed her forehead. "Come back soon. Remember, our door is always open to you. And if Smits as much as—"

"He doesn't," said Mairin shortly. "Take care, Liam. Thanks for the tea."

Harley helped Mairin off the boat. Up on the dock, he asked her, "Is Smits doing anything bad to you?"

"He's just being Smits. That's all he can be."

"But I heard my dad—"

"Liam's protective. You know how he is. Smits is a drunk, and that's a fact. But he hasn't done anything to me."

"If he ever does—"

"I'll come to the boat. I promised Liam that I would." Mairin turned and glanced toward shore. "Really, Harley. I've got to go."

"Yeah, okay. But come back soon. And do me a favor, will you?"

"What?"

"If you see that girl from the school again—if she comes into the hardware store—call me on your cell."

"Yeah, okay. But tell me, why do you think she's always there?"

"I don't know. But she's not buying hardware, is she?"

"No. And I have to admit, she gives me the creeps. Her eyes are so big, and she never blinks. She reminds me of an imp." Mairin's fingers grazed the length of Harley's arm as she slowly backed away from him. "I'm sorry about Cassandra. I mean, sorry it didn't work out for you. But those girls up there are scary. I wish they'd all just go back home."

Harley watched as she headed down the dock toward town. She didn't want him to walk with her. Someone might see them and talk to Smits. Yet it wasn't Smits he was worried about as he followed her form with his narrowed eyes across the street and past the sunlit shops. Why was Pia watching her? Why was she in the hardware store asking Mairin if she was fond of poetry?

Chapter 24

Harley was wedged between Becky and Sue at a table at Wally's Clam House.

It was seven-thirty and already the sun was slipping down. The days were getting shorter now, and the sunsets slow, a little bit sad. Farther down the table, his back to the burning harbor, Red Legs sat with his girlfriend Jane. It was official, and Harley was glad; his pirate mate had finally gotten his pompom girl. Johnny and Davy were also there. Pugwash. Lacy. Roy Boy. Fitz.

The place was filled with a noisy crowd, and Becky leaned close to Harley's ear. "What happened with Cassandra? She told me you two broke it off." And before he had time to answer: "I never heard her so upset."

"This time it's really over for good." Harley shrugged. He wasn't in the mood to talk.

Becky yelled into his ear again. "I think it's over for us as well. She's acting really weird these days." On his other side, Sue was laughing at something someone else had said.

"Weird," repeated Becky. "She's all obsessed with that ballet. I know she's the star, but really. She doesn't care about anything else."

"Yeah, I know. Something happened to her up there."

"Billy was right," Becky declared in the voice of doom.

"So Harley," called Jane from across the way, "when do you take off for school?"

"In about a week," he hollered back, glad to move on to something else.

Jane made a comment he didn't quite hear, something about how fast the summer had gone by. Yeah, he thought, a two-minute dream. What had started out so wonderful—Cassandra in the thunderstorm—had ended up in a knot of complications and horrid possibilities. He consoled himself that at least his friends were doing well. Becky and Pugs were hanging in. And Red Legs and Jane made a pretty good pair. Lacy and Sue were happy, too. They'd gotten a storefront for their salon. They were going to call it The Mermaid Spa. There'd be one more party on the beach. One last full moon. One final bash at someone's house. Then, summer would come to an end again. Harley would go back to Maine. The trees would turn, the snows would fall, and this strange, sad season, this two-minute dream, would fade into a memory.

Harley walked back on the promenade along the row of fancy stores. He stood for a while at the window of the Yankee Clipper Candle Shop, staring at the flyer on which Cassandra floated, dancing in her lover's arms. She looked like a ghost, like a girl who'd died and gone away. He gazed at her name in the swirly script. Then he noticed something strange. Where Joaquin's name had been before, there was now a strip of paper covering the spot. Harley leaned in closer. The name was definitely gone. He walked a few yards to another shop and looked at the flyer posted there. Joaquin was no longer on the bill. Harley looked at the picture again. At the blank, white faces of the girls and the strip of paper obscuring the name. What had they done with the dark and beautiful Joaquin? Something clenched inside his chest and he turned and quickly crossed the street. His footsteps thundered on the dock. The ramp rattled under his weight. By the time he reached the *Alma*, he was shaky and out of breath.

When Liam and Harley were on the boat, they rarely locked the cabin door. But tonight as Harley slipped inside, he slammed it shut and dropped the latch. He almost wished his father were there. But Liam was at his poker game, which sometimes ran till two A.M. Harley stood and peered through the window back to shore. The street was still and empty, and faint, gold light reflected in the panes of glass. Nothing moved, yet he had the strange sensation of things going on that could not be seen. Scurrying and shadows. Whispers and breath and movement in between the light. He peered through the other window over the darkness of the dock. Most of the boats were empty, all the weekend sailors gone. At the end of the pier, two dim lanterns glimmered, and here and there on the high, white piles, night lights shed their eerie glow. Harley pulled out his cell phone. There was no one to call, but he wanted to see it sitting there.

Up in the forward quarters, he changed to slouchy sweats. He came back to the larger cabin and stretched himself out on the portside bunk. He reached for his dog-eared book of poems. All at once, he was thinking of that stormy day. How he'd found Cassandra up in town, huge, blue eyes peering from the long, drenched shawl. How small and fragile she had looked, floating in his dark-blue sweats. Then he remembered other things. The sunset sail. The way the colors, the orange and pink and violet-blue, had melted in her hair. He thought of the night in Boston. How she'd made him love his own pale foot because everything was beautiful. He thought about the day he'd brought her to the cave. The silk of her skin under the blood-red rubies, the fake gold beads, the silver strands. He remembered how she looked asleep. And how the sight of her took his breath as she danced that night on the moonlit field. All the pictures crowded in, blurring to a misty dream.

But *this*, he knew, was not a dream: the patter of steps on the deck above. Not the steps of Liam. Not the steps of any man. In the porthole, he caught a flash of white. The flutter of a long, pale skirt. Harley sprang up. More rushing feet, skittered in the cockpit now, a flurry of small and weightless taps. He held his breath, his heartbeat pounding in his ear. With one quick movement, he reached for the phone. It slipped from his fingers onto the floor. The sound was dull and awful. By now, they were probably all on the boat, a chain of taut, white bodies surrounding the cabin in a ring. Something brushed against the door. A soft, protracted swishing sound. The handle jiggled right and left. Harley gasped. He tried to tamp down the panic, but it swirled inside, like a small tornado in his chest. He could feel his sweat dampening his clothing, bleeding through every pore. Maybe if he could startle them—if he burst like a shot through the forward hatch—he could break through their arms and leap from the boat. He started backing toward the bow.

Then something pounded against the door, and a high and breathless voice called out.

"Harley! Liam! Please be there!"

For a second, he froze. Then, stumbling forward as if he'd been shoved, he flipped the latch and flung the door. He was there as Mairin fell inside. He glanced beyond her onto the dock, and then pulled her into the cabin, slamming down the lock. He held her for a moment as she struggled to catch her breath. She felt small and cold and shivery. Her hair was loose and the curls were damp against his face.

"I'm sorry," she gasped. "But I had to come."

Harley held her tightly. "Don't be sorry. I'm glad you did. No one is going to find you here."

"He's too stupid to find me," Mairin said. "He thinks I'm locked inside the room." She pulled from his arms and looked at him. "Harley, God. What's wrong with you? You're totally drenched in sweat!"

"Yeah, I know. Too weird to explain." He looked at her, too. She was wearing a long, white nightgown, and he felt like a fool for thinking the crazy thing he'd thought. He wiped his face with his sweatshirt sleeve. "Did you say Smits locked you in a room?"

Mairin nodded. "What a jerk. Like I can't climb out a window. Like I don't have any brains."

"Sit down," he said, easing her over to a bunk. She was shivering still, and he drew a blanket over her. He plumped up the cushions. "Here. Lie back."

"I can't right now. I need to sit up." She perched, rod-straight, at the edge of the bunk.

"You're barefoot," said Harley, glancing down. "What the fuck did that—"

The sight of her feet, small and scratched at the hem of the gown, made him want to murder Smits.

Mairin looked up. "Can you make some tea?"

Harley put the kettle on and then went forward to get some socks. When he came back, she was still on the bunk in the same tense pose. He knelt on the floor in front of her and slid a sock onto one cold foot. "How the hell did you make it here not wearing any shoes?"

"I have clam diggers' feet. You know that."

He felt her hand as she reached to gently touch his head. A buzz ran through his body, and he carefully lifted her other foot. "Do you want to tell me what's going on?"

"It's boring and trashy," Mairin said. "Just like Smits and me."

"You aren't trashy."

"Yes, I am. You should have heard me curse him out."

"I would have liked to, actually."

"He's such a vile, disgusting drunk. Lately, it's every night with him. And then he comes home and wakes me up. I just can't stand the smell of him. I told him tonight that if he was going out again, I was, too, and I probably wouldn't be coming back."

"Good for you," said Harley.

"It wasn't good for me at all. He shoved me in the bedroom. I spit in his face, and he knocked me down."

"He *what*?"

"He pushed me. And I fell."

Harley stood up. "I'm going to fucking knock *him* down."

"The state he's in, you could probably just blow on him."

"You told us he didn't do stuff, Mair."

"He didn't. 'Til now. The last few days. Not that it matters anymore." Mairin broke off. She lowered her eyes and stared at her hands. She twirled the bracelet around her wrist. "I never used to understand why women felt ashamed of it. Ashamed that they'd got smacked around—"

"Smits hit you? That *fuck*. I mean it, Mairin. His ass is grass. *You're* not the one to be ashamed."

"But I am," she said in a wavering voice at the edge of tears. Harley stared. Mairin was not the crying type. He'd seen her cry maybe two or three times in his life. Now he really wanted blood. He wanted to break Smits's weasel face. Hear the smush of cartilage, the bony crack of punched-out teeth. "I never thought," said Mairin, "that someone would think of me like that. Like someone you could push around."

"But you're not like that!" said Harley. "That's why you're here. That's why you came to the boat tonight."

"Oh Harley, God!" The tears spilled over the edge of her eyes. "How can you even talk to me? Look what I've done to everything?" Harley sank down beside her, and her whole taut body collapsed in his arms. She cried. Dissolved. She drenched them both, as if to make up for all the years of being brave. Bee sting, bite, and broken bone. A fish hook through her small, white toe. The memories came flooding back—all the days of never-say-die and holding it together, as no other girl he'd known could do. Harley hated Denny Smits.

A half hour later, he'd gotten her settled on the bunk. She leaned against the cushions, sipping her milky tea. Harley sat at the end of the berth. They both were quiet for a while.

Then Mairin said, "You were right that night at Red Legs's house. That stuff you said about why I decided to marry Smits. Of all the losers in the world."

Harley thought back. It felt like a thousand years ago. "I shouldn't have said those things to you."

"Why not? They were true. If I couldn't have you, I might as well be with Denny Smits. I might as well have nothing at all."

"Mairin—"

"Don't tell me I could have had you. I couldn't go away with you. And you couldn't stay here. You belong out there in the big, wide world."

"So do you, Mairin."

"No, I don't. I see pictures of my mother when she was eighteen, like me. We're so alike. We might be twins."

"You are *not* your mother," Harley said.

"Yes, I am. I'm mean like her. I wanted to rub it in her face. I did just what you said I did that night. If she wanted me here—if she wanted to turn me into her, stuck in that house, babysitting all *her* kids—I'd show her good. I'd show her what she looks like. Pregnant practically half her life, married to a drunk. You were totally right. It's just what I did." Mairin's voice went trailing off. "I just didn't know it at the time."

Harley leaned slightly forward, taking the empty cup from her. He brought it to the galley, and when he came back her eyes were closed. He drew the blanket over her.

"It isn't over," he said aloud. He wasn't sure what he actually meant or who he was really talking to. But he needed to say it. It had to be true. He stood for a while, watching her face. Her cheeks were hollow. She didn't look well. In the long, ballooning nightgown her belly wasn't visible, and she looked to Harley like a child.

Chapter 25

Harley woke to the smell of food. Coffee and bacon. Pancakes. Smells recalled from a distant past when Hannah would come to cook for them. But it wasn't Hannah standing at the galley stove. It was Mairin instead, still in the long, white nightgown, her curls pinned up on top of her head. Through the cabin door Harley saw Liam busy in the cockpit, coiling some rope.

"Mairin, hi." He eased up slowly in the bunk.

"Good morning, Harley. You must have been pretty tired last night."

"This is weird. Where did you sleep?"

"I slept in your bunk up forward. Liam fixed it up for me."

"I didn't even hear him come back."

"You hungry?"

"Yeah. Do we really have food?" Harley got up and took a step forward to touch her arm. "How are you feeling? Are you okay?"

Mairin smiled. "I'm all right."

Liam poked in through the cabin door. "Good afternoon. What do you think of our galley slave?"

"I think she's great," said Harley. "Maybe we should kidnap her."

"That's just what I was thinking, too. Haul the sails and steal away."

"Oh, no!" said Mairin sharply, her attention riveted out the door.

Liam played at being hurt. "You don't want to run away with us?"

"No, I *do*!" she uttered, dropping a spoon on the countertop. "Cast off the lines. I mean it. *Now!*"

Harley followed Mairin's gaze over the cockpit and down the dock. "It's Smits," he said to Liam. "And it looks like—hell, he's with her mom."

"Please!" yelled Mairin. "Let's just go! Liam, turn the engine on!"

"Hurry, Dad!" snapped Harley. He was already springing up the stairs, ready to free the lines.

"We can't do that!" Liam barked.

"Why the hell not? Mairin wants to come with us." Harley stared at Liam. "What the fuck is wrong with you?"

Liam threw down the coil of ropes. "I'm not running away from someone's mom. And I'm sure not running from Denny Smits." He spoke to Mairin through the door. "I've got stuff to say to that little runt. It's good that he's brought your mom along. It'll keep me from punching out his lights."

"I don't want to see them," Mairin said. She folded her arms across her chest as if to form a shield.

"I promise you, Mairin," Liam said. "No one's taking you out of here. Not Smits. Not your mom. Not anyone. Not until you want to leave."

"But they—"

"Look at us. Do you think we can't handle the pair of them?"

Liam waited on the deck while Harley and Mairin stayed down below. They could hear the muffled greetings. Smits's grunts and Mrs. McConnell's mosquito whine. Liam escorted them down into the cabin, where Harley and Mairin sat side by side. Smits looked like hell. Blood-shot eyes and a red, flushed face. Mrs. McConnell looked like she was dressed for church in a lavender suit and a pair of pumps. Her short, brown hair was curled and stiff. Her eyes blinked over the ornate walls as if avoiding something lewd.

"Oh, Mairin," she said, barely moving her jaw. She knitted the fingers of her hands. "Is that what you were wearing last night? You ran all through town in your nightie like that? What on earth were you thinking of?"

"She wasn't thinking," Smits put in, shaking his unkempt head.

"Oh, she was thinking," Liam said. "She was thinking you locked her in a room, and she didn't plan to sit there while you went out to the Legion Hall and got piss-drunk all over again."

Smits's face flushed darker. There were spots of white where the blood didn't go in the center of his cheeks. He glared at Mairin hatefully. "You told these people our private affairs?" His bloodshot eye began to twitch. "How dare you go telling our private affairs!"

"Assault isn't anyone's 'private affair,'" Liam said in a withering tone. He turned to Mairin's mother. "Your son-in-law knocked your daughter down. Do you think she should keep that to herself?"

"It was an accident," Denny snapped. "I didn't mean for her to fall. She was acting all kinds of crazy." He turned to Mairin's mother. "You ought to hear the mouth on her."

Mrs. McConnell shuddered. "All the same, you can't go pushing her around. She isn't feeling well right now."

"Yeah, okay," said Smits. "Sometimes, I don't know my strength." Liam chuckled audibly, but Smits pretended not to hear.

"Now, tell her you're sorry. Tell her that it's not her fault. Go on, Dennis, so we can leave."

"I'm sorry," said Smits, looking at the cabin floor. "It's not your fault. Not totally."

"Now, you," said Mairin's mother. "Tell him you're sorry for what you said. That temper of yours is going to be the death of you."

Mairin didn't answer. Harley could see the tremor in her clenching jaw.

"Mairin," Mrs. McConnell coaxed. "Married people sometimes fight. It's not the end of the world, you know. Just say you're sorry. Dennis did."

"I can't say I'm sorry because I'm not!" Mairin exploded like a bomb. "He's a spineless, little idiot. And he drinks like a fish and stinks at night, which is something you know all about since you—"

"Shut up, Mairin! Don't be vile!" Mrs. McConnell's face was white. "Get up this minute. You're coming home."

"What's home?" said Mairin, not budging an inch.

"Your home is with your husband. That's where you have made your bed."

"Come on," said Smits. "This is no place for us to talk."

"I'm not going with you," Mairin said.

"Like hell you're not." Smits stepped forward to grab her arm, but Liam intervened.

"Mairin can do whatever she wants."

"This is ridiculous." Mrs. McConnell fluttered about.

"What's ridiculous," said Liam, "is the two of you coming to my boat, imagining she'd go with you. Home to a guy who beats her up. Or home to a mother who thinks that's okay."

"I do *not* think that it's okay. But Denny is going to change his ways. I've already spoken to Father Neale."

Liam laughed. "I'm sure that will do a world of good." Father Neale was a drunk himself.

"This is none of your business, Liam. And it isn't appropriate at all. Not that *you'd* know appropriate."

"All the same, she's staying here. Right where she is. For as long as she wants."

"Fine," Smits muttered suddenly. "If this is where she wants to be." He glared at Mairin. "I'm changing the locks."

"Dennis!" Mrs. McConnell shrilled.

"Let her live where she wants to live. She never wanted to be with me." Denny glared at Harley. "Why the fuck did you have to come back? I thought you went away for good. Why are you here? Why can't you just stay away?" His high-pitched voice had started to crack. He punched his hand against the wall, so hard that a chip of wood flew off.

"Come on," he growled at his mother-in-law. "I'm leaving you, too, if you don't just come."

Mrs. McConnell stood there, stunned. A train of thoughts paraded across her tight, dry face. She glared again at Mairin. Then she turned on her heels and followed Denny up the stairs.

Silence filled the cabin. Smits's words seemed to hang in the air, and Harley found he couldn't look at Mairin's face. They were both complicit in this, he knew. Smits was right; it never should have happened. Harley hadn't been strong enough. He'd walked away, let Mairin stay. He hadn't fought the way he should have fought for her. No wonder she'd gone with Denny Smits. No wonder it was such a mess with so many others caught in the net.

They sat at the table and picked at the breakfast Mairin had made.

"The pancakes are great," said Liam. His voice sounded strained in the somber air.

"Yeah," agreed Harley. "The bacon, too."

"I could probably stay at Becky's," Mairin said distractedly. "I mean, not forever. But for a while."

"Or you could stay here," said Liam. "I mean it, Mairin. I don't like you going back to town."

"You could stay in my quarters," Harley said. "We wouldn't bother you at all."

"I don't know," said Mairin. "I'm so tired right now. I can hardly think."

"Go take a rest," said Liam. "You don't have to make a plan right now."

Mairin looked up with the trace of a smile. "A rest sounds good. I think I will. Later on, I'll call up Becky and borrow some clothes." She slid from the bunk, and blowing a kiss at each of them, shuffled through the forward door.

After her shift, Becky arrived, a bulging suitcase in her hand.

"I really can't believe this," she whispered to Harley, climbing aboard. "I knew he was a lowlife, but I didn't know he hit her. That creep."

Mairin peeked out to greet her.

"Are you all right?" asked Becky.

"Yeah, I'm fine. Thanks for the stuff." The girls went forward and closed the door. Harley could hear them whispering, agitated and indistinct, the way girls did in crisis time in that language he would never learn.

"I'm glad Beck's here," said Liam. He flung his jacket over his arm. "I'm going to the Palmer Club. Dinner with the royalty. Order food for the three of you. Or call up Pugwash and make it four." He tossed some money next to the stove. "Keep a watch for Denny Smits."

After about an hour, Becky and Mairin came out of the room. Mairin was wearing a huge, white shirt with some leggings underneath. She still looked wan and tired despite the extra sleep she'd had.

Harley mentioned Liam's idea of ordering food.

"That'd be nice," Becky agreed. "But I've got a couple of things to do. After that, I'll pick up Pugs. Be back in an hour or so."

Harley and Mairin watched the sunset from the deck. Twilight fell, and Mairin asked, "Feel like going for a walk?"

"Not a good idea right now."

"How about just to the end of the dock?"

They climbed from the boat and ambled along the whitewashed planks. The tethered yachts hardly stirred in their quiet slips. At the end of the dock, they sat on the edge, dangling their legs. The water was calm, and the boats on the moorings gently bobbed. A bright full moon hung in the sky, and in its light the hulls of the boats looked like separate silver moons floating in the dark. Mairin was just about to speak when Harley's cell phone cut her off. He didn't bother to look at it. A few seconds later, it signaled a text. He froze as he read who it was from.

"Is it Smits?" asked Mairin, scanning his face.

Harley flashed the name at her.

"I thought you two had broken up."

"So did I," said Harley. He clicked the message onto the screen.

I know who ur with & everyone knows what u did to her I cant let this happen to me again first with A and now with u mayb I'll just kill myself. It's easy up here there are places to go.

Harley looked up. "She's crazy. I don't know what she's talking about."

"Let me see it," Mairin said, gently taking the phone from him. She read the message carefully, her eyes transfixed on the small, blue screen.

"She says she knows who you are with." Mairin turned and glanced toward town. "How would she know? Where is she?"

"She's at the school. She said 'up here.'"

"She also says that everyone knows what you did to me."

"She doesn't know anything," Harley snarled. "She's crazy. That's all. She's out of her mind."

"Wait," said Mairin. "Maybe she does know certain things. Maybe that *imp*, the one who's always in the store, has been following me around. Maybe she's seen me come to the boat. Maybe she—"

"Fuck!" exploded Harley. "That's *exactly* what she thinks. She thinks that I've been seeing you."

Mairin looked down at the baggy shirt. "And she thinks you got me pregnant, too."

"Just like with her boyfriend. That *A* in the message. Anderson."

"Text her back," said Mairin. "Before she does something really dumb."

"I have to go there," Harley said.

"No, you don't. *I'll* text her back." Mairin started typing and Harley grabbed the phone away.

"That will only make things worse." His fingers shook as he punched a rapid message in.

It's not what u think. That girl is married. She visits my dad.

Cassandra's response came shooting back:

Lies more lies u never stop

I'm coming there to talk to u.

Mairin struggled to climb to her feet. "If you're going up there, I'm coming, too."

"No, you're not," said Harley.

"I won't let you go to that place alone."

"I have to, Mairin. She's done this before."

"Done what before?"

"She's tried to harm herself before. Becky knows. She'll tell you it's true."

"Call Hannah then. Hannah's right there, and she'll know what to do."

Harley punched Hannah's number, pressing the phone against his ear. It rang five times, which seemed to take forever. Then the answering machine picked up. "Shit," spat Harley. "She isn't there. What the fuck? She never goes out."

He clicked off the phone just as it signaled another text.

By the time u get here I be gone

"I've got to go there," Harley said. "Come on, Mairin. You know I do." He took her arm and pulled her up.

"I'm coming," she said.

"No, you're not." Clasping her hand, Harley brought her back to the boat and down into the cabin. "Listen," he said, forcing her to look at him. "Cassandra might really do this. And if she does and I haven't tried to stop her, well, that makes me responsible. You can't come. You'll slow me down."

"All right, all right," said Mairin. "But call up Pugs or Red Legs. Don't go up to that house alone."

"You call them," said Harley. "I'll start off." He held her shoulders, fixing her gaze. "Just stay put. I mean it. Becky will be back here soon."

"Yeah, okay. But call me."

"I will. I promise." Harley kissed the top of her head. "Stay in the cabin. *And lock the door.* You never know what Smits might try."

Chapter 26

It was Saturday night, and some of the shops had opened again for the after-dinner strollers from the cottages and bay hotels. The promenade glittered with cozy light, and it all looked safe and pretty like a picture-perfect town. In window after window, Harley could see the small advertisements for *Giselle*, squarish blots on the shining glass. If you didn't look too closely, you wouldn't even notice the voiding of the dancer's name. He quickened his pace near the edge of town. If only Liam hadn't taken the Jeep tonight.

The uphill road was quiet. In the white frame cottages close to town, there were lanterns on the porches and voices murmuring in the dark. The languorous tranquility grated strangely on Harley's nerves. He could feel his pulse beating in places it didn't belong—the soft-skinned hollow next to his eye, the sinew behind his knee. The hill, which he'd climbed a million times, felt like Mount Everest to him, rugged and absurdly steep. Up ahead, a sleek, black car careened around the wooded bend. Harley sidestepped out of the way. The car sped on, turning into a silvery drive and down to a house at the edge of the sea, silent as a hearse. Harley approached the meadow. From somewhere deep in the curl of his ear, he heard the swish of long, white skirts. The memory made his neck hairs rise.

Around the curve, over the trees, the tower of Ocean Watch appeared, its amber light glowing like a narrowed eye. Harley realized he had no plan. Would he barge inside through the big, main door? Sneak like a thief through the shadowy rooms, whispering Cassandra's name? Then he thought of Hannah. Maybe she was back by now. It was likely she had just stepped out for a stroll around the grounds.

Yet passing through the pillars, he sensed right away that something was odd. He glanced toward Hannah's quarters. In the kitchen, a single lamp was lit. Foliage from the garden stamped a pattern against the glow. His gaze roamed up to the looming house. There was light in the downstairs windows, but the light was dim, filtered through halls and distant rooms. He realized what was different: The house was empty. No one was there.

Harley headed for Hannah's place. The girls might be out, but she'd be home. She had to be. Hannah never went anywhere except to the market and Sunday church. He passed through the humid garden, hands stretched out to clear the hair-like spider webs. Insects trilled in the dark green leaves. He tapped on the door and peered into the kitchen, trying to see around the bend to the parlor where Hannah watched TV. He turned the doorknob and stepped inside. He sensed at once that she wasn't there. Pointlessly, he called her name. Maybe just to hear his voice and break the utter silence that suddenly felt so cold and dead. He glanced inside the parlor. Returned to the kitchen and looked around. Her everyday shoes were next to the door. Her cardigan sweater hung from the hook. On the table, he saw a notepad next to an old, brown purse. Hannah's writing was big and round.

27. 8:00 The Harbor House.
7:00 Bus

The Harbor House was the restaurant in Green Banks. Eight o'clock must be a reservation time. Twenty-seven. That he didn't understand. But "7:00 Bus" was clear. The entire school had gone to dinner apparently. And Hannah had gone to chaperone. That had to be it. It all made sense. He pulled out his phone and checked for the number of the Harbor House. He was dialing when a call came in. A shock-like current zipped clear through his body as he heard Cassandra's breath-like voice:

"I know where you are. You liar. You're never going to see me again."

"Cassandra! Wait!"

The click was like a slamming door. Harley stood there, frazzled. She was not in Green Banks; of that he was sure. She was not on a bus or at a restaurant with friends. She was *here*. Right here. At Ocean Watch. He did not know how he knew this. But he knew it like he knew his name. He also knew she was coming apart. And somehow he had to find her before she did an awful thing that couldn't be undone.

He called her back, but of course she didn't answer. Clutching the phone, he passed through the door that led from Hannah's separate rooms into the large main house. In the dining room, a long, black table filled the space under a chandelier. The high-backed chairs with their knobs and spires threw eerie shapes on the dimly lit floor. Harley crossed the polished boards, each creak as sharp as a snapping branch. From here, the house expanded. Two dark rooms lay side by side, and Harley passed through one of them into an enormous space, where floor-to-ceiling windows opened to the sea. Moonlight flooded the whole expanse, and it looked to Harley like a lake, stranded chairs and couches floating on its placid sheen. The sound of the surf murmured through the thick, stone walls.

Harley wanted to call her name. But some inhibition held him back. He could only imagine how loud he'd sound. Even if he whispered, the motionless dark would split in half. With lightweight steps, he crossed the room. A doorway led to a flight of stairs. Lit by small, weak sconces, the passage headed downward, turning abruptly to the right. Harley paused, staring into the murky hole.

"Cassandra, it's me. I want to talk." His voice was weird and wavy, as if he were under water talking to himself. "Cassandra, come on. I know you're here."

The stairs were satiny under his feet. Marble or something very smooth. They led to a hall, which ended at a pair of doors. Over the doors was a glowing, stained-glass window shaped like half a moon. The window depicted a group of men, a thin, red flame suspended just above each head. Harley swallowed. He knew what he was looking at. Behind those doors was the Chapel of Air, now Madame Ravenska's private rooms. He grasped the huge, brass doorknob, his fingers slippery with sweat. Drawing a breath, he slipped inside.

For a moment he just stood there, the door behind him gaping wide. There was no one inside, not that he could see, at least, and the silence was deep like that of a church. Yet the atmosphere was anything but churchlike. Huge *chaise longues* and deep-red couches covered with silky pillows were scattered in clusters throughout the room. There were sideboards and low, carved tables and tiny, intricate chests of drawers ranged along the marble walls. On every surface, between the tall, white candles, were photos and pictures in ornate frames. There were larger images on the walls, and in one arched niche, where a statue probably used to stand, was an almost life-sized portrait of a beautiful woman dressed in black. She wore long, black gloves and a strapless gown, her hair pulled up in a tall, dark twist. Harley stepped closer to look at her. Trace of a smile. Beautiful mouth. Dark, hypnotic, mournful eyes. He glanced toward the other photographs, ranged along the gleaming shelves.

All the pictures were of her. Ravenska as a dying swan. A lavender fairy. Arabian queen. Ravenska in a white, fur cape. Floating in a gondola. Standing before the Taj Mahal. There was just one table for the man—maybe twenty photographs arranged in rows on a drape of lace. He was dark and young with eyes as tender as a girl's. Harley recognized his face from the night he'd Googled Ravenska's life. He was the South American, the one who'd had an accident just weeks before their wedding day. A trickle of sweat ran like a snake down Harley's back. The dead man in the photographs bore a striking resemblance to Joaquin.

"Cassandra!" he whispered, like a prayer.

Harley waited, but he knew. There was no one here, and nothing. Except Ravenska's memories.

As he closed the door, he could feel the first, hot, panic swirls. He had no idea where to look for her now. Maybe she had gone outside. Maybe, who knew, she was running, crazy, down the road. He was just about to go up the stairs when he noticed another archway right beyond the chapel door. Harley followed its shadowy trail. It turned again, wending its way to a place he vaguely recognized. He looked around at the bare foyer. Yes, there was the door that opened out to the side of the house. Off to the right were the winding steps that circled to the tower room.

Maybe I'll just kill myself. The words in Cassandra's message roiled around in Harley's head. *It's easy up here there are places to go.* He suddenly bolted forward, shouting her name as he started up the narrow stairs. The sound bounced back with a hollow ring. Again and again he called for her, the last "Cassandra" like a sob as he staggered through the tower door.

Details registered all at once. There was no one there. The light was off. And the center window that faced the sea opened to the vast, dark night in a frame of shattered glass. The panic filling Harley's chest spiraled upward to his throat as he plunged across the room. His mind already pictured it: the tiny crumpled body and the long, pale hair that had felt like silk, streaming out like a ribbon of light. Glass shards crushed beneath his feet, as he leaned from the window and looked below.

Moonlight illumined the jagged rocks. He could see the entire ledge of stone, the place where a body would have to land. There were complicated shadows, but Harley could not see anything breaking their dark design. Behind him, he heard a whispery swish. The sight of the moon fixed in his eye like the snapping of a photograph. Just as it looked that second, rare and white and beautiful.

When he turned around, they were already there. Their feet were so loud, clomping in the satin shoes. The skirts were like froth, like a furious mist, and petals were tumbling through the air. He couldn't see their faces through the gossamer of the bridal veils, but he didn't have to see to know. There were five in all and one was very small and quick. His heart gave a lurch as he saw that Cassandra was not in the group. Maybe she was already dead.

Something sputtered in his brain, and he lurched away from where he stood. He was sure he could evade them. They were small and thin and delicate. They were mist and smoke. They were light and air. But as he ran for the open door, they caught him in their spinning loop. When he tried to break free, he couldn't. Their fine-boned arms forged steely links, and they rushed around in circles till their veils were a blur in his dizzied eyes. They were making him move in a kind of dance. He kicked and flailed at their whirring legs. But they were too fast and agile, and he started to feel like a clumsy kind of animal being rounded up in rope. The tightening circle was traveling, too. It was edging toward the window. Toward that small, bright moon that had fixed in his eye.

Harley Martin Jamison could not believe that a thing like this could happen to him. It was much too strange and way too sad. He felt the grapple of fingers and hands. The crush of those skirts, which were scratchy and stiff and not at all the way they looked, wispy, smoky, soft as snow. He could not even scream. He would go in silent, wide-mouthed flight. How would it feel, he wondered, his thoughts slowing down as if he had forever. Maybe if he willed it, he could land in the water over the edge. Cool and green, mysterious, where the fish and the pirates went to sleep.

A shattering screech suddenly cut through the air. It seemed to come from a faraway place, from across a space that no longer existed in Harley's mind. The spinning stopped as the scream stretched out. The floor grew solid under his feet, and the blur of whiteness focused into separate shapes. One of the girls was wearing a crown. She motioned to the others, and they rushed in a whir to the open door, where a lone, white figure had appeared. No one stopped. They pushed ahead in a reckless crush, shoving the figure out of their path, not stopping as she toppled back and tumbled down the stairs. Their shoes, like hooves, clattered on the rugged stone.

Harley tore across the floor. About ten steps down, he found her. Her body was twisted, wrapped around the curving wall, her head at a funny angle, lower than her feet.

"No. Oh God. Oh, Mairin, no."

The back of Harley's knees went weak, and he sank to the stair where her head lay still and motionless in a splotch of tangled curls. He could scarcely hold the cell phone as he pulled it out and stabbed the numbers 911. His voice was weak and shaky; it broke as he spoke into the phone.

In only moments, he heard the siren's distant wail. The sound was like a ribbon, twisting, curling through the night, and help seemed very slow to come. The muted cadence of the surf marked the seconds as they passed.

"Harley." The word floated up in the chilly dark, yet he knew it could not have come from her; he had wished it out of the silent air. But when he looked down, Mairin's eyes had opened, and a small pulse beat in her smooth, white throat.

"Stay still. Don't move." He had to swallow to finish his words. She was all right, or so it seemed. But what about the—Harley couldn't think of it. The unspeakable thing he might have caused.

"How could Cassandra—" Mairin's voice was fainter now.

"She wasn't there."

"Where is she then?"

"I don't know." He reached for her hand, which seemed to dangle like a glove, clasping it to his chest. "You shouldn't have come here, Mairin. I told you to stay on the boat and wait."

"It's all right," she answered. Her fading eyes strained into his. "I've already lost the baby. It happened last week. I was going to tell you on the dock."

Harley felt his heart dislodge. Everything hazed as he toppled slowly over her, folding right in half. "I'm so, so sorry. For all of it."

For a moment, there was nothing. Just silence and dark and the empty air. Then came Mairin's quiet voice.

"I love you, Harley. I never stopped."

"I love you, too." It was all he could say.

<hr />

Harley paced in the cold foyer as the paramedics eased the stretcher down the stairs. He could hear a scraping against the walls and the careful footsteps of the men maneuvering through the awkward space. From the house itself, from the darkened hall that led inside, a heavy silence seemed to flow. A silence so deep and touchable that it almost seemed impossible that anyone could be there, breathing in the distant rooms. They had made such a racket on the stairs, clattering in those block-like shoes, but now in the soundless aftermath even the echoes in Harley's head felt like memories from a dream.

But, of course, it hadn't been a dream. It was horribly real, and the sight of the paramedics emerging from the stairwell brought that knowledge crashing back.

"Will she be all right?" Harley whispered to one of the men.

"No time for talk," he answered. "Let's get her to the hospital."

"I'm going to ride along with her."

Harley clung to the stretcher's side as they headed out the door. Mairin looked so tiny. She was wrapped in a pale-blue blanket, strapped in tight, her body bundled like a sail. Harley wanted to touch her hand, but all her parts had been tucked in. He leaned toward her face to talk to her as they jogged to the waiting ambulance. Mairin seemed to have fallen asleep.

Chapter 27

The *Alma* sliced through the midnight waves, silvered under the fading moon. The wind was high, and the boat heeled over to her port, foamy ripples splashing the deck.

"Coming about!" yelled Harley, and Pugs and Red Legs jumped. Up near the bow, Liam and Vanessa ducked beneath the swinging jib, and from down in the galley where they were working on the food, Jane and Becky squealed. In the forward cabin, something fell. Probably one of Harley's bags. There were two of them there; he'd packed last night. By this time tomorrow he'd be on a bus halfway up to Maine.

"Look at that," said Becky, climbing to the cockpit and nodding toward Liam up on the bow. "Who'd have thought he'd ever settle down again?" She passed a plate of food to Pugs.

"Hell," he said. "She's only been here for a week."

"A week's a long time for Liam." She stared at her grumpy boyfriend, his frizzy hair shaking in the wind like strife. "You have to have faith. Things can change."

"Yeah," said Red Legs. "Have some faith." Jane was nestled at his side, and he drew her close in the crook of his arm.

"There are certain things that never change," Pugwash said, harking back to his changeless theme. "Like the way the bigwigs keep the power. Like what happened at Ocean Watch again."

Harley had to agree with Pugs. History seemed to repeat itself. The police, of course, had gone to Ocean Watch that night. The girls, in fact, had summoned them, so distraught they could hardly speak. Their little group hadn't gone to the restaurant. They were practicing in the studio when they heard the footsteps on the stairs. When they got to the tower they saw the tall, male trespasser. He looked angry and crazed and had broken the windowpane, they said. They started to run, to call for help, and this girl with black Medusa hair tried to block their way. *Of course not, no*; they had no idea the girl had fallen down the stairs.

"Still," said Becky, scowling at Pugs, "other things worked out all right."

Harley coaxed the steering wheel with the pressure of one hand. With his other, he reached for Mairin, pulling her in behind the helm, her tousled curls blowing lightly against his face.

Back on the night of the incident, Harley had never left her side. He'd traveled in the ambulance and had sat by her bed as she woke and slept, in and out of consciousness. She'd had a concussion in the fall, and for several days it was touch and go. She didn't remember clearly rushing up to Ocean Watch or how she'd known where Harley would be. But she did recall thinking of Teddy Flynn that night as she breathlessly climbed the tower stairs. As for losing the pregnancy, it had happened several days before, shortly after a fight with Smits. People said it was all for the best. People in town who hated Smits. Maybe so. But something was different about her now. It was something Harley couldn't explain. He imagined a picture of her heart, and down near the pointy bottom, a tiny piece had been taken out. At least the marriage was being annulled.

"Everything's good," Jane agreed, smiling at Mairin across the space. "And you've got that great apartment, too. Did you break the news to Liam yet?"

"Yeah, he knows," said Mairin. She'd been living on the *Alma* since the night she'd run away from Smits. "He came last night to look at the place. He's going to build some shelves for us."

"And he's helping us move," said Becky. "It's happening next Saturday."

"When's the party?" Red Legs asked. "I'll order a keg of beer."

Harley moved closer to the wheel, Mairin afloat in the ring of his arms. It was strange to think of the months ahead. Mairin and Becky sharing an apartment. Life going on without him there. Mairin had enrolled in school, the community college where Becky went. To pay the rent, she'd gotten a job working in Wally's restaurant.

"You'll be back for Thanksgiving, won't you?" Jane asked Harley cheerily. "We could all pitch in and do a turkey dinner up at Becky and Mairin's place."

"My mom would freak," said Becky. "That's her favorite holiday. Let's do Halloween instead."

"I'll come as a ballerina," Pugwash said, wreathing his arms above his head. Everyone laughed at how stupid he looked. But Harley couldn't force a smile. He still felt cold in some deep-down place when he thought about Cassandra. She hadn't been in the house that night. She'd gone to the restaurant, in fact; twenty-six people could vouch for that. But Harley knew she'd set him up. She'd known what her friends were going to do. This creeped him out in a way that was hard to put into words. He knew it as a feeling, a strange sensation of being unsafe, which whispered through his body now at random moments in the day. What on earth had they done to her, that beautiful, delicate, silky girl he'd rescued in the storm? What went on at those dark *soirées*? And when would it ever stop?

Madame Ravenska had also not been home that night. She was dining at the Breeze Hotel with the parents of Brady Cameron, a talented boy, shipped from Philadelphia, who ended up dancing the Albrecht role. The performance sold out to rave reviews. "Two rising stars," the *Boston Globe* had dubbed Cassandra and Cameron.

As for the case of Anderson, that, too, was deemed an accident. For about a week, Harley had followed the story online and then the accounts abruptly stopped. Anderson had been drinking a lot, and friends who were there said he'd taken Ecstasy. Pugs with all his theories didn't even know the half. He didn't know about Julian or the boy from Boston whose face was burned. But neither did Harley know for sure. He only knew that wherever they were, these willow-tree girls, so lovely in their dresses with the wispy rosebuds in their hair, unlovely things happened and boys were hurt.

∽

The wind picked up as they headed home to harbor, southward along the coast. Liam was at the wheel again, and the rest of the group nestled in the cockpit, huddled against the gusts. Harley and Mairin sat in back at the edge of the stern, her hair unraveled in the wind. Looking out behind the boat, they could see the incandescent wake, a moonlit trail that traced the distance they had come. On the black-edged shore, the strands of light burned dimly, the jewels in the mansion windows and the great, gold eye of Ocean Watch. Yeah, Pugs was right when he said that some things never changed. They just seemed to circle round and round. Summer, as always, came to an end. The dancers returned to their winter world. Madame Ravenska went back to New York to her grand apartment on Central Park with its courtyard full of birds. The school closed down for another year, and Hannah holed up, in peace at last, and waited for the snow. Harley had come full circle, too.

"We'll be okay," he said to Mairin, drawing her close. He knew it was true as the words came out. "We're together again. That's all that counts."

Mairin leaned back against him, her face tipped upward at the sky. "*She*'s here, too. I feel her. I know she was just a tiny thing, but she had a soul, and souls go on forever, right?"

Harley's lips pressed into her curls. "That's the thing about souls," he said. For a fleeting second, he thought of Giselle. The one in the story, the soul that loved. Mairin, he knew, was his Giselle. And their love was a force as fierce as hers, stronger than hate and heartbreak or the will of any evil queen. Harley was leaving, but he'd be back. He'd come for Mairin, and off they'd fly to the far-flung places they dreamed about. Or maybe it wouldn't go like that. Maybe they'd stay in this speck of a town, this tiny world at the edge of the sea and make a life together here. It didn't matter where they were as long as he could hold her close and the wind would keep on dancing in the tangles of her wild, black hair.

∽⦿∽

Back in port, there were long goodbyes. Becky told Harley to e-mail a lot and to send her pictures of autumn in Maine. Red Legs told him not to get too goddamn smart, and Jane insisted he come for the party on Halloween.

"I'll miss you, man," said Pugwash, punching Harley's arm. "Work will be work without you there." Harley hugged him bearishly.

"I'll miss you, too. See you Thanksgiving, if not before."

Harley and Mairin waved again as the group walked slowly down the dock toward the melting lights of town.

∽⦿∽

Harley woke as a gust of wind blew through the hatch. A short ways off, Mairin slept in the narrow berth across from his. She looked beautiful sleeping, Harley thought, and he stared at her face, taking pictures with his eyes so she'd be there tomorrow when he was not. Another breeze shivered through the cabin, and Harley eased up and climbed to his feet. Under his bunk was the drawer where they stored the blankets, and he crouched on the floor to pull it out. He coaxed the drawer, careful not to let it squeak, as it opened into the narrow space. What he saw inside did not make sense.

Petals, he thought. The drawer was full of petals, soft and white, as if dozens of creamy roses had fallen from their stems. Then, with a snap, perception changed. Something shifted in Harley's eyes, and he realized he was staring down at paper scraps—a huge, white pile of torn and shredded paper scraps. With a slow, uneasy movement, he gathered a cluster in his hand. There was printing on the fragments; they were ripped-up pages from a book. Harley looked more closely. Faint, familiar details began to surface in the dark, and he recognized now a marble-like pattern on some of the scraps. And then it suddenly came clear: It was his book of poetry. Fragments tumbled from his palm as he stared at the strange, pale wreckage that still did not make sense to him. Then he noticed something else.

With a tentative hand, he reached inside, drawing out a long, pale length of gauzy cloth. Coldness flooded into his chest. He suddenly heard the swish of skirts, the clatter of shoes on a stony floor as a swirl of whiteness swallowed him and snowy petals swarmed the air. His eye remembered a small, bright moon in a shattered window filled with night.

Harley balled the fabric up, crushing it in his fist. With his other hand, he pulled a blanket from the drawer and plunked it on his bunk. He gathered the scattered paper scraps and threw them back from where they'd come. He shoved Ravenska's ancient shawl to the deepest recess of the drawer. It stuck to his hand, and he had to peel it from his skin like damp and cloying spider web.

There is no safe place. Cassandra had wanted to tell him that. It didn't even matter if you hadn't done the "wrong" they thought. You could go to New York. Or Boston. You could hide away at school in Maine. Wherever you went, they would find you there. You'd be at a party—standing on a balcony or talking near a fireplace—and they'd circle in a soft, white blur. After it happened, no one would know. No one would think it possible because they were all so *lovely*, willow-tree girls with wispy rosebuds in their hair.

Mairin stirred in the bunk below, and Harley gazed down at her half-turned face, untroubled in the quiet night. A flicker of defiance quivered up from deep inside. He wouldn't let it happen. He wouldn't let them have the power. Love won over hatred if you danced together through the night and did not let sorrow steal your soul. He reached for the folded blanket and gently spread it over her. Then, leaning close, he pressed his mouth against her cheek. Mairin dreamed on as two last petals shuddered free, dropping, soundless, through the dark.

About the Author

Celeste Conway is the author of the young-adult novels *When You Open Your Eyes* and *The Melting Season,* and the middle-grade novel *The Goodbye Time.* She is the author-illustrator of the picture book *Where Is Papa Now?* Ms. Conway lives in New York City.